THE BOSS

CHATEAU #3

PENELOPE SKY

HARTWICK PUBLISHING

Hartwick Publishing

The Boss

Copyright © 2021 by Penelope Sky

All rights reserved.

CONTENTS

PROLOGUE

Years of patience, years of virtue.

It passed with the quiet click of a clock, counting the minutes forward, but also counting backward, counting down to a date that had never been set. Because that date was a moment, not a weekday, not a weekend, not a year.

A moment.

The home was dilapidated, practically unlivable, deep in the evergreen forests of Romania. There wasn't even a road that led to the property, just a dirt path covered with leaves tinted with red and orange. Fall was bitter with cold, giving a whistle on the wind like the winter train was about to pull into the station.

The weathered wood cracked against the elements, a stair was missing in the steps, and the windows had cracks where shards had popped out of the frame. A single footstep with a heavy boot made a creak that reverberated through the house.

But a caged animal had nowhere to run, not out here.

Every step made a squeak, every movement cast a shadow across the broken walls, every moment made their hearts beat slower and slower. A narrow hallway led to a single bedroom, a cot sitting on a slab of wood, a lantern on the nightstand, a set of eyeglasses. Pictures of naked French girls were hung on the walls, decades-old and taken from outdated magazines that were probably found in the bottom of a dumpster.

The small window showed the exterior, the early morning light that broke through the trees and highlighted the gentle powder of snow that caked the branches and leaves. Like sprinkled sugar, it was on the ground, the gentle beginning of a rough winter.

He lay on his back in the small bed, a single pillow behind his head, one hand across his stomach, gentle breaths filling his lungs and expanding his body in peaceful ways. Far away in dreams, he was unaware of the two men who moved to either side of the bed, who surrounded him like the night, dark like shadows.

They both stared down at the pathetic man before them, sleeping soundly in a place he arrogantly assumed they would never find. His dark beard was now filled with strands of gray, and it grew like a brush along his chin, hung like stems of ivy down his chest. The stench wafted to their noses, causing a slight burn like the dung on a pig farm.

The shadow on the left withdrew his gun and pressed the cool barrel to the man's forehead.

Not a stir.

He cocked the gun, a little click filling the small bedroom of the shack.

Like a light switch flicked on, eyes opened, staring at the gun pressed to his forehead, the view of the shadows above him blurred. The quiet breathing quickened, panic moved into his gaze, but it faded as quickly as it came, turning into an acceptance so peaceful it almost looked like desire.

The shadow spoke, a voice deeper than hell, a voice that reverberated with power, with retribution, with the promise of vengeance. "Did you really think it would be that easy, Father?"

HIS KNEES SANK into the dry mud, his hands behind his back, viewing the forest in front of him, the birds chirping a beautiful song, like it was just another day in the world, not the day of execution for a traitor.

In a black bomber jacket that fit his broad shoulders like they were a coat hanger for a suit, he stood behind his father, watching him stare at the beautiful peace before him, the world he would leave in a very unpeaceful way.

His brother shifted his gaze to look at him, to silently conduct a deep conversation between them, with details and logistics, all passing in just a single lock of their mutual gaze. With brown eyes earthy like the trees and dirt, he watched his older brother, eyeing the knife in his hand.

Their father remained where they'd left him, breathing deeper and harder, yanking on the ropes around his wrists so he could clutch his chest and dispel the anxiety that brought him into a state of panic. There was no greater torture than the fear of the torture, of the painful moments as you waited for death's knock on your front door. All you could do was close your eyes and strain your ears to hear that sound, that sound that would end the suffering because the wait had finally ended.

He gripped the knife in his gloved hand, a knife that had never been used, sharp enough to cut through the densest bone. "There is no death that will suffice. His spilled blood will never erase the red stains on their pillowcases. The rot of his bones will never catch up to their already rotten graves."

His brother stared on and, after several seconds, gave a subtle nod.

"But his execution will be their revenge." He stepped forward.

His brother did as well, their boots crunching over the little rocks in the soil, the leaves that had dried and withered on the ground, the small ice crystals that were crushed under the tread of their shoes.

"Please...wait." Their father's pleas didn't have an echo, because they were so quiet, so disingenuous. His terror couldn't replace his defeat, knowing in his heart that this was inevitable, and no cabin in the woods would ever hide him from his sins. "I've regretted—"

The younger brother shoved his boot into his back with a kick, sending him forward onto the earth. His boot was pressed into the back of the older man's shoulder, keeping him pinned to the mud that covered half of his face as it became submerged.

"Magnus—"

"Don't speak my name." He increased the weight on his foot, submerging him farther.

Fender took a knee over him, hunching down with the knife drawn.

Their father bucked his body hard to be free of the ties that bound his wrists, but like quicksand, the more he flailed, the more he sank into the mud, covering most of his face so he struggled to breathe.

With a look of indifference, Fender jabbed the knife down into his spine, paralyzing him from the waist down. "Mother." He did it again, piercing the lung.

His father gave a gnarled gasp, a short draw of air that couldn't inflate his lungs fully.

The knife sank deep over and over, Fender speaking the names of the family that was stolen from them both. "Marie...Remy." He let the knife stay embedded in his flesh this time, pierced through the heart, and the body went limp. Whether he died from drowning in the mud, from internal bleeding, or the accumulation of all those things, didn't matter. The blood that oozed immediately mixed with the mud, creating a beautiful crimson hue, an earthy tone that almost looked natural.

Fender left the knife where it lay before he straightened once more. He shifted his dark eyes to Magnus.

Magnus stared back.

A quiet moment passed between them, a simple stare, an entire lifetime of silent worlds. It was an empty accomplishment, killing a man who was so haunted by his past that he lived in a state of ruin instead of having the strength to do what they just did for him. But it was done.

Justice had been done.

ONE

THE BOSS

MELANIE

The darkness of the cabin was pierced by the glow coming through the windows, the distant torches casting flickers of light that created translucent wisps of smoke on the floorboards. The girls were silent in their beds, exhausted from the hard work that day...and the day before that...and the day before that.

It never ended.

Perpetually sore, perpetually hungry, we were in a constant state of survival. There was little energy to devote to much else than getting through the next day... and not being selected for the Red Snow.

That was what life had become—a meaningless existence.

And it was entirely my fault.

My eyes welled with hot tears as I sat up in bed, my arms wrapped around my knees, looking into the darkness and staring at the opposite wall. Flashbacks of that night in Paris returned to me. Stupidly, I was lured by men who gave me attention, who promised a fun night that I could gloat about to my friends back home. Raven warned me, the smartest person I knew, Little Miss Perfect, but I was too resentful to listen.

It was exhausting being second best all the time.

Raised by my sister, I was nagged about everything, from doing the dishes incorrectly to not understanding how credit with the banks worked, for being inferior to her in every way imaginable. I was grateful to have her as a big sister, but her superiority made me hate myself more, and then I hated her for making me hate myself.

That was no excuse for the decision I made that night.

That decision that made us wind up here...in hell.

The tears bubbled into drops then slid down my cheeks simultaneously, warm against my skin while the air of the cabin was frigid from the winter outside. My bottom lip trembled, but I forced a cold breath into my lungs and tightened my arms around my knees to make it stop.

Raven wouldn't cry.

I had to accept the consequences of my actions, to carry the burden of this regret for the rest of my life, to beg for forgiveness when I knew wholeheartedly that I didn't deserve it. I had to live with myself every single day, live in self-loathing, to wish I'd let Raven go when she fled to Paris just to get away from me...even though it hurt.

———————

MY NOSE permanently stung from the cold. When my breath escaped my nostrils, it would rise and coat the dry skin with a steam of moisture, but it was short-lived, and in the seconds between breaths, my skin immediately began to dry and wither.

Eyes down, I measured the white sand and placed it into the bags, working like a bee in a hive with the other girls, the quiet sounds of us working as a backdrop of music to our servitude.

Sometimes my eyes would flick up to look at her.

To look at the only person in this world who ever really loved me.

Now I had to watch her pick up a box far too heavy and struggle to carry it to the table so it could be opened and processed.

Her brilliant mind wasted, she was just labor now, and she wasn't even paid for it.

Because of me.

My eyes dropped in shame like always, because it wasn't just too painful to look at her, there was also too much shame in my heart to meet her gaze, even if the rare opportunity arose for us to make contact with our eyes, our souls, and our hearts.

AT SUNDOWN, we finished up the last box. We would be discharged to our cabins to have dinner, shower, and spend our short evening in each other's company before we got up at dawn to do it the next day.

I was grateful I wasn't alone in my cabin.

I hated the fact that Raven was.

A silent hush fell on the clearing, an abrupt change in energy that was felt by every single person even though it was unclear what had caused the shift. The girls looked in the same direction, as if something was coming toward us. It wasn't Friday, so there was no Red Snow, unless there had been a change of plans.

Then I saw him.

In a black bomber jacket with gray fur down the sides, a man entered the clearing, flanked by his men. He didn't don the guard uniform—and he didn't hide his face. With dark-brown eyes and short dark hair that almost looked shaved, he scanned the area with his intelligent and cold eyes. A distinct shadow was on his jawline, the same darkness that filled the shadows in the corners of the cabin. His lips appeared then because they were pressed together tightly. He carried himself differently from the others, with a sharpness to his posture that made him stand out more than he already did. He was strong, straight-backed, his massive shoulders squeezed in the leather material of his jacket. Tall, muscular, carrying a silent power that reached every corner of this camp, he made his presence known with just his silence, showed his face like he didn't give a damn if we saw it.

He stopped in his tracks, scanned the camp, and instead of looking past me the way he did with everyone else, his gaze halted the way his boots halted in the dirt.

Right on me.

As if tentacles had wrapped around my throat and squeezed, I was unable to breathe. Like a field mouse in the wild, when an owl stared my way, I turned absolutely still in the hope that I would blend into the background, that I would be camouflaged by the girls who surrounded me, that his stare wasn't reserved for me and whatever sinister motives he possessed.

The stare continued.

My heart raced in my chest, and it felt as if the sound of drums in my ears were suddenly audible to everyone in the clearing, including him. I should drop my gaze and focus on my work. My fingertips still gripped the bag of cocaine I was holding.

But I was too scared to do that, literally paralyzed in that moment by that ruthless stare. It was like a spotlight from a chopper, and there was no hope I'd be able to run when that bright light put me on a stage.

There was a subtle shift of his eyes back and forth, those earthy-colored lenses absorbing information at such an intense rate that he couldn't keep his gaze focused for more than a nanosecond. Furiously, his mind worked, comprehending whatever stimuli flooded his thoughts.

Then it was gone.

He withdrew his gaze and continued on his path through the clearing, moving past the row of tables and ignoring the stares focused his way from both the guards and the girls. His men flanked him, one on each side, trailing slightly behind him like he was the king of this camp.

Or better yet...the boss.

AFTER DINNER AND A SHOWER, I sat on my bed while most of the girls were gathered near the fire, talking about the encounter with the man with the bomber jacket.

Petunia was a veteran of the camp, a three-year resident. Her life had changed forever when she took a different route home one night—and that was it. She was in her late twenties, strong and able-bodied, working hard every day to make sure she wasn't next in line for the Red Snow. "He's the boss. I've seen him a couple times."

"The boss?" Irene had only been there a few months longer than I had. She was still being integrated into this new world of snow-covered cabins, of torchlight that lit the pathways to and from the clearing.

The most surprising aspect of the veteran girls was their acceptance. When weeks turned into months, when months turned into years, they molded to this new life, spending their time in the cabin reading their books, playing their games, like they had gotten off work after a long day and were spending the evening at home. There was no discussion of an uprising, of freedom. They didn't even talk about the things they missed, their families and friends, the outside world that was just a few hundred miles away.

Raven could never be that way.

Not in months.

Not in years.

Not in a lifetime.

She would never forget the taste of pumpkin-flavored coffee in the fall, the lights of the Eiffel Tower, the picture of Mom on the coffee table in the living room, and she would never forget about me either...and the life I deserved.

A life she deserved more.

Petunia was in the rocking chair near the fire, drinking a mug of hot cocoa that her guard had given her. Some of the girls had special relationships with the guards, getting extra items through their obedience...or other things. Sometimes a guard would show up in the evening and escort the girls to another location for thirty minutes before he dropped her off again.

We all knew exactly why. We just never talked about it.

The only way I'd sleep with one of them was in exchange for freedom.

But freedom would never be an offer on the table.

Petunia spoke again. "He's in charge of the camp."

"How do you know that?" another woman asked.

Petunia shrugged. "You can just tell..."

She was right—you could totally tell.

Footsteps sounded outside the front door, heavy boots that announced a pair of guards had shown up to the cabin. It was normally one at a time, so this was unusual. The lock was undone, and then they stepped inside, scanning the room until his head faced my direction. His face was covered by the garb of the guards, so there was no way to discern his identity. Sometimes I could tell them apart based on their size and mannerisms, but I could never be certain.

But I was certain they were looking at me.

All the girls turned to follow his stare, to draw the same conclusion.

My body tightened in fear because I knew they were there for me, to take me away and remove my consent, to force my servitude in ways I refused to agree to. The fear was like acid in my stomach, but there was no escape from this. This was my punishment for my stupidity, for a situation that could have been easily avoided if I had just listened.

"Get your things." He stopped at the foot of the bed.

I was still on the bed, still sitting with my knees pulled to my chest, unable to understand the request.

The other guard helped himself to my dresser and pulled out my belongings, which wasn't much. He set my boots beside me and dropped my jacket over the bed so I could pull it on.

Then they both stared at me.

"W-w-why?"

The second guard scooped up my belongings into his chest and waited for my compliance.

The other just stared, but he never moved to touch me, to try to yank me to my feet and force my obedience, which was odd.

When I didn't move, the first guard spoke again. "Because he wants you."

I knew who *he* was.

The boss.

TWO

A MAN OF HIS WORD

Melanie

I was marched through the darkness to the northern part of the camp, past the flickering torches in the clearing, past the cabins with wooden rails covered in snow. The sky was dark, and delicate flakes of snow drifted down, landing on the bridge of my nose and melting instantly.

I walked between them, flanked on both sides, the sound of our footfalls crunching as we condensed the snow under our boots, grinding it into dust. Nights spent alone in my bedroom as I tried to fall asleep were never as quiet as it was now, when the tall pines of the forest shielded any sign of life from the outside world.

We reached a small cabin in the rear, a perfect square with a small patio on a rise, three pieces of wood making the stairs that led to the front door. There were windows, frosted in the corners from the cold, and a stone chimney that showed smoke rising from the top like it was occupied.

The guard opened the door and gestured for me to walk inside.

I halted in front of the wooden steps, so afraid that I was actually tempted to run. But there was nowhere to go. To face this sort of cruelty was enough to bring tears to my eyes, to experience my terrible fate before it happened, to become a slave in a new category. It was more demeaning than anything else I'd been forced to do. Crying wouldn't change that, would probably make him enjoy it more, but I couldn't control myself. I was in utter despair, unable to believe this was my life now. And when I thought about it happening to Raven, it made me cry even more.

"Come on." The guard indicated to the door. "Now."

I swayed on the spot before I rose up the stairs, passing between the two guards and entering the small cabin. My clothes had been placed on the bed, a fire was in the fireplace, and I heard the door shut behind me. Their footsteps never sounded, as if they stayed put.

I approached the bed, took a seat at the edge, and then noticed the couch, coffee table, and armchair positioned against the opposite wall. There was an empty bookshelf there as well. In the armchair sat the man I expected to see.

The boss.

He was as terrifying as I remembered.

Deep-brown eyes, hair so short I bet he shaved it whenever it became too long, a jawline so chiseled and sharp that every bone in his face was visible, even his prominent cheekbones. Through his dark facial hair, the thin beard that hadn't been shaved since yesterday or maybe the day before, his fair skin was visible, bright in the light of the flames that burned in the hearth.

The fire popped when the wetness from the wood sizzled into steam, and the light licking of the wooden pieces by the flames made a peaceful noise, making it sound like a cozy cabin over Christmas.

But it didn't feel cozy.

The longer I stared at him, the harder I cried.

He was in his bomber jacket, black jeans, and black boots. His knees were wide apart, his thick arms on the armrests, his muscular frame leaning against the back of the chair. With the same expression that never changed, he watched me cry, feeling absolutely nothing.

I pulled my gaze away because his expression frightened me. It only made it worse, only made the pain I was about to endure that much more intolerable. What was worse? What was about to happen...or the fact that there was nothing I could do about it?

In my peripheral vision, I saw his immense frame rise from the chair.

I gave an uncontrollable squeal of terror and immediately shifted farther down the bed, like the increased distance would make any difference at all. It provided me no extra protection whatsoever.

He didn't move.

My shallow breathing turned into pants, and my hand tightened into a fist and rested against my chest, my eyes on the floor, cowering in fear but also impulsively preparing to fight a battle I would lose.

His deep voice invaded every corner of the cabin, slid over every inch of my skin like a breeze from an open window on a summer day. It was warm like the fire, not cold like the piles of snow right outside. "I'm not going to hurt you."

I sucked a shuddering breath through my clenched teeth, taking comfort in the promise I had no idea if he would keep. But there was something about him that made his words unbreakable, that gave a high level of credibility. A man like that didn't need to lie...so why would he?

But his words could mean less than what I hoped for.

He wouldn't hurt me.

Didn't say he wouldn't rape me.

I remained motionless on the bed, my eyes still turned away, waiting for him to make his move.

He did—by walking out.

The door locked, and several sets of footsteps thudded against the wooden beams and disappeared.

———

THE GIRLS ASKED questions the next day on the line.

Petunia sat beside me, taking the bags I prepared and doing the final measurement before she handed it off to the next person. "Where did they take you?"

I kept my eyes down, my voice low, and did my best not to get caught by the guards. "A different cabin. I'm by myself now."

"Why?"

"I...I'm not sure." I didn't bring up the boss. Not sure why.

"They only put the really difficult people in isolated cabins," Petunia said, taking the bag from me and working like we weren't deep in conversation. "Did you do something?"

"No." I was just very unlucky.

Kiley sat on the other side of me and gave me a nudge. "Your sister..."

I looked up to see a large guard at the edge of her table, standing right over her, watching her sit across from Bethany and not take a single bite. He loomed over her, making sure she starved so her work would weaken on the line...and she would be hanged.

Tears welled in my eyes, and the only reason I didn't break down into sobs was because Raven wouldn't want that. If I drew attention to myself, I would be hanged too. And it would kill her if she had to see that, just as this was killing me now.

A GUARD ESCORTED me to my new cabin.

There was a stack of firewood beside the fireplace, but I didn't know how to get a fire going, so I didn't bother. It was cold in the cabin, so I wrapped a blanket around me as I sat at the edge of the bed. Without company or a book to read, I didn't know what to do with myself. I stared at the armchair where the boss had sat the day before.

An hour later, several sets of boots sounded outside the front door. The lock was turned, and a guard carried my tray of food to the edge of my bed before he departed. He took his position on one side of the open door, while another stood on the other side, as if they were guarding the entrance.

Then another pair of heavy footfalls sounded, growing louder and louder as the man rose up the steps and entered my cabin. In his black bomber jacket with the gray hood, his massive shoulders stressing the material at the seams and the same coldness in his dark eyes, he planted his feet.

The door shut behind him.

I didn't move for the food. A long day of work made me hungry every day, but that appetite was chased away by the terrifying man who invaded my space and took away my freedoms.

I didn't cry this time, but I was fucking scared.

His gaze had the same searing nature as before, like a hot branding iron against my skin, except his look wasn't warm, but so cold that it burned like dry ice. His jacket was open in the front, showing his black shirt underneath that outlined the discrete lines of his pecs. He was muscular beneath all those clothes; there was no doubt about it, like a bear or something. His invasive look lasted a bit longer before he lowered himself into the armchair across from me, taking the exact same position as before. His hand gripped the armrests, his fingertips curling underneath the wood. His hands were visible, monstrous in size, covered with cords of veins. He hardly blinked as he stared at me, his look constant and piercing, like a knife right between my ribs. "Eat."

I didn't turn to the tray beside me. I didn't want to drop my guard, not even for a second, even though this would be a match I could never win. My hands tightened the blanket around me, the material covering my appearance and perhaps making me less desirable.

"You're cold. Make a fire."

All I could do was shake my head.

He stared at me for another minute, having distinct characteristics of a statue. He was stony, still, solid.

I just wanted him to leave. *Please leave...*

He rose to his feet and moved to the fireplace.

I flinched at his movement and immediately scooted away, pushing the tray out of the way so I could fill the space it had once been in.

He stilled and looked at me.

I breathed hard, afraid of the repercussions.

His stony expression didn't change. It never seemed to change. It was impossible to gauge the thoughts of a statue, something lifeless, something created with knives and sharp tools. He continued his movements and grabbed the lighter sitting on top of the fireplace. He bent down, piled the wood into the hearth, lit it on fire, and then stepped back.

The flames came alive and immediately filled the cabin with warmth, lighting up the darkness and chasing away the shadows...except his shadow.

He returned to his armchair and took a seat once more.

The staring continued.

My eyes remained on the floor, waiting for the assault to begin.

It never came.

Thirty minutes of silence passed, my food got cold, and his eyes never strayed from my face.

I cleared my throat and forced myself to speak. "What do you want?" I kept the blanket bundled around me even though I was actually too warm from the fire. But I held on to it like a life raft in the middle of the ocean.

"You to eat."

My eyes returned to his. "Please...leave me alone."

"I said I wouldn't hurt you."

"But that doesn't mean you won't—" I couldn't even bring myself to say that disgusting, grotesque word. A word that should be eliminated from society because the act had been eradicated. It should be like smallpox, something that had been wiped from the face of the earth, so it wasn't even discussed anymore.

His brown eyes were the same color as the cabins, a dark, earthy color, with gentle flecks of different colors, like gold, amber, and other subtle hues that could be found in the forest. But the intensity of his gaze was not from this world, but deep below...in a place where he would return when his time on this earth expired. "I want you." Every word that came out of his mouth was deliberate and simple. He spoke plainly, but very little. "But that's not the way I want to have you."

Every muscle in my body relaxed a little, holding on to his words like he'd just pardoned me from an execution. I clung to those words, felt the air slowly leave my lungs, felt my eyes close for a brief moment as the relief I felt entered every single inch of my face. My reaction was uncontrollable, and I could feel the hint of moisture that rose from my throat and entered my eyes. I looked at him again and almost thanked him...but I didn't because I shouldn't have to.

He held my gaze for only a few seconds before it was gone. He then shifted his gaze to the fire. It was the first time he broke contact first, the first time he severed that connection. "Eat."

THREE
NEGOTIATE

MELANIE

Raven was getting worse.

With every passing day, she grew weaker.

She struggled to carry the boxes to the table, starved until she turned white and weak, a translucent ghost.

And there was nothing I could do.

I was in my cabin, sitting in the dark and the cold, knowing the boss would visit me once more. He didn't come yesterday or the day before. My food was brought by a faceless guard, and I shivered through the night because I still didn't know how to make a fire. When I tried, I couldn't get the flames to stick to the wood, not the way he could or the other girls in my old cabin had.

I knew when he arrived before the door even opened.

There were several sets of footsteps. They thudded against the wooden beams as they approached. The door was open, the tray was served, and then the guard took his post outside my room.

The boss entered, making the same quiet but powerful entrance as with any time he stepped into the vicinity of other people. His eyes went to the fire first, then shifted to me. He didn't sink into his armchair.

The door shut behind him.

After several long seconds, he spoke. "Why do you not use the fireplace?"

I was a little less scared of him, so I spoke. "I...I don't know how." I was still in my work clothes because they were a lot warmer than my lounge clothes, and they were warm on the inside from my body heat through the day.

His stare lingered before he grabbed the lighter, kneeled, and did it for me. When the fire grew into flames, he rose to his feet and set the lighter on the stonework. "Light the deepest part of the logs. Not the corner." He moved to his usual spot and sank into the armchair, the glow from the flames blanketing his face with golden light. It made his eyes a little brighter, like freshly tilled soil on a spring day. His gaze was reserved for my face. He always wore a stoic and intense expression, but whenever his eyes were on me, it was more pronounced. Slight, but deep.

He was in charge of this place, had the power to do anything, so if he said he had no bad intentions toward me, I believed him. There was no reason to give me a false sense of security, to make me drop my guard when he could just tear it down. I grabbed the tray and started to eat.

With his arms stretched out in front of him and his body still, he watched me eat the food the guard had provided. A lot of men weren't talkative, but he took it to a new extreme. He seemed to enjoy silence more than a good conversation.

I didn't know what else to do besides eat, so that's what I did. I was starving after the long day. We didn't get break-fast. We got two meals a day, and that was why the girls slept with the guards to get extra sustenance. I'd never had much of an appetite, so I didn't need to go the extra mile.

The thought of the girls made me think of Raven.

She was being starved on purpose—so she would be the next candidate for the Red Snow.

I didn't know what had caused the guard to focus on Raven, but knowing her, she probably refused a request or pissed him off, and now she was at his mercy. My mind suddenly became clear as a sunny day after a rain as I looked at him. "I have an offer."

It seemed to be too much effort for him to react, and his face stayed the same.

"I'll let you have me the way you want to have me...if you let my sister and me go."

His face was a slab of gray concrete.

An eternity seemed to pass, and there was no response. A silent no.

"Okay...if you let Raven go." If I could get her out of here, I would be able to live with myself again.

He didn't even blink.

"Her guard is starving her—"

"I don't negotiate." The look on his face told me the conversation was over. The request had been denied. We were finished.

At least I tried. "You said you wanted me..."

"Still do." A man had never looked at me like that before, like he could touch me with just his stare, wrap his fingers around my neck and slide his hand gently up my shirt over my soft belly—when there were twelve feet between us.

"I just offered you a way to make that happen—"

"That's not how I want to have you."

"You don't have any other option." He either forced me, or he gave me something in return.

He touched me again with just his look, his big hands in my hair, his body guiding me flat against the bed, his narrow hips sliding between my parting thighs. His weight pressed me into the mattress, and he looked down at me like I was a newfound paradise he would claim in his name. "I do."

I shook my head. "No, you don't." I was terrified to defy him, but the words fluttered out anyway. If he really forced himself on me, I'd just give in and allow it to happen because a fight would be pointless. But knowing that he wouldn't gave me some courage to disagree. He gave me a power that no one else in this camp had given me. I took it and ran with it.

He turned his gaze to the fire. "I don't need another option. I just have to wait for the option I want. And I will."

I WORKED IN THE CLEARING, my fingertips callused from the constant toil from sunrise to sunset. With our heads down, each one of us worked as if our lives depended on it—because they did.

It was Friday. That meant someone would be selected.

I hoped it wasn't Raven.

Everyone looked up when they saw the boss approach, flanked by his men, striding through the clearing carrying his massive shoulders beneath his bomber jacket. His breath escaped his nose as he exhaled, creating a cloud of white smoke in front of him. His eyes didn't land on me until he began to pass.

He looked at me just as he did in the cabin.

The look lasted a moment before it was gone—and he departed.

All I should feel was relief at his departure, but there was a flare of disappointment. Ever since he'd taken an interest in me, the guards stopped manhandling me every time they escorted me anywhere. They didn't say a word to me either, didn't taunt me. I'd clearly been designated as off-limits, and I suspected that respect would continue even when he was gone. My nights in the cabin gave me a bit of normalcy, where I had the power to make decisions that were accepted.

I shouldn't feel grateful for that, not when he was the reason this camp existed in the first place, but I was.

Night descended. My worst nightmare began.

Torches were lit, the noose was readied, and the block was set in place for the next victim. The executioner made his way down the aisles, staring down all the women who kept their heads bent in the hope that they would escape his notice.

Not Raven...not Raven.

I didn't want anyone to die, but if it had to be someone... please, not her.

Then she stood up.

The executioner wasn't even in her aisle, but he stopped to turn to her.

"No..." *Raven, stop.*

Raven stared him down fearlessly, as if she wanted death to come. "I'm the one you want, so let's cut the shit."

"No..." Tears sprang to my eyes, and I instinctively rose to my feet.

Petunia yanked me back down. "There's nothing you can do for her. Stop."

All I could do was mask my tears with quiet whimpers, feel the warmth of the liquid coat my cold cheeks.

The executioner marched her to the block, secured the noose around her neck, and his eyes shone with mirth, as if claiming the life of someone who deserved to live more than the rest of us were some kind of accomplishment.

If only the boss had accepted my offer.

"Don't look." Petunia turned my face to her to shield me from the pain. "I'll tell you when it's over."

I could hear the moment Raven's weight dropped, hear the tension of the cord, but I didn't hear a sound come from her. I held on to Petunia and sobbed, knowing that my sister was about to be gutted because of me.

Because of me.

"Stop!" A man's voice rang out in the clearing.

I immediately turned away from Petunia to see something I never expected.

A guard cut her down, told off the executioner, and saved my sister's life.

My fingers wiped the tears from my cheeks as I watched the rope be cut from between her wrists. "What?" There was a mark around her throat where the rope had burned into her skin, and she coughed into the snow, trying to catch her breath after nearly suffocating. When the guard was finished berating the executioner, he leaned over and extended his hand to her, like they were equals. The look in her eyes was one I'd never forget, like she was looking at more than her savior...but her friend.

"She must be sleeping with him," Petunia whispered. "And it paid off...because he just saved her life."

WHEN I RETURNED to my cabin, my body was numb.

I didn't even see what had happened, didn't lose my sister, but the incident was traumatizing, nonetheless. The guard opened my cabin door and ushered me inside before he shut the door behind him.

I stood in the middle of the cabin and looked at the fireplace.

The stonework wasn't cold, gray, and dark. The inside of the cabin wasn't partially illuminated by the limited light from outside the windows. It was bright and warm, a roaring fire burning in the fireplace, waiting for me. The room was cozy, like it'd been burning for a while.

Like it'd been set up just for me.

WHEN THE BOSS left the camp, nothing changed. He still had dominion over the place, even in his absence. There was no Red Snow that night. My sister was spared —but not because of me.

When he returned and heard the events that transpired, would he execute her?

If he really wanted me, he knew he would have no chance if killing her was his decision.

A blizzard came into the camp, a powerful wind that blew a storm of snow that blanketed the grounds with small mountains that were impossible to circumvent. It was impossible to work in the conditions, so we remained in our cabins until the worst had passed.

When it did, we were handed shovels and told to get to work.

We were spread out everywhere, digging into the snow and carrying the powder to the edge of the clearing. I copied what the other girls did, but I'd never held a shovel in my life. It was heavy and cold, even through my gloves, and my entire back was sore from the work. I was used to sitting in the clearing and doing processing tasks with my hands, not real work like this.

"Like this." Raven appeared beside me and shoved the shovel into the snow, stepped on it with her foot, and then scooped up a pile of powder.

I slowly straightened as I examined her, looking at her neck in the small opening between the metal of her zipper. There were hints of redness, but the bruising had disappeared considerably.

She held my look for a moment before she moved. "Keep working, Melanie."

I gripped the shovel hard because all I wanted to do was hug my big sister. I wanted to apologize a million times, to tell her I wished it had been me instead of her. But there were guards everywhere, and we were never allowed to be near each other except for a random occasion such as this.

I did as she taught me and scooped up a pile of snow.

We walked together to the edge.

I threw the snow onto the growing pile. "You okay?"

"I'm fine." She spat out the answer like it was an automatic response. Even if she wasn't fine, she would never admit it—not even to herself. "What about you?" She turned her head to look at me, her brown hair pulled back in a bun, her blue eyes fathomless pools of pain that reached deeper than the deepest ocean.

The boss immediately popped into my mind, the man who'd taken one look at me before he'd claimed me for himself. My new residence was an upgrade compared to the old one, but without company, I spent my time in solitude—and that was a lonely experience. Maybe he did that on purpose, so I would actually look forward to his visits. "Yeah, I'm fine."

FOUR
CHÉRI

FENDER

Nightfall.

I entered the camp with my men on either side of me. Torches lit the pathways through the cabins. A storm had passed over the Alps and blasted the setup, but it'd been shoveled back to its original form. My eyes scanned as I moved, making sure the place was run to my expectations. It was quiet after a long day of work, the girls locked in their cabins, the drugs safely stored in the guards' cabin.

I gave no warning of my visits. There were days when I left, only to return the very next evening, just to remind my guards that this was my camp—not theirs. Their lives were just as expendable as a pig on a goddamn farm.

One of my men led my horse by the reins, while the other carried my bag as I was escorted to my quarters.

I halted in the clearing and turned my attention to the little cabin in the north, where a glimpse of the firelight was visible through the frosted window. I redirected my route to her cabin. "My dinner will be served here."

Silently, the men attended to my horse and carried my belongings to my residence.

My boots crunched against the packed snow as I passed through the light of the torches, my eyes focused on the front door of the little cabin. A shadow emerged from the right, but I continued my pace without bothering with a glance.

"There was no Red Snow. Magnus stopped it." It was the executioner, in the guard's uniform, his face visible because the women were locked away in their cabins.

I stopped in my tracks, but my eyes remained on my target. "There's nothing that happens in this camp that I'm unaware of." I turned my head to stare him down, to dismiss him from my presence. "You should know that by now."

He gave a curt nod then excused himself.

I continued on my way, approaching the little cabin that held the woman who'd caught my attention the instant I laid eyes on her. The light-brown hair, the bright-blue eyes, the fair cheeks that were as white as the bones of winter.

My route was interrupted once more.

"Fender."

White smoke left my flared nostrils as my right boot rested on the bottom step of the stairs. Like tearing flesh off bone, I dragged my gaze away from the door and looked into brown eyes identical to mine.

His hood was pushed back, his short hair tousled from the wind and the cold, his lithe and athletic body leaner than mine but packed with a speed I could never produce. White smoke left his nostrils too, increasing in intensity as our eyes held each other. "Return Melanie—"

"French." I didn't want her to hear a word of this conversation.

Magnus spoke again, obeying my request. "Return Melanie to her cabin."

He was the only one who could speak plainly to me, who could say or do anything and escape my cruelty. They say water could be as thick as blood. A lie. Blood was always thicker than water. There was no man who could earn more loyalty than Magnus had as his birthright. "That's rich."

His brown eyes shifted back and forth as he held my gaze, the quiet night acting as a buffer around us. "Raven is our best worker—"

"That's not the reason. And I don't care what the real reason is." Like the rest of the guards here, Magnus had found a concubine to facilitate his needs while he was away from his French whores.

His shoulders tensed as a long trail of vapor left his nostrils.

"No woman is worth making enemies, Magnus." I turned away and put my weight on the bottom stair.

"Fender."

I turned back to look at him.

"Let her go." He tried again, even though it was pointless to argue with me, but this woman must have clawed her nails deep into his back.

I left the step altogether and came close, my breath moving into his face. "What did I just tell you about making enemies, brother?" It was an idle threat, we both knew it, but I wanted him to give up his endeavor.

"This is not who we are." He continued to stand his ground, continued to defy me—like a fucking idiot.

"Our ideologies have always been very different. They will remain different."

Magnus stayed for another moment, eyes locked on to mine, the vapor dissipating from his nose at a slower pace, a sign of defeat. He abruptly turned and walked off, disappearing into the darkness.

I rose up the steps, unlocked the door, and stepped inside.

Melanie hadn't been expecting me, judging by the stark white paleness of her cheeks. She was in her lounge clothing we provided, a black tank top with gray pants. Her hair was slightly damp, like the fire hadn't dried it fully since she'd stepped out of the shower. With no makeup on her face, her skin was a blank canvas of artwork. Subtle freckles like stars, lips full and curved like a bow, beautiful long hair that didn't need hours of preparation and product to shine.

She slowly scooted to the edge of the bed as she kept her eyes trained on me.

I dropped my jacket and threw it over the couch before I sank into my armchair, planting my feet wide apart, one elbow propped on the wooden armrest so my fingers could cup my chin. It'd been a long ride on horseback, and while the tense muscles of my back craved a shower and a soft bed, this beautiful woman was the first thing that required my attention. My hungry eyes needed to soak in her appearance, to remind myself that she was real, that her memory when I was away wasn't an exaggeration.

She was still as I stared, staring back at me.

The door opened, and the guard set my dinner on the coffee table, along with a tall glass of scotch. He silently excused himself, not looking at Melanie because I'd threatened to emasculate every man in this camp if they so much as glanced at her.

I scooted forward, pulled the coffee table toward me, and then proceeded to cut through my well-done steak and take big bites before moving to the roasted potatoes and grilled asparagus.

She watched me eat.

I cut into a piece and held up the fork to her.

She eyed it before she switched her gaze to me.

I turned the fork in my fingertips and extended it to her.

As though she thought it was a trick, she remained reluctant, but then she left the bed, came the closest to me she'd ever come, and placed the meat in her mouth. She chewed slightly, a flash of pleasure coming into her gaze as she handed back the utensil.

The girls were fed well so they could work well, but they weren't given steak.

I was the only one who was.

She sat at the edge of the bed again, this time looking at the fire.

I ate my dinner, wiped the plate clean, and then took a deep drink of the scotch, letting that familiar burn ignite then subdue my nerves. I extended the glass to her in offering.

She shook her head.

I finished it off.

"Please don't punish my sister." Her hands were together in her lap, but she held her back straight as she sat at the edge of the bed, like a Parisian noblewoman. Watercolor paintings were hung in my residences, fine pieces of art that showed French aristocracy, and beautiful lords and ladies were on display. That was exactly what she reminded me of, one of those gorgeous women who should be preserved in an oil painting created by an artist talented enough to capture her surreal beauty.

I could stare at her for hours but always find something new to appreciate. The length of her slender neck was engrossing, the way her collarbone sat on her frame, the way her chin was so sharp in her face that it made a prominently curved line, showing just how perfect every angle of her profile was. My art collection had started as a status symbol, an ode to my noble roots, a history that filled my walls and reminded me of what I'd reclaimed. But in time, I'd begun to appreciate those multimillion-euro paintings, begun to appreciate the famous artists whose work filled my homes and apartments. And that made me appreciate this one-of-a-kind woman. Her work clothes were unflattering, her hair was pushed out of her face so she could focus on her tasks meticulously, and her skin was bloodless because of the cold, but somehow, she made Parisian models look like trolls. She made my whores unremarkable.

"Please..."

The desperation in her quiet voice brought me back to her request. "I don't think about your sister." I was well aware of the situation because I'd been briefed. The situation was over now. Nothing left to think about.

She inhaled a breath of relief as she played with her fingers in her lap. "Thank you...for the fire."

I relaxed into the armchair with my fingers wrapped around my glass, choosing to spend my evening winding down to the presence of her beauty, the sweet sound of her gentle voice, pondering how I would have her when she wanted me to have her.

"Where did you go?" Her guard visibly lowered in front of me. She was finally beginning to realize I was no threat to her.

"Paris." The women in my bed were of a specific caliber. Models, whores, socialites. Beautiful women in every category. This was the first time I'd ever taken an interest in a woman in the camp. I couldn't buy her a drink, take her to an estate outside of Paris, couldn't get between her legs in any conventional way. So, I sat in my chair and waited for something to happen, for her to want me like the others...because they always wanted me.

"Is that where you live?"

I gave a nod before I brought my glass to my lips.

"What did you do there?"

"Work."

"What does work entail?"

It required too much effort to answer, so I chose not to.

She seemed to understand I wasn't much of a talker, so she stopped asking questions.

There was only one way I wanted to communicate with her. My hand in her hair, my hips between her thighs, my arm hooked behind her knee to keep her open so I could thrust time and time again, make her wince in pain then moan in ecstasy. I wanted to communicate with fire, with grunts, with the taste of my sweat on her tongue, with the lock of our blazing gazes.

She stared at the fire, the dancing flames reflecting in her eyes. "Why me?"

My palm rested on the top of my glass, and I listened to the fire pop when it became so hot that it burst. I stared at her cheek, saw the way her light-colored hair fell from behind her shoulder and hung down her chest, fully dry. "I like beautiful women."

She turned away from the fire and met my look. There was no surprise there, but there was also no arrogance. She would have to be blind to dispute her beauty, but she clearly didn't view herself in that regard either.

"And you're the most beautiful woman I've ever seen."

A small burst of surprise exploded in her eyes.

"I will have you." I would have her as another item in my collection, a living and breathing piece of artwork. A painting in my bed, a piece of jewelry on my arm, a different kind of wealth that other men would envy.

Her stare remained on my face. "Why would you have me when you have nothing to offer me? You're a bad man..."

The women in my bed knew I was a drug kingpin, but that made them want me more, not less. These circumstances were very different. "You want to be taken care of. I can take care of you." She couldn't start a fire even though she watched me do it more than once. Her intellect wasn't the hindrance. She'd just been spoiled her entire life, and as a result, there was no drive to figure things out on her own. "I can elevate you to Parisian aristocracy. I can bring you to my estate outside of Paris, where a butler can attend to every need you didn't even know you had. Gowns, designer clothing, diamonds on top of diamonds on top of diamonds..." She was my diamond, the most expensive piece of jewelry I could ever wear. "Michelin-star meals daily, lingerie more expensive than a Bugatti, sexual satisfaction you've never known. Old lovers will feel like inexperienced boys after you've had me. I can give you everything. Literally everything."

Her expression glazed over as she pictured everything I described, the luxuries that her imagination couldn't even produce. Just a single taste of me would ruin her palate forevermore, and there would be no going back. She would live in my home and share me with my whores, because even a piece of me was more satisfying than the entirety of another man.

I glanced at the bed. "Let me show you now." A night was all I needed. A night of my heavy body on top of hers would change everything for her. She would want more. Her addiction would turn to obsession.

A tiny flash of temptation crossed her gaze with the speed of a shooting star. It happened so quickly that she probably thought I didn't notice.

I did notice. "Chérie." *Sweetheart.*

She pretended it never happened. "You're a drug dealer... you're dangerous."

I brought the glass to my lips, tilted it to get the last of the scotch, and then set it on the coffee table. "If I'm the most dangerous thing out there, then there's nowhere safer you could be." I was the big bad wolf in the woods. I was the monster in the dark. I was the boss that no one wanted to cross. I owned the police, the government, and the addicts on the streets of Europe. "If you think you left an innocent world and descended into the shadows, you're wrong. It's on every corner, it's in the back room of your favorite restaurant, it's on the other side of your camera on your laptop. You walk past it every day, brush up against it on the metro, listen to its footsteps down the hallway outside your apartment door. I can protect you from all of that. You were taken from your home on a dark night, but with me, you'll never have to worry about that again."

Her chin tilted down to her hands in her lap.

"I'm everything you want. Everything you deserve."

A sarcastic burst of air came from her throat, along with a slight shake of her head.

My eyes narrowed on her face.

"You might be right about that second part..."

My fascination with her only grew. "Come with me."

She lifted her chin and looked at me.

"When I leave. Come with me." I could take her away from this place. Instead of a cabin, she would have a palace. Instead of a guard, she would have a butler. Instead of these weathered clothes, she would have the finest material kissing her skin. "Let me give you what I've promised."

The temptation returned again, staying a little longer this time, but it faded too. "No."

I gave her a way out—and she said no. "Why?"

She shook her head and looked down again. "I won't leave my sister here...alone. You take us both, or you don't take me at all."

Disappointment flushed into the veins of my hands, and I resisted the urge to allow my fingers to curl into fists. I'd just opened the door to a life she could only dream of, but all she could think about was that unremarkable woman. "I don't negotiate."

"Then don't expect my answer to change."

FIVE

THE SMILE OF A BOY

Melanie

Days blurred together. Just like when the wind kicked up and blew snow everywhere, it made our surroundings blurry. Everything was out of focus. Everything was an opaque combination of faded colors. The only reason we knew the days of the week was because of the weekly Red Snow. It was our archaic form of a calendar.

I sat at the bench and worked like I did every other day, glancing across the clearing to see Raven carrying the boxes to the table. Adequate nourishment had made her strong once again, and her throat seemed to have healed completely. It was a calm existence, work, sleep, repeat.

If it weren't for the Red Snow, it wouldn't be that bad.

But it constantly hung over our heads, lingered just behind our shoulders, haunted each of us every Thursday night. I never slept well on Thursdays. Not because I believed I would be next, but because someone would be next. It would happen—and there was nothing we could do about it.

The boss stopped coming to my cabin.

He was either busy...or I'd pissed him off.

Probably pissed him off.

I couldn't lie and say I wasn't tempted by his offer. I was...deeply. To get out of the cold, to descend into a life of riches and luxury, to have a warm bed made up with satin sheets, have gourmet food whenever I wished... Who wouldn't want that? When he looked the other way, I could run.

But where would I go?

Even if I never ran, it was better than being here.

But I could never leave my sister behind. I could never enjoy any of the amenities he described when I knew she was stuck out here, her only ally the guard who seemed to care whether she lived or died.

There was nothing I could do for her. I should just take the offer and run.

But I'd rather work my hands bloody every day in the cold and look up to see my sister there.

To see her face.

Another blizzard came into the camp, howling outside the cabin with shrieks that couldn't be drowned out by the fire. Every day after work, my fireplace was roaring with flames, my dinner was delivered, but it was different from what I used to have.

It was steak, potatoes, corn, asparagus, fresh bread, a glass of wine, and a slice of pie.

I imagined he was eating the same thing—so we were still connected even when he didn't come to me. He tempted me with breadcrumbs, with fine delicacies the other girls could never have. The guards couldn't even have them.

I continued to work in the clearing, but I felt like one of the most powerful people in that camp. I was never touched, the guards never looked at me, my cabin was always prepped for my arrival, and he continued to prove that he could give me so much more.

If I said yes.

When the blizzard passed, I was given a shovel and put to work with everyone else. Digging the shovel into the snow and hauling the powder away was much more physically demanding than sitting on the bench and processing the cocaine, so I dreaded doing it. It gave me a workout that I'd never had in my life, leaving me sore for two days afterward.

Hours into the day, Raven found me.

Discreetly, she came closer and closer, moving into earshot. "You okay?"

She always checked on me first. "Yeah, I'm fine. What about you?" I got a pile of snow in my shovel and carried it to the edge, while she did the same.

"I'm going to get us out of here, okay?"

I believed my sister was capable of anything, even the impossible, but I didn't believe that. I kept my mouth shut because I didn't want to sabotage her hope. It was probably the only reason she was still going, the fantasy of freedom.

"I've been gathering supplies. When I've got everything, we'll go."

I did my best not to have a reaction so the guards wouldn't realize we were talking. "Raven, what do you mean—"

"We're going to run for it, okay?"

"Run where?" I dropped my head as I shoved the shovel into the snow, covering my reaction by letting my hood tilt then cover the back of my head. "We're in the middle of nowhere. We'll die out there—"

"I heard a bell."

"A bell?"

"Yes. On the wind. I know it's there."

I lifted the shovel out of the snow and stared at my sister, seeing the fearlessness in her eyes. "We're going to get caught."

"We've got to try, alright? I'd rather try and die than live like this for god knows how long." She lifted her shovel from the snow and carried it to the clearing. "Where's your cabin?"

"Raven, I—"

"Melanie, I'm not leaving unless you come with me. Be brave, okay?"

I carried my shovel to the edge of the clearing and tossed the snow onto the pile. I'd done my best to convince the boss to take my sister too, but he wasn't just stubborn, but uncompromising. If Raven didn't at least try to escape, she would stay here until her neck was in that noose. "Is your guard helping you?"

"Kinda...in a way. You need to be prepared at a moment's notice. You need to be prepared to run like our lives depend on it—because they do."

———

WHEN I RETURNED to the cabin at sundown, I stepped into the room and immediately shed my coat, because the hard work had actually made me warm, made me sweat throughout the day. The fireplace was burning, and my dinner was on the bed. I pulled off my jacket and tossed it on the floor. Then I reached for my shirt to pull it over my head.

"Be aware of your surroundings."

I dropped my shirt back down then clutched my chest as I turned to look at him in the armchair behind me, sitting there in his long-sleeved black shirt and black pants. His bomber jacket was thrown over the couch. It took me a few seconds to catch my breath.

He grabbed his glass of scotch and took a drink, his deep-brown eyes glued to my figure. His eyes were almost the same color as the contents of his glass, like automobile oil with an earthy hue. His eyes roamed over my figure as he licked away the drop that he missed. "Continue."

My hair was caked with sweat, and my clothes were uncomfortable because they were soiled with a hard day's work. As hungry as I was, what I really wanted was a shower. There was a lone tub in the corner with a shower curtain. I used to take baths when I couldn't figure out how to get the fire going. "I'd like to take a shower."

He raised his glass and slightly gestured toward the tub. He was exactly the same each time we interacted, possessing a quiet hostility with clipped responses. There were no good moods or bad moods.

"Do you mind coming back later?"

His only response was taking a drink of his scotch.

"Then can you at least look away?"

"No."

I released an annoyed sigh, because I was so uncomfortable in my own skin that I really wanted to rinse off.

He drank his scotch and watched me.

I grabbed my towel and did a quick change, dropping my clothes next to my bed then moving to the tub, a black towel wrapped around my body. I turned on the shower head and waited for the water to get warm.

He held his glass but didn't take a drink, his eyes piercing me like my appearance in that towel was enough to fuel his attraction. His desire was palpable, somehow in the air like the steam from the shower. It was just a piece of cotton, but he looked at it like it was lingerie.

I got behind the curtain and draped the towel over the edge. The warm water hit me, and I felt all my muscles relax with the heat, felt the clumps of sweat leave my scalp and the roots of my long hair. With the curtain closed shut, I could forget he was there, have a moment to myself after the long day.

When I was finished, I dried off as best I could before I grabbed the clothes I brought with me. I put on the gray pants and the black tank top before I wrapped my hair in the towel. Then I opened the curtain and stepped out.

His look had only intensified in the meantime. His eyes were borderline angry, and one hand had tightened into a fist on the armrest. It was so startling that I actually stilled before I continued to move to the bed.

His eyes followed me.

I sat on the edge then combed out my wet hair so it would be free of tangles.

"You have a beautiful silhouette."

My eyes immediately went to the curtain, imagining the light from the fire creating a distinct shadow of my body, like it was film on a projector. That was something I hadn't considered.

It didn't seem that erotic, but he looked at me like it took all his strength to stay in that chair.

He was the most dangerous man on this planet, but I somehow felt safe in his presence, even when I was wrapped in a thin towel. He had the physical authority to force me to do whatever he wanted, but he never tried. He always asked for permission, and when he was denied, he respected that decision. He was the reason I was there in the first place, but he also gave me more power than anyone ever had in my life. When he'd first come in here, I sobbed because I thought I was about to be raped. But I was given more respect than any other man had shown me.

If they could get away with it, most men would do the unthinkable. Without the law and the police, without retribution, they probably would regularly force women against their will. The boss had nothing to keep him accountable, no repercussions whatsoever, but he still didn't do it. That actually implied a lot about his character.

I pulled the tray of food toward me. "Why won't you do it?"

He repositioned his head slightly, but his gaze never flicked away. One hand remained on the empty glass, which he must have consumed while I was in the shower. "Rape and sex are two different things. Rape is about taking. Sex is about giving. I want to give you things, chérie."

It was a question I shouldn't have asked, but his answer put me further at ease.

"I want to make you feel beautiful. I want you to give yourself to me completely. I want to make you come. I can't do those things if it's not mutual. We can't have the passion or the fire unless you want me too."

"I'll never want you."

A subtle smile moved on to his lips. It only lasted for a few seconds before it disappeared.

I knew what that look meant.

He didn't believe me.

WHEN I ENTERED my cabin the next evening, I made sure to take in the entire room.

My tray of food was there, filet mignon with a cream sauce and a side of pasta with veggies. There was also a thick piece of chocolate cake and madeleine cookies. A stack of books was on my nightstand.

He was there too.

Sitting in his armchair, his empty plate on the end table beside him. A bottle of scotch was next to him, along with a half-empty glass. The most striking thing about him was his bare chest.

His big, strong, muscular bare chest.

His pectoral muscles were each the size of a plate, the muscles defined and wide, cut into his flesh with a sharp knife. Now that he was shirtless, it was easy to see the way his strong body came together, the way his bulging arms connected to his powerful shoulders, the way those connected to this enormous chest that looked like the concrete wall of a parking garage. He was relaxed in a seated position, but his stomach was so naturally tight that it was flat as a board. The grooves of his eight-pack were just as deep, as if an artist had taken a knife and dragged it through his flesh, cutting into his body like it was the trunk of a tree. He was in sweatpants instead of jeans, low on his hips, showing those deep lines over his hips. He'd just eaten his dinner, and his stomach was still a flat surface.

I flinched at his appearance. I was used to seeing him decked out in black, used to discerning his strength through the tightness of his clothing. Now I could see his slightly tanned skin, a golden color to his complexion. His jawline didn't have a shadow, and his hair was a little shorter like he'd gotten annoyed with the length and shaved it off.

His eyes were the same as always. Dark. Angry. Authoritative.

I moved to my bed, where my tray sat, feeling timid all over again.

His chin was propped on his closed knuckles. Veins like rivers flowed from the back of his hand, along the mountains and valley of his arms, over his shoulders, and then up his neck. Thick like a horse but cut like a marathon runner, he was the strongest man I'd ever laid eyes on. There had never been a man in my life who looked anything like him, even the best ones. He was a different cut of premium meat, composed of a substance harder than steel.

I couldn't look away because I was both intimidated and mesmerized.

He didn't reach for his drink. His eyes were reserved for me, like I was the one half naked. After a few minutes of the fire burning in the hearth, of the rising intensity of his presence, he spoke. "Let me take you to bed, chérie."

I shifted my gaze away and forced myself to stop staring.

He grabbed his glass and took a drink.

The more time I spent with him, the less I viewed him as the boss, the man in charge of this hellhole. He became someone else entirely. Now he was this sexy stranger I should stay away from, but his magnetism continued to draw me in, deeper and deeper, into an invisible black hole from which there was no escape. Even if I could run out the door and hide in the wilderness, his pull would still reach me, because it was innate. His branding iron had seared me, and that mark would be implanted in my skin forever. Without touching me, he had felt me everywhere. Without sharing a kiss, he had tasted me everywhere. His fingertips were deep under my skin, wrapped around my bones. "Let my sister go, and I will." His desire was the only leverage I had. It was a sacrifice I'd make for her, especially since it didn't feel like that much of a sacrifice.

"I will say this once more and never repeat it. I don't negotiate. This—" his eyes burned into me further "—is irrelevant to the world outside this cabin. My rules are not broken. Your sister is stuck here forever. There is nothing you can do to negotiate her freedom. You should take my offer and save yourself."

I looked at him again, feeling powerless once more. He gave me that power, but then he also took it away. "Why would I want to bed the man who's keeping my sister captive?"

"She was never a target of the Hunters. You were. The only reason she's here is because you two were together. Blame me for her captivity if you must, but I had nothing to do with it. I can't let her go because it will cause chaos in this camp."

"Then why can you let me go?"

He dropped his hand from his chin and straightened. "I said nothing about letting you go."

I shifted my gaze away, the heat burning my throat, the overwhelming weight suddenly hitting my shoulders and causing my back to bend. It was on my chest, making it hard to breathe, and the pain was so sharp that it made me whimper. Tears sprung to my eyes as my body faced what my mind couldn't.

She would never forgive me.

And she shouldn't.

My hand cupped my mouth as I started to cry, seeing the flames begin to blur as the moisture coated my vision. Flashbacks of that night came back to me, me with the two men who'd bought my drinks throughout the night, and Raven standing there...telling me not to go. I basically told her to fuck off. *Girl, you need to chill. Your mind is playing tricks on you.* I cried harder, remembering the look on her face as I said that. *Stop telling me what to do. I'm a big girl who doesn't need you to take care of me anymore.*

Her response to that sealed my fate, because then I just went with them out of spite. *Obviously, I still do need to take care of you because these guys have got psycho written all over them, and you're too stupid to see that. I'm sick of this shit, Melanie. I'm sick of you making stupid decision after stupid decision. I'm telling you, I saw that motherfucker outside our apartment, and he's gonna put you in an oil barrel or something. There're a million guys out there, you'll find someone new tomorrow.* I covered my face with both hands, sobbing harder, hating myself more as the memory haunted me.

The bed dipped beside me, and the air was instantly different. It smelled like pine, like fresh air, like the woods after a rain. He was on the opposite of the fire, but he brought his own heat as if he were engulfed in flames. "Chérie." He didn't touch me, kept a foot of space between us.

I was swallowed whole by my pain. I wished my next breath would be my last.

"Chérie." His hands gripped my wrists and pulled them from my face. "What did I say?" He leaned toward me, closer to me than he'd ever been before. "Tell me what I said." He grew more demanding as I didn't answer, even angry.

"It's all my fault..." I pressed my eyes tightly together, so more tears squeezed out. "She tried to save me, but I wouldn't listen. She tried to warn me, but I was a fucking brat. I'm the reason she's here. And she won't...she won't forgive me." I lowered my wrists to my thighs where his hands remained, three times the size of mine, exerting the gentleness of a feather, like he knew exactly how to touch someone so delicate.

His coal-colored eyes looked at the side of my face, drilling deep into my core. The light from the fireplace brightened his face, sharpening the lines of his jaw by deepening the shadow behind the edges.

"I've tried to apologize a few times, but she won't hear me out." I gave a loud sniff then reached for a napkin on my tray to blot the tears away. The material balled up in my closed fingertips. "She's right about me...she's always been right. It made me angry with her, made me resentful. Not because she was wrong, but because she was right...and I hate that she's right."

"Right about what?"

I gestured to the fire. "That I'm worthless. That I always need someone to take care of me. That I'm an idiot who constantly makes bad decisions, so I need someone to make decisions for me."

"Doesn't mean you're worthless. Means you have a different kind of worth."

I patted the napkin against my cheek again, absorbing the final trail of tears.

"I can take care of you."

My eyes stayed on the fire, his hands cupped underneath mine, letting mine rest inside his like they were pillows.

"You will never feel worthless with me." He moved his face to the crook of my neck, his warm lips coming into contact with my skin. A soft kiss was pressed to my flesh, the same gentleness he showed with his hands. He let his mouth linger awhile before he shifted upward into my hair, smelling me, breathing against me. He turned a little bit more and pressed a kiss to the shell of my ear.

I closed my eyes and automatically interlocked our fingers. I was at the beach, and my fingers dove into the soft sand, the grains surrounding me until I was buried. His hand gave me a gentle squeeze in return. "The events of our lives that shape who we become are out of our control. Accept who you are."

"That's hard to do...when I'm the reason she's here."

"She's the one who decided to be responsible for you. Never should have taken on the role if she couldn't handle every aspect of it."

My eyes started to water again. "I knew she moved to Paris to get away from me. So, I kinda forced my visit... just to be spiteful. It hurts that she moved to another continent just to be rid of me. I meant to confront her about it, but I never did." He was now my confidant, my friend, the man who held my hands and listened to me cry. He was the only person who accepted me as I was... the exact opposite of Raven.

His hands continued to cradle mine, keep them warm next to the fire.

"If I hadn't been a brat, she would still be in Paris, drinking her coffee and going to school. But like always, I came in like a fucking hurricane and destroyed everything." Being trapped in this camp gave me time to self-reflect in a way I never had before. It forced me to look inward, to pick myself apart and acknowledge all my flaws, my mistakes.

"I like hurricanes."

My eyes left the fire, and I slowly turned to look at him, to see his face so close to mine that his gentle breaths spread across my skin. Instead of pitch-black darkness of space, his eyes were warm like coffee, the fire highlighting the little flecks of gold in his gaze.

"Tornadoes, earthquakes...I like them all. And I can handle them." He came a little closer then purposely looked down at my lips. Like they were my eyes, he gazed at them with the same intensity. His hand left mine then gently grazed my cheek before sliding into my hair, pulling it back from my face so he could see all of me, take in the watery eyes, the blotchy cheeks, my ugliness. His eyes lifted to mine. "Let me handle you."

My mind was empty of consciousness, and I felt like part of the elements. I felt like the fire, the air, the snow on the ground outside. There was a contentment to my heart that felt so comfortable, a peace that was stronger than an entire bottle of wine. My hand rose automatically, and with my fingertips outstretched, I inched closer to him, like I was feeling for something in the dark. My palm flattened against his strong chest, hitting a slab of concrete that had been sitting in the summer sun all afternoon. A rush gave me a nanosecond of vertigo because so much was channeled into my body at once. Lust, desire, raw and unbridled attraction. But there was more. Safety, security, peace, trust, friendship. How could I trust this man when he was the reason I was there? How could I have complete faith in his word when he broke the law? How could I feel...*this*?

Now, his eyes were dark again, the restraints in his gaze tightening as he resisted. His breathing sped up, his breath blanketing my face more often, his chest rising and falling at a quicker rate. But he continued to give me all the power, the final say in the matter. A no, while it would make him flush with disappointment, would also make him depart.

My hand slid up his chest to his shoulder, feeling the mountains of muscle there, the hot skin. My fingers slid down his arm, over the individual hills, valleys, and the rivers of his veins. My hand followed one vein in particular, tracing it all the way to the hand that was sunk into my hair.

His stare was unmoving like the mountains, as if time had paused and everything was frozen. Then he pulled me toward him slightly as he moved the rest of the way and planted his mouth directly on mine, his kiss warm like the one he pressed to my neck, gentle and soft, a direct contradiction to his hard nature.

He was a big man, monstrous, with callused fingertips, short hair, and intense eyes, but he knew exactly how to touch a woman like she was a teacup in a china set. He allowed our lips to greet each other with soft tugs and caresses, his eyes open and on mine, watching my reaction to the burn between our mouths.

My fingers returned to his arm and then his shoulder, touching the strongest man I'd ever felt. He was thick like a tree trunk, but powerful like a wild bear that sometimes approached the camp in search of food.

His kiss deepened, his hand fisting my hair, giving me a breath that expanded my lungs. His head turned left to right, taking my mouth at different angles, giving me purposeful kisses that he'd practiced in his mind as he'd sat across from me in that armchair. When his tongue met mine, it started off gentle too, getting to know my mouth little by little, his breathing increasing the more acquainted we became.

The sound of the fire drowned out the sounds of our kisses and breaths, but soon it faded into the background as our passion cupped our ears like headphones, throbbing like the bass from a loud concert.

He lowered me to the bed as he moved on top of me, pressing me into the thin mattress with his immense weight, dwarfing me with his size. He pulled his mouth from mine and looked down at me. His eyes quickly shifted back and forth between mine, his gaze dark once again, with a burning intensity that almost made him appear angry. With a single arm, he scooped me up by the waist and repositioned me on the bed, so my head hit the pillow at the top.

The world faded away, and it was just the two of us. I watched him stare at me in a way a man had never stared at me before. It made me feel transparent, like he could see completely through me, see my heart, my flaws, my shortcomings, and didn't care about the information he found. Whatever I lacked, he would provide.

I didn't think about anything except the two of us.

In this moment.

Man and woman.

His hand slid underneath my top and lifted it as he planted his face against my belly, kissing my soft stomach, dragging his tongue over it as he moved farther up, to my chest and then the area between my tits. His hand spanned my entire stomach, could crush me if he decided to squeeze.

My eyes naturally closed at his touch because I'd never been worshiped by a man like this, as if every part of my body deserved to be kissed, as if there was more to my body than the area between my legs.

The bed dipped farther and farther as he positioned his weight directly on top of me, his hand pushing my top higher until it rose above my breasts and revealed my large tits. My nipples were hard, my skin sensitive, and I sucked in a loud breath as I felt him drag his tongue in the little valley between my nearly nonexistent cleavage.

He kissed me like I was perfect.

He dipped his head as he kissed one nipple, flicking it with his tongue before he gave a harsh suck, making me wince in both pleasure and pain. He lifted his head, brushed his nose against mine before he kissed me, his eyes open and deep with desire, and then he moved to the other tit that required his attention.

I hadn't even had him yet, and he was the best I'd ever had.

His kisses became more aggressive, treating my second tit far more harshly than the first, his hand cupping my rib cage like it was my waist. His thumb pressed into my sternum, testing my petiteness, memorizing the measurements of my body.

My hands explored his body as I arched my back to give him more of me in his mouth, my unclipped nails dragging into the searing skin of hot muscle, of the beast that pinned me to the mattress and devoured me like his dinner of steak and potatoes.

When he held his head over mine again, he pressed his forehead to mine, his eyes on my lips, and his fingers unbuttoned my pants and got the zipper down, breathing hard with me, his arousal growing.

His lips returned to mine and kissed me as he gripped the material over my hip and yanked it down. My hips lifted off the bed automatically, and he moaned as he got the pants loose over my ass and down to my thighs. My cooperation turned him on, made him moan again when I helped him kick the material away and leave my ankles.

His hand gripped the inside of my thigh with his big fingers and slowly positioned it. His kiss ended so he could look at me, stare at my face in the firelight, his fingers trailing to the area between my legs, over my underwear, and then down the front.

When his fingertips reached my clit, I released a loud moan, and that was when I realized how much I'd been waiting for that touch. My hands automatically held on to his arms for balance even though I lay completely still, and the increased desire in his eyes only made my desire increase more.

He rubbed my clit with the perfect pressure, with the perfect touch, like he knew exactly what my body wanted.

I breathed deeply as the sensations made my hips rock automatically, letting out quiet moans because every time he touched me, it felt so good. My nails started to claw, and I looked into his eyes and felt his pleasure as I felt mine.

His features hardened the longer he touched me, his jawline turning sharp like the edge of a knife, his eyes turning into black abysses that knew infinite depth. His fingers shifted farther back to my entrance, and he moaned as his fingers became coated with my flooding arousal.

When he knew I was ready, he pulled out a condom from his pocket and dropped his pants.

My eyes took him in, seeing his bottom half match the top half. His thighs powerful and toned, full of the same muscle definition he had in his torso and arms, and his narrow hips had that prominent V that segmented two levels of muscle.

His dick was exactly what I expected—and it matched everything else about his body.

Humongous.

He got the condom on then moved between my legs, his arms pinning my legs back so he could sink inside my pussy with the least resistance. He left my shirt pushed up to my shoulders with my tits on display, and the bed shifted and moved again as he repositioned himself. "Just for tonight, chérie. I will give you all of me." He pressed his head covered with the stressed latex between my lower lips and slowly pushed to get through.

Completely absorbed in this moment, nothing could pull me out of it. Our surroundings, our reality, nothing could break the trance between our eyes, our bodies, and our hearts. I'd never wanted a man more, never wanted to give myself to someone like this, never wanted someone to take me, all of me.

He slowly sank inside me, patiently waiting for my body to accept him inch by inch, giving quiet moans as he claimed my body further and further.

My hand cupped his neck as I moaned at his entrance, winching at his size but appreciating it at the same time. His size was part of his nature, and I would never change it even if I could. I took the bad as well as the good. My other hand planted against his chest, and I breathed harder as he moved farther inside me, stretched me to full capacity, making this time somehow feel like my first time.

His intense eyes were glued to my face, his jaw tenser than it'd ever been, razor-sharp. When he reached a dead end inside me and could go no farther, he released a moan as he gently rocked his hips. *"Chérie, tu es à moi."* With his eyes on me, he rocked into me at a quick and steady pace, his eyes burning into my fiery ones with lustful flames. *"Si belle."* He spoke to me in French as he had me, enjoying me in a way a man had never enjoyed me, like I was the best he ever had when I just lay there and enjoyed it. *"Je suis ton homme. Il n'y a que moi. Tu comprends ?"*

HE DIDN'T CLIMAX and leave.

He changed his condom and kept going, taking me again in the exact same position, speaking to me in French. His powerful body was slick with sweat, glistening in the light of the fire, making my sheets smell like him and our spent bodies combined. A pool of arousal had dripped down my ass to the sheets beneath me because he didn't take me in another position, and that moisture grew until I could feel it coat my lower back.

Frenchmen fucked differently from Americans. His passion was unbridled, wild and free, and once, twice, even three times wasn't enough. He was ready to keep going, to kiss me hard, to please me so thoroughly that my body actually ached. The fire burned down without either of us noticing, and the heat we made together kept the cabin warm despite the snow that fell out the window. He didn't even want me to do any work. He just wanted me there, underneath him, taking his pounding dick. My only responsibility was to lie there and come, to scratch his skin with my sharp nails, to watch him fuck me like he'd never wanted a woman more.

I was about to come again, for the fourth time, when I didn't think that was possible. Once was a miracle sometimes. Twice was a fluke attributed to my hormones. But three and four times...that was all him. I tugged on his lower back as I pulled him flush against my clit, ready to come again, my lips trembling and incoherent mutterings coming from between them. I reached for a word I couldn't find, begged for a name to enter my throat so I could say it out loud.

He supplied it, as if he knew I was desperate to say his name in gratitude for the night he'd given me. "Fender. Say my name, chérie." He pounded into me harder than before, filling the cabin with his grunts and heavy breaths, driving me into a final explosion as he reached his. "Say it."

My eyes blurred with tears as I came around him, looking at him above me, saying the name in worship. "Fender... yes." I said it again, like he was a god, like I should be nothing short of utterly grateful for the way he made my toes curl, the way he made everything hurt and feel good simultaneously. "Fender."

He came with a loud groan, filling the condom that separated us, shoving himself as far as he could go without hurting me as he finished. His forehead rested against mine until he was completely finished, the gentle rock of his hips coming to a standstill. His moans died away, and all that was left behind were breaths.

My nails released his scratched skin.

He opened his eyes and gave me a passionate kiss like he still had a little bit left in his engine. It had tongue, breath, possessiveness. He pulled himself out of me and rolled off me.

I winced when he left my body, aware of the soreness now that the passion was gone.

He pulled off the condom and tossed it aside before he immediately got dressed, like he had no intention of sleeping beside me.

I was so tired that all I did was turn over and pull the sheets over me. I didn't even care about the stain that my wetness had left behind. My body and mind were both exhausted, and I just needed sleep.

He didn't seem to have brought a shirt or a jacket, so he pulled on his boots and prepared to leave. But he hesitated.

I heard him stop, my eyes on the dead fire, unsure if he was looking at me or had something to say.

His bootsteps sounded as he moved to the fireplace. He kneeled, added more logs, lit them on fire, and made the cabin brighten once more so I would stay warm for the rest of the night. "Goodnight, chérie."

SIX

SOFT GRAVES

FENDER

I stepped into the infirmary and stared down the only doctor I had on duty.

He looked at me from his chair then quickly rose to his feet. "What do you need, Boss?" He approached the table between us, his eyes slightly fearful like he didn't know if I was there to berate him for something.

"Birth control."

He didn't have any reaction at all, even though I'd never made that request before, and the only people who did were the guards that had relationships with the girls. Not romantic relationships. Barter relationships. They gave them medicine, desserts, books in exchange for pussy. It was the only currency used in the camp. Wordlessly, he unlocked one of the cabinets and pulled out a pack before he set it on the table between us.

Footsteps sounded behind me from the door that I'd left open.

I took the pack and slipped it into the pocket of my jacket before I turned around.

Magnus stood there, his hood up and his face unseen.

I didn't need to see his face to recognize him. I could feel him, could discern him based on his energy alone. His emotions and thoughts were like visible words in the air, and they were palpable, absorbing directly into my skin.

He knew exactly what I'd placed in my pocket.

And he disapproved.

A wordless conversation passed between us. I stared at where his eyes were located, and his invisible stare drummed into my face. When he didn't speak, I stepped around him and exited the cabin.

He came after me and joined my stride, but he didn't address what he'd seen.

I didn't give her the pills beforehand because I knew she wouldn't take them. Pills were unreliable unless she *wanted* to take them. After last night, I knew what she would do. We walked past Alix, and I stopped to look at him.

He immediately stilled and waited for orders.

I pulled the pack out of my pocket and extended it. "Cabin #44."

Alix took the pack and walked off without questioning me.

Magnus and I continued on our way. "What is it?" I asked the question as we walked side by side.

He was quiet as he headed into the headquarters.

I stopped in my tracks and stared him down.

He looked at me through the darkness of his hood.

"Have something to say to me? I have shit to do today."

Magnus looked away and continued to walk.

I joined him.

"The Hunters want a bigger shipment since we don't need their services for the time being."

Business. All I wanted to talk about was business. "Alright."

"How much can I distribute?"

"Double."

"We don't have enough for double."

I halted again and looked at him. "I told you to increase the shipments."

"And you know that's not easy."

"Then make it easy, Magnus. When I leave, I will speak with Bartholomew."

Magnus nodded.

"And when I return, I expect the shipments to have been increased. Do whatever is necessary." I moved forward.

"We can't compromise the quality of the product. If we demand—"

"Then don't compromise." I stopped again and stared him down more aggressively, because he was wasting my goddamn time with these excuses. "We don't negotiate, Magnus. Get it done."

WHEN I HEADED to her cabin, I went alone.

I didn't need my men anymore.

I didn't need them to stand outside and listen to her come.

I unlocked the door and stepped inside.

She was on the floor, leaning against the bed, her legs out and her ankles crossed, reading one of the books I'd had the men drop off for her entertainment. I provided everything she could possibly need to be comfortable.

She looked up from her book, her expression different than it used to be, as if she'd been expecting me, and if I didn't show up, she would have been disappointed. Her fingers gently pushed the book closed.

My eyes went to her nightstand, seeing the packet that had been dropped off earlier. A pill was missing.

Good.

I moved to the couch and dropped my jacket before I took a seat and loosened my boots.

She sat in the light of the fire, the glow of the flames painting her in a golden hue that made her even more beautiful than she was. Her blue eyes were like sapphires, her slender neck a landing strip for my tongue. Her beauty was timeless and special, once in a lifetime, so hypnotic that a night of passion was barely hors d'oeuvres.

When the boots were gone, I pulled my long-sleeved shirt over my head.

Her change of expression was subtle, but there was a flush of her cheeks, a desire to repeat what we had the night before.

I got to my feet and dropped my pants, letting my cock free. I stopped in front of her, my hard dick pointed directly at her face, waiting for that mouth to open and that tongue to stick out. "Why are you still dressed, chérie?"

IT STARTED with me on top, my hips between her soft thighs, my bare cock inside her wet and perfect pussy, her cream building up behind my crown and at the base of my dick. My arms were hooked behind her knees, and I fucked her exactly the way I did last night, like that didn't even happen, like I didn't need her in another position because I loved to look at her face.

Her eyes watered every time she came, and the convulsions she made were sporadic and uncontrollable, as if my dick gave her so much ecstasy that her body could barely tolerate it. Her tits shook slightly as I thrust inside. And now she looked at me like I'd successfully claimed her as mine—and I deserved her.

We were skin on skin, and it was so good, as if I hadn't fucked her for hours the previous night. It felt like the first time I had her, the first time I really got to feel her at this intimate level. My dick memorized her channel like a blueprint, and I knew it like the back of my hand.

I came inside her with a deep grunt, filling that tight little pussy with every drop of my seed, and then I thrust through my own come and kept going, adding another load a short time later...and then another.

We ended up on the floor, my back against the bed, her little body bouncing on my lap, moaning and screaming in pleasure, dropping down on my dick over and over as if she could handle my dick like my favorite whore.

The fire roared in the hearth nearby, providing heat we didn't need, and that made her beautiful skin shine with sweat, highlighted the sexy curves of her perfect body.

My hands gripped her ass and guided her up and down when she got tired, when she ran out of air and had to pause to catch it once again.

One hand moved to her neck, and I held her there as I moved her up and down, my eyes on her, smelling her come, my come, and the slick sweat all over our bodies. Sex was always hot, always sweaty, always a workout for every muscle in my body. But it'd never felt this goddamn good.

She rocked her body the way I showed her, moving up and down but also doing this sexy shimmy with her hips that I liked, and it felt good for her too because she clawed at my chest as she came again, more tears dripping down and then landing on my chest.

I'd pictured this moment the first time I saw her. I'd pictured this heat, this passion, this very moment before I heard her speak. Beautiful women were a dime a dozen in my world. They were everywhere in Paris. But none held a candle to this woman riding my dick now. She became a fantasy I was desperate to turn into a reality. She became a prize I had to earn. She became the one thing I didn't have, the one thing money couldn't buy.

Her breaths slowed once she was finished, her nails slicing into my shoulders less. She flipped her hair and kept going, wanting to drive me into giving her another mound of come that would just drip out once more.

"Slow." I gripped her hips and controlled my thrusts, taking it down to a fraction of what it'd been before, our bodies slowly gliding past each other. My arm circled her lower back, and I pulled her into me, making her arch her back farther, stick out her ass. My other hand covered both of her ass cheeks, gripping them together in a single grasp because she was the size of a twig compared to me.

Her arms hooked around my shoulders, and she brought herself closer, our faces just centimeters apart, her hips giving long and exaggerated rocks to take my dick at this pronounced angle.

I rested the back of my head against the bed as I looked into those soft eyes, saw the moisture glimmer on her eyelids, saw a woman so satisfied but still so desperate. This was how I wanted to come, nice and slow, looking into her gorgeous features as I filled her with a final load. I breathed a little harder, a little deeper, and clenched my jaw as I felt the momentum approach.

She started to moan when she felt it coming, when she felt my dick harden just a little bit more because it released.

I pulled her down as far as she could go while I gave it to her.

She moaned louder, like my come inside her made her want to come too. She loved taking my loads, loved feeling me inside her, loved feeling it drip between her thighs.

"You like that, chérie?" I asked with a grunt.

Her arms circled my neck harder, and she released a quiet moan. "Yes."

I finished with a moan and continued to stare at her. My dick slowly softened, but I didn't move her off me. I didn't wait for her to move because I didn't want her to leave. I wanted to stay this way...just like this.

She stayed in place, her pussy not wanting to release the best dick she'd ever had.

I was a man of my word—and I proved that a million times over.

She dropped her gaze and ran her hand down my chest. When the heat passed, the glaze over her eyes faded away, and reality slowly came back to her like a slow fog rolling in over the mountains and into the valley. Her eyes watched her hand, watched it press against the solid wall that guarded my heart.

"I leave in two days."

Her chin lifted again, her eyes looking into mine with a kaleidoscope of emotions. Surprise, fear, disappointment...all of it. Whether she would admit it to herself or not, she was attached to me. A woman didn't fuck like that unless she was.

"Come with me." Her answer had always been no. This time, it would be yes. Without me here, her fireplace would still be lit every afternoon. Her dinner would still be the best in the camp. The men still wouldn't look at her. But she wouldn't have me. She wouldn't have this. And this was just the beginning.

Her hand slowly dragged down my chest, and her eyes fell to my chin. A stretch of time passed, a silence that amplified the sound of the fire. Then her beautiful, light voice spoke. "I can't..." She got off me and reached for her clothes.

I remained on the floor, staring at the place where her face had been just a second before. My jaw clenched in irritation. The muscles of my arms twitched. A silent outburst took place inside my chest, a roar that never left my throat. There was nothing that money and violence couldn't buy for me.

Except Melanie.

I left the bed and pulled on my clothes without looking at her.

She sat at the edge of the bed, uncertain like she was the first time I'd come to her cabin. Like we hadn't just spent the night together in a passion that made the fire in the hearth look tame. I stood in front of her, in my boots and jacket, ready to depart. "Chérie." A strong temptation to force her overcame me, but I beat it back. I thought our passion would be enough to sway her decision, to leave her sister behind and be the woman in my bed every night. If that wasn't enough, what would be? "There's nothing you can do for her."

She turned her gaze to the fire. "It's not about what I can do for her. I just can't imagine not seeing her face every day, even if it's from across the clearing, even if it's in the snow. If you had a sister or a brother, you would understand."

My eyes drilled into her face, watching her watch the fire, her cheeks still flushed because of what we'd done for the last few hours. Her blue eyes had this unique brightness whenever she looked at the fire. It was never replicated in the clearing when the sun was shining, when I stared at her from the window of my cabin. For a brief moment, my anger was quieted. But then a horrible memory came to me, a winter night with rain on the streets, the echo of a gunshot from a silenced pistol. Beds turned into graves. Home turned into a homicide scene. There was only one soul I could save—and it nearly cost me my own.

She looked at me again, her entire body tightening like she knew she'd said the wrong thing. Her eyes shifted back and forth quickly as she looked into mine.

I turned to the door.

"Fender?"

I shut the door and locked it.

Her voice came through the door. "Fender, wait..."

I ignored her and left.

SEVEN

BLIZZARD'S WHISPERS

MELANIE

I'd never met a man who could be so furious without raising his voice.

Without saying a single word.

It was something I'd said. Was it my refusal to leave with him? That was the most obvious explanation, but it seemed like my comment about having siblings triggered him more.

I would never know.

When I worked in the clearing the next morning, I expected Fender to walk by on his departure, but he never did. He was supposed to leave tomorrow, but maybe he would just leave now. It seemed like he'd gone a different route—just to avoid me. My eyes were down on my work, lost in the memories of the two of us together, hot and sweaty, saturating my sheets with the scent of sex.

A part of me felt dirty for what I'd done.

How could I sleep with the man who ran this camp?

But more importantly—how could I like it?

A cloud of guilt rose up inside me. I looked across the clearing at my sister, her voice in my head. *Melanie, what the hell are you thinking? How could you sleep with him? What the fuck is wrong with you?* I knew exactly how that conversation would go without even having it.

But when he returned, I knew it would happen again.

And again.

Whenever we were together, it was easy to forget the context of the situation. Maybe he was just a phenomenal lover, maybe Frenchmen fucked like they were making love, and made love like they fucked. But it felt like more than that, at least to me. I'd never gotten so lost in a man that I forgot reality. I'd never been so satisfied and desperate for more at the same time. In the breaks in between, I wanted to curl up and sit right inside that expansive chest, like it was the safest place in the world. His strong body looked bulletproof. If someone shot him with a machine gun, the bullets would ricochet right off him.

"One of you has stolen from us." The executioner's booming voice echoed in the clearing.

I dropped the bag of coke I was holding. It hit the table and tipped over, powder spilling out.

The executioner looked right at Raven. "If anyone knows anything about this, come forward. You'll be rewarded."

My eyes shifted to Raven, seeing the same stoic expression she always wore, her poker face. But I saw what others couldn't see from a lifetime of experience. *Raven... what have you done?*

The executioner walked forward. "Every cabin will be searched. When we find what belongs to us, you'll hang." He departed the clearing, but no one got back to work right away. The girls all looked at one another, like the accomplice was right beside them.

My eyes stayed on Raven.

Then she looked at me.

That look told me everything I needed to know.

RAVEN WAS STILL at the clearing throughout the day, and the executioner didn't mention the stolen items.

I had no idea how she managed to pull it off—but she did.

That told me our escape was imminent. Any moment, it could happen.

Fender didn't come to me again, even if he was still in the camp, and that told me he was truly pissed off by what I had said.

Was it over?

For good?

There was a twinge of pain in my chest, and that made me hate myself more.

The lock clicked, and then the door opened.

Fender stepped inside in his typical attire, and his expression was as hard as ice frozen solid. His jawline was covered in thick facial hair like he'd stopped shaving the last time he saw me. It gave him a wilder look, like he was part grizzly. The clothes didn't come off, he didn't take a seat, and he seemed to have no intention of staying. "I'm leaving."

"But it's dark outside—"

"Change your mind." With an unblinking gaze, he stared me down like an enemy rather than a lover.

My heart was split in two because of my conflict. Raven was about to run for it, and let's be real, I wouldn't be able to help her odds. If she died, I'd die too. I may as well take Fender's offer. He promised me a beautiful life, but that wasn't the only reason I wanted to go.

He was the reason I wanted to go.

All I did was give a subtle shake of my head.

His eyes hardened deeper than they ever had.

Even though we'd probably die out there, I'd rather die with her than leave her behind. "How long will you—"

He left. The door locked, and his footsteps faded.

I closed my eyes and hated myself for wishing I could go with him. I hated myself for missing him. I hated myself for the fact that there was even a choice, two things I wanted at the same time.

I looked at the fire and took a breath, unsure what would happen in the next few days or weeks. Whether I'd be alive. Whether I'd be dead. Whether I'd be free—

A knock sounded on the door.

No one ever knocked.

My neck actually ached because I turned my head so quickly. "Raven?"

"Shh." Raven's hushed voice was on the other side.

Oh. My. God.

I rushed to the door.

"Come on, don't be a bastard right now..." She used some kind of tool to pick at the lock. A click sounded, and the lock came free. "Oh, thank god." She opened it and looked at me, a bow slung over her back with a pack, two flashlights in her hands, her hair pulled back. She was ready to take on the wilds, to leave this camp and run to her freedom...or death.

"Oh my fucking god." I couldn't believe my sister had managed to accomplish all this, and while I was terrified in that moment, I was also proud. I was proud that she never gave up. Ever.

Raven kept her voice low even though she was inside the cabin with the door closed. "We've got to go. Got to get a head start before the storm hits."

"I..." I looked around my cabin, feeling the hesitation like chains on my ankles. If I stayed there, I would be warm and comfortable. Fender would come back and take me with him. I wouldn't be out there in the snow with nearly no chance to survive. And if we got caught, Raven would be killed, and I... I wasn't sure what would happen to me. There were a million reasons to stay put. But my love for my sister was a stronger reason than all those other ones.

"I'm not sure if this will make you feel better or not, but I'm scared too." She didn't look scared, not when she was decked out for the wilderness, not when she broke in to my cabin just minutes after Fender left.

My eyes shifted back and forth as I looked into hers.

She pulled the flashlight out of her pocket and placed it in mine, along with a bottle of water and a plastic bag of nuts. "We can do this."

"Did you get a horse?"

She shook her head. "It's bolted."

"How far can we get on foot?" I whispered even though no one was around.

"We just have to hide from them. They'll eventually give up, and we can take our time."

"Raven, we won't survive long enough to take our time—"

"I'm going. Are you coming with me or not?"

I hesitated again.

"Don't make me leave you here...but I will." It wasn't a bluff. If there was a chance of freedom, she would take it even if I wouldn't. I watched her look at me like she assumed my answer would be no, like I wouldn't be brave enough to do this.

I would never be brave. Not in my nature. But she made me brave. "Alright." I put on my boots, pulled on my jacket, and then opened my drawers to stuff my pockets with the extra food I had, since Fender gave me everything I could possibly want. I had extra water, so I took that too. "Okay...let's go."

Raven wrapped her arms around me and hugged me for the first time since Paris, giving me that maternal warmth, giving me love that I didn't deserve. She squeezed me tightly. "We're gonna make it."

I clutched her harder and felt my eyes water. All I could do was nod.

"Let's go home."

THIS WAS A MISTAKE.

The snow slapped our faces in the wind. It was so dark we couldn't see our noses. My lips instantly cracked because it was so cold and dry. We continued to move forward, but we had no idea where we were going. Raven pretended to know, but I knew it was a lie. She would fake it until she made it.

She'd always been that way.

The snow was different from the mounds that arrived in the camp after a storm. It was as tall as we were sometimes, and we had to push through it and hope we wouldn't suffocate. Our flashlights were practically useless. Clouds covered the starlight because we were in the middle of a blizzard.

A fucking blizzard.

But Raven said it was our best chance because they wouldn't be able to find our tracks.

They wouldn't be able to find our bodies either.

"Raven, we have to go back—"

"We aren't going to die." She screamed into the wind so I could hear her. "And even if we do, we'd die if we went back anyway."

"Not if they don't know we've left—"

"I'd rather die out here than die there." She kept going, pushing through the snow, trying to conquer the unconquerable.

———

IT WAS impossible to gauge the passage of time.

We seemed to be out there for days, but the sun never came up. Minutes felt like hours. We were moving so slowly that I doubted we were gaining much ground. When they realized we were missing, they would catch up to us in an hour. "We shouldn't have done this..." I faltered behind her because I didn't have the strength or the grit to keep up.

"We're going to make it, Melanie."

"We're going to die, and you know it!"

She turned back to look at me, her hair blowing everywhere in the wind, but she still wore that ruthless expression. She wouldn't admit defeat, even as she experienced the final beat of her heart. Her eyes flicked past me, and her face changed.

I followed her look.

Torches.

"Fuck." She grabbed my arm and tugged me. "Come on!"

We moved as quickly as we could across the field of endless snow, waist-deep. Our flashlights were turned off so they wouldn't see us, so we blindly pushed through the snow, getting closer to the dark outline of the trees.

We finally breached the tree line, and the snowdrifts were a little lower here since most of it was caught up in the branches above.

"Run!" Raven led the way, leaving a trail of footprints that they would see when they arrived.

I kept up as long as I could before a stitch entered my side. "Wait...I can't." I stopped and bent over, heaving for air.

"Yes, you can." Raven came back to me and tugged on my arm. "Come on, Melanie."

I pushed her hand off and breathed through the pain in my waist. I'd never been athletic, never been one for a hike, barely went to the gym. I was a couch potato, and now I was out in the middle of nowhere, in a fucking blizzard, and she acted like I was weak.

I knew we would be captured. I knew we would be taken back to the camp. Fender would probably protect me, but she would be hanged. She would be stabbed until her guts spilled onto the ground and stained the snow. The image brought me to tears. "I'm so sorry—"

"We don't have time for this." She flashed me an angry look, immune to my tears.

"Raven." I wiped them away and straightened. I couldn't die without earning her forgiveness. Or worse, I couldn't survive if she didn't...and carry that for the rest of my life. "I just—"

"We need to keep moving." She grabbed my wrist and yanked me, forcing me up and forward.

I yanked my hand away, heartbroken and angry. "You're never going to forgive me, are you?" We were on death's doorstep, and we both knew it. We had an hour, if we were lucky, before we were captured, and she was still so angry with me that she couldn't forgive me, not even if it was the last chance she had. That was how deep her hatred went. She'd rather die with her resentment than let it go.

She turned around, her eyes unsympathetic. "Melanie—"

"We're going to die out here." If we managed to escape the men, we'd die in the snow. If we were captured, the result was the same. "I need you to know how sorry I am." I needed her to understand it haunted me every night, every day I looked at her in the clearing, every waking moment...except when I was with Fender. He was the only thing strong enough to give my heart a break from its mental torture.

"I do know you're sorry." She still didn't have the look she gave me in the cabin, when she hugged me, when she loved me. Her expression now was packed with endless layers of resentment and pain. It was full of accusation, and even worse, shame.

I was on the verge of tears, afraid this would be the last meaningful conversation I would ever have with her. "I need you to forgive me..." My eyes watered and tears dripped, hot for just a split second before they turned ice-cold and slid down my cheeks.

Raven turned around and continued to walk away.

Leaving her answer in the wind.

EIGHT

A BROTHER'S PLEA

FENDER

Two flashlights attached to my horse lit the path to the main road.

But I could make the journey in the darkness if I needed to.

I'd done it before.

The blizzard was approaching from behind, so I was unaffected by it as long as I made it to the road before sunrise. The wind did pick up subtly, stinging the back of my neck above my collar and below my hairline.

My satellite phone rang in my pocket, the only source of communication from the camp when I was in Paris and elsewhere. I fished it out and answered it. "What?" I held it to my ear, one hand on the reins.

"Boss, two girls escaped."

My hand immediately tugged on the reins and forced my horse to a stop. There was nothing to look at except the circles from the flashlights and the darkness that surrounded them, but I stared like there was something there. "Which girls?" I already knew the answer before I asked the question.

But I needed to hear it anyway.

"The sisters."

I inhaled a deep breath of rage, the exhale coming out as steam from my nostrils. I released a loud growl into the night, loud enough to make my horse neigh and jolt in fright. I yanked on the reins and forced him to turn around, to face the wind and the blizzard that had been on our tail. I kicked my boots into the sides and urged the horse into a sprint. I screamed into the phone. "Find. Them. Now."

I SAT in the armchair in my cabin. A glass of scotch was on the table in front of me. I was in desperate need of a drink, but I was too angry to do anything other than stare. "Do you know anything about this?"

Magnus sat across from me, his hood pushed back, his brown eyes locked on my face. His brown hair was tousled from the wind, and his skin was pale white from the cold. His stare lasted a long time. "No."

I trusted no one in this world. Not a soul. Eyes were in the back of my head because I expected to be stabbed in the back by my own men. My butler had served me for years, but I kept tabs on him too. There was only one exception to that.

My brother.

So I accepted his answer without doubt. He wouldn't lie to me—especially for a woman. "How did she escape?"

His forearms rested on his knees, and he leaned forward, massaging his hands so the ice in his knuckles would thaw. "She must have taken something from the clearing to allow her to pick locks. The doorknobs aren't busted."

"She's the one who took the bow and arrow." That fucking cunt was sneaking around in my camp, right under my fucking nose, making a fool out of me.

"We searched her cabin and found nothing."

I clenched my jaw as I thought about Melanie. She couldn't be forced to leave her cabin. She went willingly. She went out into a fucking blizzard with her dumb-ass sister to get away from me.

When I asked her to come with me, she said no.

Did she say no because they had planned this?

I stared at nothing as I waited for news. The men had been sent out with horses and hounds, and they would find them—dead or alive.

Magnus bowed his head and continued to rub his palms together.

The door opened. "They've returned." Alix stood in the doorway, his face hidden.

"Dead or alive?" I was on my feet instantly, already moving for the door.

"Alive." Alix stepped aside.

Before I got to the door, I turned to Magnus. "You. Stay." I spoke to him like a dog because that cunt had turned him into a dog for pussy.

His eyes shifted back and forth as he looked at me, his face indifferent but his panicked eyes giving him away.

"You don't want to watch your whore hang, right?" I turned away and listened to Alix close the door behind me. I marched through the snow and approached the clearing, desperate to hang that bitch who dared to mock me. No one escaped this camp—and I would prove that now. I wouldn't let my brother's interference change her fate, not this time.

The girls were pinned to the cold ground, their wrists bound behind their backs.

I approached Melanie on the ground, her cheek against the snow with her eyes on her sister. My boots thudded against the earth then I stopped directly beside her. She could sense me before she even looked at me. It was obvious by the change in her breathing. She was scared... and she should be scared.

"We'll hang the other girl first." One guard gave a gentle kick to Melanie's foot. "And make this one watch."

"No!" Raven sobbed. "Please..."

I almost didn't speak because her tears brought me some satisfaction. "Just this one." My eyes burned into Raven's face, her round face, her plain lips, her plain everything. It was hard to believe the two of them were related because she was a fucking hag compared to Melanie.

Raven's eyes shifted to mine, and the hatred in her gaze was volcanic. She writhed on the ground like she'd do anything to break free of her ropes and lunge at me. "Don't fucking touch her!" Her screams were mixed with angry tears, and she yanked so hard on her wrists that she rubbed red marks on the surface of her skin. "You motherfucker!"

One of the guys kicked her hard and made her gasp for air.

I'd love to do that myself—but I had more important shit to do.

I kneeled and placed my hand to Melanie's cheek. My eyes bored into hers, sharing an entire conversation with her with just my look. It was one of those rare times when I was so angry, I was actually speechless. My look said it all.

She breathed harder because she knew.

"Get her up." I rose to my feet and watched my guards yank her to her feet.

I grabbed both of her wrists and yanked her into me, her back hitting my chest, and I leaned over her slightly, looking down at her, my lips near her ear. I'd never manhandled her like this—but she'd forfeited her rights tonight. "You trying to leave me, sweetheart?" I squeezed her wrists hard before I released her. "I'll take you with me tomorrow, then. Take her to the cabin."

The guards took her away.

She fought the whole way. "Raven!" She dragged her feet and sobbed, looking at her sister on the ground, knowing it was the last time she would see her in this life. "No! Please! Please don't do this." She was dragged away against her will, pulled across the snow, her cries becoming quiet when she was far enough away.

Melanie could beg all she wanted, but I wouldn't spare her sister—not after this.

When she was gone, I moved to Raven, my boots close to her face. "Congratulations." I kneeled and got a closer look at her, seeing dull eyes that didn't sparkle like Melanie's, seeing nothing appealing whatsoever. Disobedient. Opinionated. Annoying. Fucking pain in the ass. Not the least bit attractive. "You've made it farther than anyone. I hope it was worth it...but I imagine it wasn't." I nodded to the men.

They pulled her to her feet.

The executioner approached her, ready to take over and do the dirty work. "I'm really going to enjoy this." He slammed his fist into her chest and knocked her back to the ground—where she belonged.

I turned away to head to the cabin where Melanie was waiting for me.

"Up." The executioner continued his taunts. "I said up, bitch."

But I halted in my tracks when I saw someone approach.

Magnus.

He'd disobeyed my order and come here anyway.

His eyes locked to mine as he spoke. "We aren't hanging her." He held on to my look of fury with his own, silently making a stand that would result in his death if he were anyone else.

The executioner turned to Magnus. "Not this time."

He broke contact with me and walked over to the executioner. "She's the strongest worker we have—"

"No." The executioner stepped toward him. "She stole from us. She tried to escape. She killed two of our own. How dare you stand there and ask for her to be pardoned." The other guards stayed back, watching the two of them stare each other down.

I stayed silent, watching the scene play out, floored that Magnus stuck out his neck for her—again. It made him weak. It brought the two of us shame, and he knew that, but he fucking did it anyway.

"I'm not asking for her to be pardoned. She should be punished."

The Executioner stepped closer to him. "She deserves to be executed. Your dick is not part of this discussion."

Magnus hadn't blinked once. "She'll be whipped."

"No." The executioner turned back to grab her. "You can't save her this time." He snatched her by the back of the hair and yanked on her scalp as he forced her to her feet so the noose could be wrapped around her neck.

Helpless, Magnus just watched.

Then he turned around and looked at me.

I didn't say a word because I didn't need to. My answer was on the wind, in the air we breathed, as obvious as the darkness that surrounded us. It burned white-hot like the torches that flickered around the clearing.

But he continued to stare anyway, silently begging me.

No. I would not lose the respect of my men by sparing her. I wouldn't do it for Melanie. I wouldn't do it for him. Raven had already evaded one Red Snow. She stole from us. She ran from the camp. Some of my men were killed because of her foolishness. *I do not negotiate.*

Magnus took a breath before he stepped closer to me, so we could converse without being overheard. They prepared Raven for her execution behind him. His eyes burned into mine with a desperate intensity that I'd never seen before. "Fender, a whipping will suffice—"

"No. Your request insults me."

He took another deep breath, pathetic and frantic.

"You're asking me to humiliate myself in front of my men —for *her*." I glanced at her behind him, showing all of my disgust for that bitch that had been the bane of my existence. If she weren't in the camp, Melanie would have agreed to come back with me a long time ago.

Magnus held his silence.

That had better be the end of it.

But it wasn't. "Please..." He made his voice louder, so people could hear him beg, so the men would know he was the weak one, not me. He threw himself on his own sword, humiliated himself...for her.

My respect for him just dropped by half.

I turned to the executioner and gave a sight nod.

The executioner gave a loud sign in pure frustration, but he obeyed.

I gave Magnus a final look of disappointment before I walked away.

NINE

THE COLDEST FIRE

MELANIE

I sat on my bed, the fire gone because it'd burned out in the hours after I'd left with Raven. My chest convulsed with sobs, so grief-stricken I couldn't take a sip of water or a bite of food. My body was frozen solid and a hot shower would be perfect for thawing, but all I cared about was Raven.

She was probably dead by now.

When I went to the clearing tomorrow, I would see her blood on the ground.

I would see her lifeless body... just hanging there.

"No..." I clutched my stomach as the sobs physically pained me.

Heavy boots sounded outside the door, the lock turned, and then Fender stepped inside.

I immediately went still, my sobs stuck in my throat.

He shut the door behind him and stood over me.

Livid. Psychotic. Maniacal.

Just a look was far scarier than anything he could actually say.

He came closer.

I instinctively backed up.

"You're afraid of me."

I started to breathe hard again.

"Good." He went to the armchair, but instead of plopping down into it, he carried it to my bedside and took a seat. Right across from me. His dark eyes were colder than the blizzard raging outside. We went back in time to our first interaction, and I was even more scared now than I was then. "You're leaving with me tomorrow. You don't get a choice. You forfeited that luxury when you betrayed me."

It was too intense to look at him, so I dropped my gaze.

"Look. At. Me."

I immediately obeyed, my eyes still watering in grief. "I... I didn't betray you—"

"Did I say you could speak?"

Now I realized just how well he used to treat me. He'd never been this callous, even when I rejected his advances or told him no when he expected to hear yes.

"You ran off into a blizzard with no chance of survival." His voice rose slowly, climbing like a spark growing into a flame. "You could have broken through ice and felt your heart stop from shock before you even had a chance to drown. You could have been attacked by wolves, your flesh ripped off your face piece by piece. You could have fallen into a crevasse of snow and suffocated. You could have done any of these things—and I wouldn't have been able to save you. That's betrayal."

I breathed hard as I stared, not expecting that to be the reason for his wrath.

His eyes narrowed. "You would rather die out there than be with me?"

I shook my head. "I...I didn't want my sister to be alone. I didn't want her to die alone—"

"So, you wanted to die with her?" he snapped, his voice growing louder.

"Do...do you have a brother?"

His eyes narrowed in a way they never had before. "Yes."

"Then wouldn't you rather die with him...than leave him to die alone?"

He processed that question for a long time. A really long time. With his unblinking gaze, he stared at me endlessly, like he could read the words written across my eyes, found something new to look at as the seconds passed.

He rose from the chair. "We leave in the morning." He left the chair where it was and moved to the door.

I started to sob again, knowing Raven was out there, dead.

He opened the door then turned back to me. "Your sister will live."

I gave an involuntary gasp, and new tears flushed my eyes. "Thank you...thank you so much—"

"Thank Magnus. If it were up to me, she would have hung." He shut the door, locked it, and left. He didn't make a fire for me like he usually would. He let me sit in the cold and the dark...like I deserved it.

ONCE I KNEW my sister was okay, the tremors and tears stopped. I took a hot shower to thaw my fingers, to get the dirt out of my hair that had been transferred from the snow. My clothes were dropped on the floor, and I slept in my bed naked. I didn't even need a fire because the inside of the cabin was still considerably warmer than the blizzard outside. The wind made the windows rattle, waking me sometimes because it was like a witch shrieking right next to my ear.

By morning, it was over.

Silence.

I sat up in bed, the sunlight coming through the windows because it was a clear day now that the snow clouds were gone. Last night felt like a bad dream, a cold nightmare. My lips were still dry because the moisture had been sucked out of my skin by a sponge made of ice. I barely moved my legs and felt my muscles resist because they were sore.

The lock turned in the door.

I tugged the sheets to my chest even though it was just Fender, and there was no reason to worry about modesty with him.

But it was a guard with my breakfast.

When he realized I was naked in bed, he stilled, like he shouldn't be there. He didn't even bring the tray to the bed like usual. He left it on the armchair by the front door and hurried out. "Boss said be ready in thirty minutes."

DRESSED IN MY WORK ATTIRE, I sat at the edge of the bed next to my empty tray.

Several pairs of boots thudded against the wood. The door was unlocked and opened. The two men there took their usual posts on either side of my door.

And then Fender made his entrance.

Dressed in all black, his eyes matching, he stared me down. His muscular arms hung by his sides, the veins visible on the backs of his hands and along his neck. The rest of him was covered.

His anger hadn't faded after a good night of sleep.

He actually seemed angrier.

Wordlessly, he turned around to depart, expecting me to follow him.

"Fender." I approached the front door and looked outside, the sunlight making my eyes squint and water.

He pivoted slightly toward me but didn't completely turn around. He could only see me in his peripheral vision.

"Can I say goodbye—"

"No." He continued forward.

I ignored the men on either side of the door and caught up to Fender. "Please. What if I never see her again—"

He spun around and gave me a look that was the gateway to the underworld. Eternal flames burned, the threat unmistakable. "I allowed her to live, and you dare ask me for more?" He took a step closer to me, an audible crunch of his boot against the snow. "After what you've done to me, you dare ask me for anything else?"

I instinctively stepped back, my nostrils exhaling the moisture from my lungs. His eyes seared mine, so I dropped my chin and looked away. The contact was too painful, too blazing hot. It was like looking directly at the sun.

He took the lead, walking ahead of me, his two men positioned on either side of me from behind. In a perfect triangle, we walked, moving through the camp, past the clearing. Blood wasn't visible under the noose because none had been spilled last night. The girls weren't at the benches yet because they were still getting ready for the day. I should only feel relief that I was departing this place forever, but since a part of my heart was still there, it was like leaving home.

Because my sister was home.

We moved to the front of the camp where I'd arrived all those weeks ago. A black horse was there, saddled and ready to go. Fender climbed on then looked down at me.

I just stood there. "I...I've never ridden a horse."

He stared down at me for a couple seconds, his hostile look exactly the same, and then he climbed back down. "Left foot here." He tapped the metal opening where it was supposed to slide in. "Grip the horn." He instructed me by putting my left hand on the horn of the saddle and my right on the back of the saddle. "Swing your leg over. Go." He gripped my hips and lifted me, guiding me up like a father putting his daughter on a pony at the fair.

Now, I was on top of the horse, having a clearer view of the camp because I was so tall.

Fender guided me to the back of the saddle then climbed in front of me. He took the reins of the horse in one hand. "Hold on." He dug his heels into the sides of the horse, and we took off at a run.

"Oh my god." I squeezed him hard and pressed my cheek into his back, holding on for dear life. "Can you slow down?"

"No. I'm late—because of you."

AFTER A LONG RIDE, we made it to a main road.

There were men there ready to take the horse into a stable to rest. There were also cars tucked inside a wooden structure covered with ivy and bushes. On the left were two expensive sports cars. The rest were work trucks and cars I used to see on the road every day.

Gray like rain clouds, the car Fender chose was sleek and curvy, a type of car I'd never seen before. I didn't even know what kind it was. We got into the seats, and he started a powerful engine that was like a small explosion in the beginning before it faded into a gentle purr. He turned on the radio, carefully backed out until he made it to the main road, and then floored it.

It was like riding the horse all over again.

Fender took the road hard, pushing the car to a speed that would kill us instantly if he lost control of the wheel.

My arms covered my chest, and I disappeared into the seat, watching the world fly past us so quickly, it was just a blur. The trees, the grass, the sky, it was all a streak of color. "You might get pulled over..." If I asked him to slow down, he wouldn't, even if I was scared.

He glanced at me, one hand on the wheel while the other relaxed on the center console. He gave that slight smile, like he knew something I didn't, and then focused on the road again.

HOURS LATER, we were in Paris.

I couldn't believe it.

My visit had been short, but the beauty had been so profound, the culture potent, the food exquisite, that it felt like home now. It was the last time I was normal—so it held a special place in my heart.

There wasn't snow on the ground here, but a light rain dotted the front windshield. People walked on the sidewalks with umbrellas over their heads, a hot coffee usually in their other hand. We took a bunch of smaller streets and maneuvered around roundabouts until we headed away from Paris, into the countryside, into a landscape as beautiful as the city—just in a different way.

Then we approached tall, iron gates that immediately opened as we got closer. Armed men were on the inside, and they stepped aside when they recognized Fender's car. The view of the property had been obstructed by high walls made of stone, green ivy growing over the surface with resilient white flowers drinking the drops of rain.

A long road wrapped around the property and approached a three-story palace.

Palace might not be the right word, but that was how it looked to me.

A pond was in the center with a fountain, and large lily pads floated over the surface, raindrops making indentations in the smooth water like bullet holes. Fender slowed down as we took the car around the pond and approached the grand front entrance to his home.

Was home even the right word?

He brought the car to a stop but left the engine on.

I looked through the raindrops on my passenger window and saw a man standing underneath the front portico in a tuxedo. Another man in a suit immediately went around the front of the car as Fender went around the back, like he was the valet. I opened the door and stepped into the rain, my hair immediately losing volume from the moisture on my scalp. I walked up the stone steps and underneath the portico roof, approaching the man in the tuxedo.

He gave a slight bow. *"C'est merveilleux de vous revoir, Sire."*

Uh...what?

Fender barely gave him a glance over before he nodded to me. "English. Melanie doesn't speak French."

The butler turned to look at me, and his greeting was not warm or kind. He pressed his lips tightly together and looked at me like a wet cat that had shown up on his doorstep. He sucked on the inside of his lip before he met my gaze again. "I see."

Fender stepped through the grand doorway. "She's the lady of the house. Service her the way you service me." He disappeared farther into the house until he was gone from view.

I stayed outside like I needed approval from his butler to step inside.

Based on the look he gave me, I wouldn't get that anytime soon.

He crossed his arms over his chest and rested two fingers against his temple. Like he had a migraine, he gave a long and drawn-out sigh. "His Highness did not tell me he was bringing a guest. I'm quite unprepared for—" he pointed down at my clothing "—*this.*"

I dropped my gaze, feeling embarrassed by my appearance. I'd gotten used to it during the course of my captivity and didn't think twice about it. But out here in the real world, I really did appear homeless. Wasn't sure what Fender's fascination was if his butler didn't even want me in the house. "You want me to take off my shoes?"

He gave a nod. "That's a good start, yes." He stood there and watched me remove my muddy boots, pure disgust on his face. "We need to get you some clothes..." He released another annoyed sigh. "Immediately."

GILBERT ESCORTED me to my bedroom on the second floor.

But it wasn't really a bedroom as much as private quarters. A four-poster bed made of gold was against the wall, with a blush-pink duvet and ivory sheets. A mass of decorated pillows were on top, and a nightstand was on either side, matching the bed. Curtains of the same material as the duvet covered the windows, and floral wallpaper was on the walls. A private living room had a tea set on the coffee table, which didn't have a speck of dust even though Gilbert hadn't expected me to occupy this room. There was a TV, a shelf of old books, and a grand bathroom with a bathtub the size of a small swimming pool.

"Undress and shower. I will dispose of your clothes."

I turned to look at him, not even having enough time to absorb this unbelievable room, a space suited for French royalty.

Gilbert continued to stand there, his arms behind his back, staring at me expectantly.

I waited for him to leave.

"Please." He nodded to me.

"You...you want me to undress right now...in front of you?"

"Yes. I want to get those...I don't even want to call them clothes...out of this estate as quickly as possible. It's insulting to the history in these walls just to have them here. And I'm not buying what you're selling, Melanie... even if I didn't prefer men for my lovers."

I did as he asked and stripped down until I was completely naked.

He took it a step further and actually put on gloves before he rushed them out of the room, muttering in French. "Disgusting...absolutely disgusting."

———

IT WAS the first time I'd showered with real hair products, high-end stuff I hadn't even heard of. I scrubbed myself down, shaved everything, massaged my scalp with the quality shampoo, and let the camp rinse off my body.

When I dried my hair, there was an assortment of brushes and hair products available, prepped for any guest who might stay. But I couldn't imagine Fender having a guest...unless it was a woman, and she would probably have her own clothes.

For the first time, I was actually able to style my hair, give myself a blowout, get the shine back into my strands. My face was free of makeup, but I actually could see a glimmer of my old self in the reflection. I stared for a while, my thoughts immediately going back to what I'd left behind.

I hoped she was okay.

I stepped back into the bedroom and found clothes on the bed. Gray sweatpants and a black t-shirt were there, big enough to make a poncho for a horse, so I assumed they belonged to Fender. I put them on and had to tighten the drawstring and make a double knot just to keep them up. The shirt was more like a blanket.

But it felt like heaven against my skin, because it was the first time I was able to feel clean cotton against my skin. Our work clothes were only washed once in a while, so it was rare to feel a shirt against my skin that felt this weightless, that smelled like nothing except the faint hint of soap.

I took a seat on the edge of the bed, unsure what else to do with myself. Leaving the room didn't even cross my mind because I hadn't been allowed to vacate mine at the camp, ever. The door was always locked.

But my bedroom door was actually open, and I could see the hallway.

I still didn't move.

I wondered where Fender was. Would he come to talk to me soon? Or would he ignore me for a while because he was still angry with me?

Voices sounded from down the hallway, Gilbert's French-accented words loud and booming. "Thank you for coming on such short notice. Most gracious."

A woman's deep voice responded. "When Fender calls, we come."

Gilbert stepped into the room first. "Melanie, come here. Stand straight."

I hopped off the bed and approached them.

The woman walked in with a younger man behind her, who held a clipboard and a pen. She looked at me the exact same way Gilbert did, visibly disturbed by my appearance, which was saying something because I looked a lot better than I had earlier. She turned to stare at Gilbert, as if this was some kind of mistake.

Gilbert shook his head.

She rubbed her hand absent-mindedly into her chest as she looked at me. "Oh dear..."

I stood there, humiliated once more.

She pulled out a measuring tape from her pocket and wrapped it around my waist, taking a series of measurements. "We'll need everything, Pierre. The full makeover."

Pierre started to take notes. "Already on it."

I SPENT the day in my room, sitting on the terrace and admiring the grounds of his estate. There were always a dozen men down by the front entrance, guarding the premises with guns. The lawns and grounds were immaculate, with freshly trimmed bushes and beautiful flowers, bright even in the coldness of winter. It was like a watercolor painting.

When the sun set, it turned frigidly cold, so I returned to my bedroom.

Gilbert knocked on the door before he entered with a silver tray. Without looking at me, he carried it to the small dining table in the living room and set it down. He poured a hot cup of tea from the teapot and removed the silver lid over the plate.

I walked over to take a look.

It was fresh pasta with red sauce, an entire loaf of bread, and a side of cookies. The smell hit my nose with a burst, and it was the best-smelling thing I'd inhaled in a long time. "That looks really good."

As if that was all Gilbert had been waiting for, a compliment, he departed.

"Gilbert?"

He turned back around, his hands behind his back, standing tall, straight, and proud. His nose was slightly upturned, like I was still beneath him even though he was the butler. "Yes, Melanie?"

"I'd like to see Fender." We'd arrived that morning, and I hadn't heard from him. I imagined he had been served the exact same dinner just minutes before mine.

"Absolutely not." He shook his head. "He's very busy with work. Can't be disturbed."

I felt like I was still in the camp, only able to see him when he wanted to see me. "Could you tell him I'd like to see him?"

"I can pass along the message, but as I said, he's very busy. You can expect to hear from him tomorrow." He gave a slight bow before he took his leave. "Place your tray outside the door when you're finished."

He departed and left me alone.

I was in a palace now, surrounded by luxury and gourmet food, but it felt the same as the camp.

Like nothing had changed except the one thing I didn't want to change.

Seeing my sister.

THE NEXT MORNING, I had barely finished my breakfast when Gilbert stepped through the open door. "Put everything in the closet. Makeup in the bathroom."

I left the living room to see what the commotion was.

A dozen people, all finely dressed, entered my bedroom, carrying designer clothes and heels, placing them in my empty walk-in closet. Another group of people entered my bathroom, setting up makeup stations and an array of skin care products.

One woman walked up to me, carrying a couple makeup brushes in her hands. Her eyes absorbed my face, like she was dolling me up without even touching me. "Let's take a seat. I'm going to teach you how to do your makeup."

"Oh...I already know how—"

"No, she doesn't," Gilbert interjected. "Please show her."

I was placed in the chair in front of my vanity in the bathroom while the makeup artist placed all of her supplies in front of her. "Always put a primer on your skin. It's sunscreen, and the number one enemy of your skin is sun exposure." She talked me through everything, from concealer and then powder, the brushes to use when blending eye shadow, how to create the perfect lip liner around the mouth to give my lips a fuller appearance. It took her an hour to explain everything to me, to go through each step.

I recognized all the brands of makeup on my vanity, all items I could never afford in a million years. I used to get my makeup at any walk-in retailer because I didn't wear a ton of it in the first place. Now I was getting a personal tutorial from a woman who knew what she was doing, judging by how beautiful she looked.

Another girl did my hair, curling my strands into spirals before brushing it out, adding more product to give it that bounce and shine. Over the course of an hour, my appearance was transformed until I could barely recognize myself. I'd been looking at my plain face at the camp for so long, my eyes washed out without eyeliner or mascara, my lips blending into my cheeks because they were cold and lifeless.

"What do you think?" She smiled at me in the mirror, like she knew she'd created a masterpiece.

"I...I barely recognize myself."

"Couldn't agree more," Gilbert said as he walked by, holding a pink dress in his hands.

"But yeah, it's lovely." I'd never felt prettier, never felt cleaner, never felt...more privileged. I looked like those models on social media, on the cover of magazines at doctor's offices. People had always said I was the pretty sister, but I never saw the difference between us the way other people did. But with my makeup like this, I really did look far more beautiful than I ever had.

"Put this on." Gilbert held up the dress behind me.

"Am I going somewhere?" That looked like a dress for a special occasion.

Gilbert's eyes narrowed as if I'd said the wrong thing. "A lady is always dressed to go somewhere, even if she has nowhere to go. Now, up."

I left the chair and moved to the center of the bathroom. "Can I get dressed alone this time?"

"Yes. But we want to see." Gilbert waved everyone to the door. "Everyone out."

They filed out, and I shed Fender's clothes before I put on the pink dress. It had subtle designs inside the material, indistinct florals that gave the dress texture but not an obvious pattern. It was sleeveless and tight over my stomach before it flared out slightly. It'd been altered to my measurements perfectly, and with my hair and makeup done this way, I looked like I'd stepped into a completely new life.

I looked like a...countess or something.

"We're coming in." Gilbert opened the door and came first, looking me up and down with that critical eye. Then he raised his hands in celebration. "We did it, ladies and gentlemen. Look at her." He flipped his finger in the air. "Spin. Now."

Awkwardly, I turned in a circle.

He gave me a look of approval as he crossed his arms over his chest. "Miracles do exist..."

I WAS all dolled up with nowhere to go.

Not even outside my bedroom.

I hoped Fender would come to me, but he still hadn't. I sat on the couch and looked out the window into the darkness, sitting in my pink dress, legs crossed. Diamonds were in my ears, and a sparkling necklace hung down my chest. I was lavished with the finest things in life, but it only made me feel lonelier.

At the camp, I could talk to the girls in the clearing. Fender visited me at night. Occasionally, I'd get a short conversation with Raven. But now, I was totally alone. All I had was Gilbert, who chose to spend his time ripping me apart like I wasn't good enough.

Gilbert's voice sounded from the door. "Your dinner is served." He rounded the corner then carried the tray to the dining table. It was another gourmet meal with hot tea and dessert. He lifted the silver lid to display it to me.

I barely looked at him before I gave a nod.

He stilled, visibly offended. "Is there a problem with the meal?"

"No." I looked out the window even though I couldn't see anything except the outdoor lighting on the lawn. "It's lovely, Gilbert. Thank you."

He sighed before he placed the silver lid back on top. "Then what is it, Melanie? You're unhappy with everything you've been given today? A dress that cost five thousand euros. Diamonds worth the price of a car. Makeup created by the greatest designers in this world. You're that ungrateful?"

I turned my gaze on him, feeling a kind of anger that I couldn't express. I'd just been a prisoner at a camp for weeks and weeks, survived a blizzard, had all my rights stripped away, and he acted like he was either unaware of that or didn't care. "I want to talk to Fender."

"He's unavailable."

The outburst came out of nowhere. "Why the fuck did he bring me here, then?" I flashed him an angry look. "I'm just supposed to sit around and wait for him to come fuck me? That's my life now? Because that's not what he promised when he offered to bring me here." I silently excused Gilbert by looking out the window again.

He stood there for a few more seconds before he left. "Enjoy your dinner."

I DIDN'T TOUCH my dinner.

I wasn't used to having three meals a day, so I didn't need that much food. Everything was delicious and I wanted to eat every crumb on my plate, but my stomach had shrunk during my captivity. I was thinner than I'd ever been, realizing how petite I'd become when one of the personal shoppers said I was a double zero.

I remained on the couch, sitting in the dark, when I heard the door open and close.

Gilbert didn't announce himself.

That was how I knew it wasn't Gilbert at all.

I rose from the couch and turned around.

There he was.

In black sweatpants that hung low on his hips, bare feet on the hardwood, his chest muscular and strong like the last time I saw it. He'd had dinner, but his stomach was chiseled and tight like his muscles were permanently flexed. He was like a grizzly bear, his size doubled just by his muscle mass alone. That meant he must dedicate hours to the gym every day because no one just looked like that without sacrifice. A man didn't have ripped arms the size of my head unless he pumped iron like his life depended on it. He was a behemoth because he chose to be.

The hostility in his gaze slowly evaporated the longer he stared at me, as he took in my new appearance, my curled hair, my flawless makeup, the dress that had been altered to fit me like a second skin. There was still anger behind his eyes, but it was impossible for him to hold on to when he loved the way I looked. He said I was the most beautiful woman in the world when he saw me at my worst. What did he think of me now, when I was at my best? "I'm here."

I half expected him to bend me over the couch and fuck me mercilessly. I was actually disappointed when he didn't.

He clearly wasn't interested. "Speak."

"It's been three days. How are you still mad at me—"

"Because I don't let shit go. Ever." His eyes started to turn maniacal once more.

"I chose my sister over you. That's an unforgivable offense?"

His eyes were open and cold, bringing the camp right into my bedroom.

"Fender."

"Getting yourself nearly killed is an unforgivable offense. And no, I'm not over it."

I wouldn't apologize for it. "I don't know what you expect me to say—"

"What do you want from me?" His fire rose, like I'd just drenched him with scotch.

"I..." I really didn't know what I wanted from him.

"You demanded my attention...for that?" His eyes seared me, like I'd committed a terrible sin. "My time is valuable. Don't waste it again." He turned around to depart.

"Wait."

He ignored me.

"Fender." I grabbed on to his arm. "Please."

He didn't yank it out of my grasp, but he didn't turn around either. He halted in his tracks, giving me another opportunity to speak my mind.

I rested my forehead against the back of his arm and closed my eyes, feeling his warm skin, thinking of our nights together and the comfort it brought me, even when it shouldn't. "You're all I have..."

He was still, letting me hold on to his arm, letting me rest my lips against his skin. "I'm not ready." He pulled his arm free from my grasp and walked out, leaving me alone, the shadows closing in and hiding the beautiful moldings, the fine furniture, the golden sconces, and bringing me into a dark cabin without a fire to keep me warm.

TEN
SMALL TALK

FENDER

My presence at the camp was about accountability.

The real work took place in Paris, with my men, distributors, logistics, dinners with the people I paid to look the other way. That was where my most important work happened. The only pleasure I took in the camp was the unbelievable landscape. Quiet. Isolated. Timeless. It was a place very few people had ever seen.

My week had been spent running a drug empire.

It wasn't just that I didn't want to see Melanie. I also didn't have the time. And I was unwilling to make the time after what she did.

I pulled up to the front of my estate and handed the car over to the valet before I approached the open doorway where Gilbert stood, hands behind his back, his appearance immaculate as ever despite the late hour.

"Welcome home, Your Highness." He gestured for me to step inside before he shut and bolted the door behind me. His shoes tapped against the hard floor as he followed me. "A brand-new bottle of opened scotch is in your office. The dinner I served this evening is still fresh if you'd like that as well?"

"No." I walked into the main sitting room, which I rarely used unless guests were present.

"Of course. I've also given Melanie a tour of the house and grounds. I was thinking—"

"We'll speak tomorrow." I took the stairs without looking back.

Gilbert's voice reached me from the foyer. "Of course. Have a good evening."

I made my way to the third floor and approached my bedroom door, which was open. I stepped inside and shed my clothes, tossing them on the floor for Gilbert to fetch tomorrow while I was gone. My gun was placed on the dresser, and I loosened my watch and set it next to it.

"Always be aware of your surroundings."

I didn't flinch as I pulled out my phone and set it on the dresser. A slight smile slid on to my lips as I dropped my jeans and walked across the room in my boxers. *Thinks she caught me off guard. Cute.* "What do you want?" I moved to the flask at the bar and poured myself a glass of scotch so I could take a drink before bed, get that burn in my veins so I could skip the nightmares tonight.

When she didn't answer, I looked at her, where she sat on the couch. The second Gilbert told me he gave her a tour of the house, I knew she'd be waiting for me. A week had passed, and we hadn't had any interaction.

She was in a black nightgown, her curled hair pulled over one shoulder, her makeup still on. One strap gently slipped over her smooth skin, falling to her elbow. She didn't seem to notice, her brilliant blue eyes on me, even brighter than they used to be with the dark smoke around her eyes. She was a beautiful woman naturally, without a drop of makeup to accentuate her features, but with a face full of makeup...there were no words. She looked photoshopped even though she was real. She would be the item people envied me most for. It wouldn't be the money, the power, the whores—it would be this single woman. *My woman.* "You didn't keep your promise..."

I watched the resentment in her eyes, the disappointment. A life of luxury wasn't enough—not without a critical component.

Me.

I entered the living room and lowered myself onto the couch across from her, a coffee table between us. I set the glass on the surface, my elbows resting on my thighs, leaning forward as I examined her.

"I'm alone in my room all day, have no one to talk to, your butler hates me..." She crossed her legs then wrapped her arms around her shoulders, her hands gently rubbing her skin, as if she were cold. Her eyes wandered out the window for a brief moment before they came back to me.

"He doesn't hate you."

A quiet, sarcastic chuckle escaped her lips.

"He just expects the best at all times. That's why I hired him."

Her arms went still as she gazed at me, looking me deep in the eye the way she did when we were naked and sweaty. She'd tried to run from me, but my hook was in her flesh, and she was permanently attached to me by an invisible line. Despite our differences, our ideologies, our morals, she couldn't deny the all-consuming connection between us. If that weren't the case, she wouldn't come to me at all. "This is worse than the camp. At least I could go outside..."

"You can go outside."

She released a quiet sigh then looked away.

I studied her accentuated cheekbone, her almond-shaped eyes, the way her hair shone like the snow in direct sunlight. There were evenings when I could stare at a painting for hours. She was a painting I could stare at for a lifetime. "I promised you gowns and diamonds. I promised you a butler, albeit one with attitude. I promised you gourmet meals, a palace—"

"And you promised me you." She finally spat it out, her expression tightening in a stark look of self-loathing. Her eyes immediately dropped in shame as she swallowed, her throat shifting slightly at her actions.

A small smile moved on to my lips.

She kept her eyes down for a long time. Her thick eyelashes stretched down her cheeks. Her plump lips were pressed tightly together, trying to suppress the words that had already flown out of her mouth.

"You want me, chérie?"

Her chin quickly lifted when she heard her nickname. The satin of her gown tightened and shone differently every time she took a breath, and that shine appeared more often because her breathing had quickened. The brilliance in her eyes had disappeared, and now she was vulnerable, a meal for the taking.

One of my hands enveloped the other, sheathing my knuckles. The smile was gone, my eyes ripping that dress to shreds. She was mine even when I didn't touch her. She was mine whether I was right beside her or hundreds of miles away. I'd claimed this woman as mine, and she needed to be reminded that I hadn't claimed her by force —but acceptance. "Then don't cross me again."

"I—"

"Don't. Cross. Me."

HER NIGHTGOWN WAS a small bundle over her stomach. The straps had fallen down her arms and revealed her tits, and I shoved the material over her hips when I got her on her back, my hips between her thighs, my arms pinned behind her knees. I pushed her into my sheets, fucked her hard like a whore, slamming my wooden headboard into the wall and scraping the wallpaper.

It didn't matter how hard I gave it to her. She always took it. She was always wet. She winced in pain sometimes but never complained once. Her nails anchored into my flesh and held on, making me bleed whenever she came, and the tears that streaked from her eyes to her ears made her makeup run.

She handled my size like she was paid to enjoy it. Her hand cupped my cheek, and she kissed me, tasted the sweat that dripped from my forehead to my jaw, gave me her tongue as she moaned into my mouth. The cuts on my back burned when the sweat poured in, but the pain got me off because of the woman who inflicted it.

I could have her any way I wished, but I was so eager to fuck her every time I looked at her that this always happened. I got between her legs and looked at her face as I conquered her, like I was bedding a queen after I'd killed her king—and she liked it. My eyes drank in her appearance, watched the tears streak every time she came, watched her lips tremble before the uncontrollable moans rose to my ceiling. I watched her open like a flower, drop her walls, and give me her complete vulnerability. When we were together like this, the camp didn't exist. Her sister didn't exist. We were just a man and a woman, burning in each other's fire, scarring our skin with third-degree burns that we didn't even feel in the moment.

I came inside her for the final time, my ass tightening as I shoved myself completely within her, my spine tingling when I dropped another load inside her body. Skin-to-skin with her, it felt like pleasure in its purest form, the ecstasy that could only be created when there was nothing between us.

She winced and gave a quiet cry when I forced myself deeper. There was nowhere for me to go, but I did it anyway, my dick out of my control. But she drew me into her body like my release was more important than her temporary discomfort.

I finished with my face pressed into her neck, kissing her as the last wisp of pleasure faded, as my dick softened because it'd finally had enough. I pulled out of her then rolled over, getting to my side of the bed and immediately closing my eyes.

Her breathing quieted over the next few minutes. She continued to lie there, her skin shining from my sweat, my come between her thighs and on the sheets beneath her. When her breaths became quieter and drawn-out, I knew she'd fallen asleep.

My eyes opened, and I looked at my lit bedroom, the windows a mirror because they reflected the light coming from the sconces and chandelier. A million things went through my mind—all the shit I had to do tomorrow, an email I got from Magnus right when I walked through the door. My head turned farther to look at the woman beside me, in the exact same position I'd left her, as if this were the first time she'd truly slept since arriving here.

Dark makeup had stained her pillow, and my bed smelled like sex with a hint of her floral perfume. Her lips were neutral because the color had disappeared on my chest and neck. Her fair skin was unblemished, like she hadn't just spent weeks as forced labor in the camp in the middle of the wilderness near the French Alps. Her perfection was eternal.

I left the bed and put on my boxers before I scooped her into my arms and carried her down the stairs to her bedroom. She was barely covered by the black night-gown, her perfect curls now messy from my possessive fingers. My arms were used to lifting bars with weight plates stacked to capacity, so she literally felt like a feather to me, a single barbell.

I placed her on the bed and draped the blanket folded at the corner on top of her before I left.

"Fender?" Her quiet whisper was cracked, as if she'd been asleep for hours rather than minutes.

I turned back around at the door, prepared to flip off the light and depart.

She took a quick scan and realized she was in her bedroom. "Why...why did you bring me here?"

I was in no mood to explain myself. I walked out and ignored her question.

———

I SAT in my office across from Liam, one of my top guys. With blond hair and blue eyes, he was a young guy, nearly seven years younger than me, but he was eager, obedient, and most importantly, quiet.

I stared him down. "Explain." I sat in my leather armchair with gold buttons in the stitching along the sides, my large carved desk in front of me, windows all along the wall from one corner to the next. A full sitting area was on the rug in the center, several couches and armchairs, a large mantel with a fire that was big enough to roast a whole pig on a spit.

"Charles said he's been having issues with his men—"

"No." I straightened in my chair and leaned forward, one of my heavy arms resting on the shiny surface of the preserved wood, a relic of my noble ancestors. "Don't explain why he hasn't paid. Explain why he's still alive."

Liam stilled at my command, his blue eyes showing a brief hesitance. "It's only been a day—"

"If it'd only been a minute, that would be enough. Tell me when it's done."

"He's one of our biggest distributors—"

"You think I give a damn?" I instantly blew up, spittle flying from my mouth and sprinkling the desk with my outburst. "Everyone wants to do business with me. You know why? Because I don't fucking play games. If I say I'm gonna do something, I fucking do it. You don't pay me, you die. That simple. I made that very clear when he signed his contract."

"His men were hit by somebody. Bad blood—"

"Don't. Fucking. Care."

Liam finally shut his mouth.

"Now that you're done wasting my time, go do your job."

MY ELBOWS WERE on the desk as I stared at my laptop, my hands together in front of my mouth, my eyes combing through the columns to make sure every single ounce was accounted for. Magnus did his own measurements at the camp and sent them to me securely, so we would always be able to track every single grain from start to finish. If someone was disloyal, we would find out. It'd only happened once, and it never happened thereafter because the men never forgot that brutal execution.

People were only honest if you gave them no other option but to be honest.

The door opened without a knock. My eyes immediately glanced up to see Melanie standing there, wearing a beautiful dress and heels with a sparkling necklace and bracelet, her hair straight and shiny, her makeup ready for a formal event.

She kept one hand on the door as she stared at me, trying to gauge my mood.

That was pretty easy to do—since I was always angry.

She took the risk and stepped farther into my office, scanning the elegant room as she approached my desk, her heels were muffled on the rug and then loud against the hardwood floor as she made her way across. She stopped in front of my desk, her fingertips fidgeting together at her waist, having an elegant poise that I found so attractive. Even when she was in the clearing, she had this graceful posture that gave her an unspoken power despite her situation. She was both confident and timid at the same time...especially around me.

I waited, in the exact same position as I'd been in before, except my eyes were on her instead of the screen that required my attention.

"Will you have lunch with me?"

I ate lunch alone, right here at my desk, so I could keep working. My dinner was usually enjoyed in the same way. I hardly ever dined with anyone except at social events, and without company, there was no reason to sit alone at a dining table, my thoughts my only conversation. I didn't want to spare the time to eat with her now, but when her appearance was so hypnotic, it was difficult to say no. I could stare at a bright screen with spreadsheets and emails, or I could stare at the most perfect thing ever created. My only answer was a nod.

WE SAT at the dining table in the garden room, where the windows showed the rose bushes and tulips. The different seasons gave birth to different kinds of flowers, so new ones were constantly cycled in to mask the dead ones. Right now, the pink roses were in full bloom despite the winter season. It was a clear day, so the sun came through and highlighted the water drops on the petals and leaves from the rain that came in the middle of the night.

She sat across from me, eating with proper manners Gilbert must have drilled into her, her back perfectly straight and off the padding of the chair. Lunch consisted of sandwiches, a salad, and a side of fruit, along with homemade bread.

Melanie must have enjoyed tea because Gilbert had placed a teapot in the center of the table and gave her a vintage teacup to enjoy it. He didn't bother to bring me one because I only drank tea on formal occasions.

She ate quietly across from me, her eyes down most of the time, sometimes on the garden outside the window, which she clearly admired.

My eyes stayed on her the entire time, grabbing my sandwich without looking, taking bites as I took in her features for the hundredth time. It was the first time she and I had had a meal together. In her cabin, sometimes I would eat, sometimes she would eat, but never at the same time.

"How's your day going?" She buttered a piece of bread with the homemade jam my pastry chef made then took a bite.

I wasn't a fan of small talk, so I shrugged, doing the bare minimum to participate.

"You seem to work a lot."

"What else is there to do?"

She stilled at the question and stared for a while, like she didn't know how to answer that.

I picked up the other half of my sandwich and took a bite.

"What are you working on right now?"

I chewed my bite as I stared her down. "I don't want to talk about work." She would never understand any of it, and I wasn't happy about the way things were going at the moment.

"Okay..." She took a drink of her tea. "Does your family live in Paris?"

I paused at the question momentarily, flashbacks playing across my mind. As much as I tried to scrub those memories from my brain, they were permanent. They didn't live in Paris...but they were buried in Paris. And my father's body had been thrown into the ocean, to be forgotten, not to be remembered by anyone. "I don't want to talk about that either."

Disappointment filled her eyes. "My father abandoned us after I was born. I don't remember him." She shared that information unexpectedly, like she just wanted to talk to me, even if I was only listening. "My mom raised us until she got sick...and then Raven took over."

I finished the bite in my mouth as I listened. My eyes dropped for a moment as the clarity struck me. Raven was like me—taking care of her sister the way I took care of Magnus. Dead mothers and worthless fathers. "I'm sorry."

Her eyes softened at my comment, because I would never say something I didn't mean. "Thanks."

I took a piece of bread and slathered it in butter before I took a bite, eating with polite manners since she did as well. If I were alone, I wouldn't bother. Too much work when my energy was reserved for more important things. "How did you spend your time in America?" I knew nothing about her as a person. I knew her body like my own, knew her subtle reactions, her presence, but nothing substantial. That information was irrelevant because it wouldn't change the way I felt, so it had never been important to me.

"I was a bartender...going to cosmetology school," she said with a slight twinge of embarrassment. "Raven is the smart one. After college, she moved to Paris for her graduate studies—"

"I don't care about her." Her only relevance was their relation. Outside that context, I didn't give a damn about her life and accomplishments. "Being educated and being smart are two different things. The only reason you live in her shadow is because you choose to stand there. Move."

She rested her fingertips on her teacup as she absorbed my words.

"If she were smart, she wouldn't have been picked for the Red Snow. She wouldn't have run into a blizzard. She would have kept her head down instead of pissing off every single guard in that camp. She doesn't belong on the pedestal where you've placed her."

Her eyes shone a little brighter as she stared at me, words sitting on her tongue that she struggled to say. "You think she's stupid for trying to be free. Your definition of smart is submission." Melanie caved to me in every way imaginable, but this was the one thing she wouldn't bend for.

Instead of keeping her mouth shut, she defended her sister.

"I believe in working smart, not hard. Every choice she makes harshens her conditions, makes her existence more unbearable. Her outcome won't change, so instead of trying to improve her quality of life like the other girls, she chooses to attempt the impossible. Idiotic. Her time could be better spent." I took a drink of my water and stared at Melanie, wondering if she would make the wrong decision and push this conversation.

She dropped her gaze.

Good.

AFTER LUNCH, I returned to my office.

I approached my desk where my laptop remained. A cup of hot black coffee was waiting for me along with my mail. I grabbed it and sifted through it, opening each piece and glancing through it before tossing it into a pile on my desk.

Footsteps sounded behind me.

With an open letter in my hand, I turned around to see her.

Melanie took a seat on the couch and got comfortable with a book in her hands.

I stared.

When she felt my look, she turned to meet my gaze. "I'll be quiet."

My eyebrows furrowed, and I lowered the letter to my side.

Her body became more rigid under my gaze because she knew I was pissed.

I approached the couch and stared down at her. "Get. Out."

She got to her feet. "I said I'll be quiet. I just don't want to be alone—"

"Too fucking bad. Take the car and go into the city."

"How do you know I won't run away—"

"Try, and see what happens."

She gripped the book to her chest, her breathing elevated.

"The only way you leave me is if I let you leave." My hand shook at my side the longer she didn't cooperate, when my men would have fled. "Go."

She stayed. "Why do you want me here if you don't—"

"That's my business."

She turned away, her eyes starting to water.

Tears didn't affect me. Empathy was something I'd never learned. The pain and suffering of others was white noise, because no one cared about my suffering. But watching her struggle to combat tears made me feel inadequate, like I'd allowed my trophy to rust over instead of taking care of it. "Chérie."

She wouldn't look at me, her lips tightly pressed together in restraint.

I set the letter on one of the tables and came closer to her, my hand moving to her waist, my thumb over her belly button while my fingers stretched across her back. My thumb squeezed her stomach slightly as I moved farther into her vision. "I need my space. I need to work."

"I'll be quiet..."

"My men stop by throughout the day. It's not a place for you."

She still didn't look at me, but she eventually gave a nod in agreement.

I could read her pretty well, but in this instance, I struggled. "Why is it hard for you to be alone?"

"I...I don't know," she whispered. "When I'm with you... it drowns out the thoughts I don't want to have. You see me so infrequently that I'm just left to my own voice, my regrets, my pain. I live in a palace with beautiful clothes, while my sister is—" She couldn't bring herself to finish. "It's just hard."

My hand cupped her face, and my thumb caught a tear that slid down her cheek. Her eyes were subdued, as if she were scared, and the sheen on the surface of her eyes reflected the brilliant chandelier above. Whether she cried or smiled, her beauty was the same, but this was a sad beauty. Her words from last week came back to me, an echo. *You're all I have.* Her father left. Her mother left. And then her sister left, and Melanie crossed the ocean to chase her, hurt that she was left behind. Every single person had come and gone. My fingers moved to her chin, and I forced her to look at me. "I will never abandon you, chérie."

Her eyes started to water more.

As if that was exactly what she needed to hear.

WHEN I DIDN'T HEAR from Liam by that evening, I texted him. *Is it done?* I shouldn't even have to ask, and I was tempted to order his execution next.

There was no response. No dots. No activity.

I sat at my desk, staring at the dark screen of my phone, growing more furious by every passing second.

Then it rang.

It was Magnus, using the satellite phone at the camp.

I answered but didn't speak, my mood too foul for a conversation.

He was used to my silence, so he knew I was there. "I've agreed to give Charles forty-eight hours to get the money."

My body immediately tightened when I heard what he said, and without a second thought, I was on my feet. I moved to the windows, looking out into the darkness like I could somehow see him hundreds of miles away. My anger was so fucking loud through the phone that I didn't need to say a goddamn word.

"He lost over half his men in the hit. The money was taken. But he will have it for us in forty-eight hours."

I could see my own reflection in the glass, see the fire in my dark eyes. "I will slit Liam's throat for this."

Static came over the line because the connection was weak, but his words were strong. "It's forty-eight hours, Fender."

"Doesn't fucking matter."

"That's how we treat our partnerships? I've verified that his story is true, that the hit was real, that he even lost his wife and eldest son. Your response isn't just cold, but maniacal."

"We have our rules."

"No one has to know—"

"People talk, Magnus. They'll know we're soft."

"I think it's better to appear soft than fucking insane. It's bad for business. Charles has been our partner for years, has always paid us on time, and to ignore that is disloyal. We would lose more respect doing it your way instead of mine."

"There is no *your* way. It's *my* way. I'm in charge here—not you."

He turned quiet for a while. "My job is to make you see clearly, to see past your anger and stubbornness and make the best decision for yourself as well as the business. I will do that job whether you like it or not."

I clenched my jaw so hard my gums ached. "If you were anyone else, I'd kill you. Personally."

"Trust me, I feel the same way."

———

I SAT in the sitting area in my bedroom, looking at the TV above the fireplace, nursing my anger with a glass of scotch. The screen was showing a replay of the game, but I didn't pay attention to it.

Fucking Magnus. He had a lot of goddamn nerve.

We disagreed on almost everything, from the business to personal ideologies. We were enemies in every way but blood. But that connection was so strong, so innate, that it conquered everything else.

I made threats I would never execute.

He did the same.

My own man went over my head and snitched to Magnus, and I should kill them both, even if they were right, but I couldn't. All I could do was sit there and simmer, infuriated. My hands squeezed my glass so hard that I almost shattered it a couple times. But I'd learned my lesson from doing it so many times. A shard of glass in the hand was a bitch to get out, and Gilbert would lose his goddamn mind if the blood stained any of the furniture.

My bedroom door opened.

It was behind me on the other side of the room, but I knew exactly who it was. "Not tonight." Her beauty wouldn't pull me out of this mood. Her sweet voice wouldn't make me think of the roses in the garden. My fury was unconquerable.

But she came to me anyway.

Wearing lingerie.

A black bodysuit covered in diamonds.

I stared at her, still angry, but a bit less. "I'm not in the mood." I turned my gaze back to the TV and took a drink.

She remained next to the armrest, in sky-high heels, smooth legs, big hair. "What happened?"

I rested my arm over the back of the couch. "Doesn't concern you."

She studied me for a while before she moved to the couch and straddled my hips. Her fingers moved between her thighs and unclasped the bottom so it would open, her sex easily accessible.

My eyes were forced to look at her, to smell her, to feel the tension ebb away just from having her on top of me. Images of us together in front of the fireplace on the floor of her cabin came back to me, her body covered in sweat because she worked so hard to fuck me, to get the two of us off repeatedly.

When she pulled on my boxers, my hips automatically rose so she could get them off. My hand set the glass on the table beside me, and my dick went from soft and angry to hard and eager.

Her hand cupped my face, and she kissed me, her hair falling down around me and blanketing me in a curtain of her smell, and she directed me inside her as she slid down over my length, her pussy perfectly coated with arousal to take me without foreplay.

Like she'd been thinking about me all day.

I closed my eyes and moaned against her lips as she sheathed me with the best pussy of my life.

Her arms hooked around my neck as she kept her face close to mine, and she fucked me the way I liked, good and slow, rocking her hips exactly how I'd shown her.

All the bullshit with my brother went out the window as I enjoyed my woman. And fuck, did I enjoy her.

"You make me forget." She breathed against my mouth as she continued to force me inside her, grinding her hips at the end of every drop to let me feel her more intimately before rising once again. "I can make you forget..."

ELEVEN

FIDELITY

MELANIE

We spent most of our nights together, but I always woke up alone.

He would either carry me to my bedroom, or he would leave mine after I fell asleep.

I didn't demand a change because I knew I would never get it.

When he'd brought me here, I'd expected something more. I expected him to want me all the time, to have me by his side constantly. But our relationship was the same as it'd been in the cabin, where he would visit me when he felt like it, then ignore me the rest of the time.

I should be grateful to be spared, but my solitude was far more horrific than his company. Everything had been taken from me, and even if he was the one who took my sister away, I couldn't bring myself to hate him.

My relationship with him somehow felt separate from my captivity, which didn't make any sense. I shouldn't feel affection for him, but I did. To everyone else, he was the boss, the man in charge of a vile camp that claimed the freedom of innocent women, including my sister and myself. But to me, he was the man who didn't force me to do anything. He waited for my consent. He took care of me when other men would consider me high-maintenance. He was surprisingly soft at times, always caring about the tears I shed, when he didn't seem to care about anything else.

He always had something nice to say about me...when no one else ever did.

Fender left that morning, and he hadn't returned. He never told me where he was going, and I didn't try to ask. I tried to keep myself busy by taking a walk through his grounds and admiring all the flowers he bothered to upkeep. He seemed like a man who didn't care about that sort of thing. Then I walked through the house and admired all the paintings on the walls.

There were a lot.

His home had to be twenty-thousand square feet, and every wall had some kind of piece, something evocative and beautiful. I moved from one to the next, seeing watercolors and lily pads that reminded me of the pond in the front of his estate.

"Melanie, lunch is ready." Gilbert was never pleasant toward me. When he spoke to me, it was like giving an order. When he spoke to Fender, there was more than just an employee kissing the ass of his boss. There was genuine affection there, genuine respect. He immediately walked off without waiting for a response.

I looked at the painting for a moment longer before I walked to the dining table in the garden room, my favorite place to have lunch. Gilbert set the plate in front of me, and the serving was different from usual. It was much smaller, and there were no desserts.

He must have noticed my quizzical expression because he said, "You're gaining weight." Like that wasn't rude at all, he grabbed the teapot and set it on the table along with my lunch.

"Did...Fender say that?"

"No. I am. How do you expect all your clothes to fit if you're getting bigger every week? You can always take something in, but never out." He shook his finger. "And you shouldn't wear those beautiful designer clothes unless you're worthy of them."

"Why do you hate me so much?" I blurted out the question because I was exhausted by his hostility. "Fender told you to service me the way you service him, but you're constantly insulting me when I've done nothing to you."

He looked down at me over his nose, like nothing I said meant anything to him. "He said to service you. Said nothing about liking you." He walked off and left me there to sit alone, to stare at my small lunch of a salad and a side of fruit. Everything I ate was wonderful, something to look forward to, but now I didn't have an appetite.

GILBERT BROUGHT dinner to my room.

"Is Fender home?" There were other workers in the house, housekeepers and chefs, but they only spoke French. I had no one to talk to besides Fender, so days without interaction felt like an eternity.

He set the tray on the dining table. "Yes. But he can't be bothered right now."

I stayed on the couch and swallowed my disappointment.

"Enjoy your dinner." He excused himself.

"Wait." I rose to my feet and turned to look at him.

He turned back around and didn't hide his annoyance, but he obeyed my request.

"Can I have dinner with you...sometime?"

A slow, bewildered expression came into his face. "Staff never dine with their masters. And even if I could, I wouldn't." He turned around and walked off.

I shouldn't care what he thought about me, but since he was the only person I interacted with, it really brought me down, made me feel worse about myself than I already did. I'd been nothing but polite to him, but he continued to treat me like I was worthless. Maybe I should take a drive to the city, have dinner in a café or something...just to be around people who would have no reason to hate me.

WHEN I MADE IT DOWNSTAIRS, I searched for Gilbert to ask for the keys to a vehicle. I'd never driven in Paris, but as long as I drove slowly and took my time, I should probably be fine...I think.

Gilbert was nowhere to be found.

Footsteps sounded behind me on the stairs.

"Bring my car around." Fender's deep voice sounded from the very top, and his footsteps became louder as he descended toward the bottom floor.

Gilbert was behind him. "Of course, sir. Which vehicle would you like this evening?" Cheery and kind, the excitement was in his voice, like he lived for these interactions with Fender.

"Surprise me." Fender made it to the bottom, dressed in all black, in a sleek black leather jacket. His hair was styled when it was normally ignored, and he wore a black watch with a gold case around it.

When he noticed me, he walked up to me but didn't embrace me. He had this look on his face that clearly said, *"What do you want?"*

I got better at understanding what he said when he didn't say anything at all. "Wanted to take a car into the city..."

Gilbert joined us and walked past, trying to disappear.

"Not tonight." As if the conversation was over, Fender headed to the front door.

"Why?"

He continued to the entryway and ignored me.

Something about the whole thing pissed me off, so I followed him. "Where are you going?"

He reached the front door but didn't open it. "Out."

He wasn't dressed like he was doing something for work, but some kind of social event, and that made me feel betrayed. He was going out without me, and the only reason for that would be because of women. "I'm talking to you." I was tired of the back-and-forth, of his affection and then his coldness. He could be so good to me and then so indifferent.

He stilled then turned around, giving me his gaze and attention. His muscular arms rested by his sides, and he took a step toward me, his eyes showing their annoyance at the interruption.

"Why won't you answer me?"

"Because I don't have to." Like that was final, he said nothing else.

My eyes started to water against my will, my throat beginning to burn. I felt so alone here, felt betrayed by him when he owed me nothing. I hated myself for feeling this way, feeling something I didn't quite understand.

As with every other time I shed tears, it softened him. His eyes dropped the hostility. "What do you want from me?"

"Are you with other women?" I dropped my restraint and spoke my mind.

His eyes narrowed. "None of your business."

"Because if we aren't going to use anything—"

"Is that really your concern?" He stepped closer to me, his eyes shifting back and forth as he burned his look into mine. "If you want my fidelity, all you have to do is ask for it."

My eyes were still wet with tears, but they were old now, and there were no new ones to replace them. "I ask you things all the time, and you ignore me or say—"

"Yes or no."

"Yes or no, what...?"

"Do you want my fidelity?"

Out of pride, I should say no, but I couldn't do that. The idea of him going out and being with another woman made me sick, and not because I wanted to stay clean. It was much deeper than that. "Yes."

He turned to the door again, like the matter was settled. He opened the door and stepped outside, where his car was waiting.

My unease had been swayed, but there was still a gaping hole of confusion inside. "Why will you give this to me but nothing else?" I went after him, ignoring the valet who stood there and Gilbert, who appeared out of thin air.

Fender turned back to me once more.

"How can you give that to me so easily but dismiss me all the time? When you ignore all my questions? When you treat me like I mean nothing to you? Explain to me how that makes any sense."

He considered me for a long time, those hostile eyes infinite pools of darkness. He had a sinister energy and radiated constant coldness, but he was the strongest, most handsome man I'd ever looked at, and the idea of sharing him...made me irrational. "You said you would never abandon me." But every time he left, he did. Every time he excluded me from his life, he did. "I want more than that."

"And you would have had it if you hadn't run from me." His voice deepened and turned angry. The sting of betrayal was obvious in the burn of his eyes. Even after our conversation about it, he was still furious. He said he never let anything go—and he wasn't kidding. "You fucked my brains out, and then the next day, you threw yourself at death."

"For my sister," I snapped. "And you wouldn't have done the same?"

All I got was a staredown.

Gilbert slowly stepped away, nodded to the valet, and they excused themselves somewhere on the grounds so we could talk in private.

Fender didn't seem to care whether they were there or not. His look continued to pierce through my flesh and to my skull. "If I let you go right now, would you leave?"

I stilled at the question.

"Answer. Me."

"I don't understand why—"

"Answer the fucking question."

If Fender really let me go and I could walk out those front gates and return to a normal life...I wasn't sure what I would even do. The only thing I'd want to do is go to the police and tell them about the girls at the camp so they could rescue my sister, but my limited time with him taught me that he was invincible, that he dared me to escape because he was untouchable. The authorities would do nothing. And if I couldn't do that, then I didn't know what I would do with myself. I didn't know how I would adapt to normal life, not after what I'd been through. No one would ever understand, and the men I met wouldn't understand either. And they wouldn't compare to Fender anyway, the man who made other men undesirable. If I couldn't save my sister, then an existence out there felt pointless, not when I had everything I could ever dream of right here—including him. "No."

His eyes remained rigid for a few seconds before they released me. It took him time to absorb my answer, but when he got it, his hard body began to soften everywhere, not just in his eyes. "I haven't been with anyone since you, nor did I ever intend to. I'm meeting someone I work with. And I'll see you when I return."

TWELVE

BARTHOLOMEW

FENDER

The club was dark. Music blared overhead, the bass thumped, the walls were covered with red velvet that smelled like decades of smoke. The leather chairs sagged in places because they hadn't been replaced since the place opened decades ago.

I sat alone, the glass of scotch in front of me, my eyes surveying the idiots who danced to the music, took shots, flirted with people they would never see again after the next morning. A group of girls seemed to be celebrating a bachelorette party because one had a fake veil on top of her head.

With police cars in the streets and cameras everywhere, people assumed the world was a safe place. Well, I was sitting just twenty feet away from them, and I could shoot each of those girls in the back of the head with no consequence.

And they had no idea who was about to join me.

He appeared through the darkness and the smoke, dressed in all black, wearing his signature military boots. As he passed the girls, one reached out to grab him by the arm. His head wasn't even turned her way, and he side-stepped the touch and kept going.

He fell into the booth across from me, and before his ass even touched the seat, the waitress was there with his drink.

He gave a nod without actually looking at her.

Now we were alone.

He tilted his head back and took a big drink, like it was a shot rather than a glass of whiskey. He wiped his mouth on the back of his hand just behind his thumb then got comfortable in the leather chair, leaning back, looking at me with dark eyes that reminded me of shadows. He wasn't much of a talker.

Neither was I.

No wonder we got along so well.

After a long staredown, he spoke. "On behalf of the Chasseurs, I demand a cut." He picked up his glass and held it lazily, almost like it was a cigar between his finger-tips. "You need fewer girls, you need to supplement us with something else." Bartholomew was the leader of the Hunters, an underground criminal organization that was connected to every aspect of the underworld.

And his headquarters were literally underground.

The Parisian Catacombs.

"I don't have the room."

"Make room." He turned colder when he didn't get the answer he wanted.

"Not possible. You can thank Magnus for that." We hadn't spoken since that last conversation, and I had no desire to have another. He was already on thin ice, and then he decided to stomp his foot.

A long stare transpired, everlasting. "What'd your brother do?"

"One of our partners was unable to pay. I ordered his execution, but Magnus decided to spare him because of the circumstance."

"The circumstance?"

"He's got a blood feud with someone, and they decided to hit him hard. They took the money, half his men, and even his wife and one of his kids. Said he would produce the money in forty-eight hours."

"Did he?"

"Deadline is tomorrow. But I don't care about his sob story. Despite what many people may think, rules aren't meant to be broken—especially mine."

Bartholomew gripped his glass as his elbow rested on the table, and his direct eye contact lasted a long time, both hostile and indifferent. He was one of the few men I'd met who was truly impossible to read. It wasn't a poker face either. He was just complicated. "No, they're not. I wouldn't have spared him either."

"I've always liked you, Bartholomew." I raised my glass before I took a drink.

He didn't crack a smile. "Magnus has been dead weight for a long time. Cut him loose."

I took another drink.

"And replace him with me." He set his empty glass on the table then relaxed in the chair, giving me the floor to respond to what he said—because he was dead serious.

My eyes immediately flicked away and surveyed the scene of the club, seeing the girls cast interested glances our way but never making their way over. Maybe they knew we were the kind of men that would ruin their lives.

"He's not cut out for this. You know it."

My eyes moved back to him. Magnus had been pissing me off for a while now. He questioned every decision I made, tried to convince me to change our entire operation even when I explained to him dozens of times his suggestions would never work. When I wanted to scale up the operation, he was full of excuses.

"If he were anyone else, you know you'd kill him."

Yes, he would have been dead years ago.

"You know what I'll bring to the table." His arms rested on the surface of the table, his long sleeves gripping his muscles. His eyes pierced into my face as he stared me down, forcing an answer. "What does he have that I don't?"

I sucked in a long, slow breath before I finished off my glass. Melanie's beautiful voice echoed in my mind. "He's all I have."

THIRTEEN
TAKE THE FALL

Melanie

I looked at the clock.

Two a.m.

Fender said he would see me when he returned, but he hadn't appeared. I spent my night on the couch watching TV in a language I didn't understand and failed to learn, and when my eyes grew heavy from waiting, I decided to go to bed.

My room was cleaned every day when I had lunch in the garden room, so it was always a five-star hotel experience when I walked inside. The flowers were changed regularly, the sheets always so soft, and the vaulted ceilings made it seem like a palace—just my bedroom alone.

I pulled the sheets back and slipped inside before I turned off the lamp on my nightstand. A little bit of light always came into my bedroom because I kept the curtains parted. I hadn't had curtains at the camp, so I was accustomed to looking outside as I closed my eyes and went to sleep. I was used to the moonlight, the distant flickers of nearby torches, the sound of the wind as it rattled the glass in a storm.

It felt like I'd just closed my eyes when footsteps sounded on the hardwood. They were muffled when he reached the large rug around my bed. Clothes dropped, boots hit the floor. My eyes opened as I sat up to look at him in the dark.

He stood beside my bed, shirtless, his immense size making him appear like a monster that had crawled from underneath my bed. He dropped his jeans and boxers. He hadn't changed into his sweatpants in his bedroom before he appeared, which meant he came straight here.

He threw the sheets off me then yanked me to the edge of the bed, dragging me with a hard tug that made me suck in a breath in surprise. I was in my nightgown, my makeup off because I'd assumed he would never come.

He shoved my dress to my hips then dragged my panties over my ass and off my legs. "When I say I'm going to do something, I fucking do it." He positioned me on the edge, leaned over me, and shoved himself inside me, making me gasp in surprise. "Be ready for me. Always." His hand slid into my hair, and he fisted it as he fucked me that way, his eyes on mine, his look hard and possessive, his dick pounding into me like this was the first time he'd had me since we'd left the camp.

I grabbed on to his tree-trunk arms and shook with his thrusts. "Oh god..."

He fucked me to a record-breaking climax before he released, giving a loud groan in my face. But like always, that wasn't the end of it. His dick stayed hard as if he took pills on a regular basis, and he kept going, slowing it down, his fist relaxing in my hair and moving to my neck, touching me gently, his eyes turning soft and tender. He came closer to me, his body warmer than the sheets that had rested on top of me just minutes ago. "Chérie." He started to speak to me in French again, which he hadn't done in a long time. "Tu es vraiment magnifique." His thumb brushed over my bottom lip as he looked at my mouth, still pushing himself inside me. His fire had rekindled, his passion roaring like a forest fire that destroyed everything in its path. Every touch was searing hot, his kisses purposeful and full of gentle caresses, his deep breaths filling every inch of my enormous bedroom. "Tu es à moi. À moi." He thrust inside me. "À moi." He did it again. "À moi."

WHEN THE SEX WAS OVER, he usually got out of bed immediately.

This time, he stayed.

His arm was wrapped around the small of my back, keeping me flush against him, my leg hooked over his hip, my wet sex against his stomach. His face was pressed against mine on the same pillow and his eyes were closed, but his pull on my back remained, like I might slip away if he let go. My tits were against his powerful chest, and he smothered me with his masculine warmth and scent.

It felt even better than sex, to close my eyes with him next to me, holding me. I'd slept alone in that cabin, and there was always a little anxiety because a guard could open the door at any moment and demand something from me. But with him there, I knew no one was getting through that door.

There wasn't a single thing in the world that could touch me now.

I shouldn't feel safe with him; I understood that. But in reality, I'd never felt safer in my entire life.

His hand left my back and slid between my shoulder blades, into my hair, and he gave me a soft kiss on the mouth.

I opened my eyes and looked at his dark eyes, saw their special softness, saw the way he looked at me like I was the single most important thing to him. My entire body softened to a deeper level, invisible weight leaving my shoulders.

Then he left the bed.

Grabbed his clothes.

Headed to the door.

"Where are you going?" I sat up in bed, my skin forming bumps because the cold hit me like a winter breeze coming through an open door. My nipples hardened, and all the relaxation I'd felt a moment before disappeared.

He turned back around. "I don't sleep with people." As if that was final, he headed to the door again.

"Wait."

He didn't stop this time. He opened the door and looked at me over his shoulder. "It's not you, chérie."

I SPENT MY MORNING READING, and when lunchtime arrived, I went to the garden room to eat alone.

Once I took a seat, Gilbert silently placed everything in front of me, still hateful as ever. He didn't give me a greeting the way he did with Fender. He didn't even try.

I would just eat in my bedroom, but the view of the garden was so beautiful, and I needed a change of scenery. Otherwise, I would lose my mind stuck in my bedroom all day. Gilbert lifted the teapot and poured the lavender-flavored tea into my teacup before he excused himself.

Footsteps sounded behind me, loud and quick, moving with purpose.

"Your Highness?" Gilbert's voice turned a little frantic at the unexpected visit. "I was just about to bring your tray—"

"I'll take lunch here." He moved to the seat across from me, in a long-sleeved black shirt, his eyes immediately absorbing my face like he hadn't stared at it for hours last night. There were no bags under his eyes, like he never got tired, even when he hardly slept. "As I will every day from now on."

Gilbert looked like a cat thrown out into the rain. The unexpected change in schedule and setting made a fuse burn in his brain. He took a moment to recover himself before he headed into the kitchen to grab the tray.

I watched Fender stare at me, hardly recognizing the man right in front of me. One conversation had changed everything, brought back the man I'd missed since the camp. His eyes didn't burn with resentment and bitterness. Now, he looked at me openly, like he could stare at nothing else but me and be perfectly content.

Gilbert returned a moment later and placed Fender's lunch in front of him, which was different from mine. He had a big portion of pasta, a salad, more bread, and desserts. A glass of water was placed next to his food since he didn't drink tea. "Anything else I can get your, sir?" Gilbert had composed himself once more, over-coming the shock of Fender's decision.

Fender dropped his gaze to my meal, which was a salad with a small piece of salmon on top. "Gilbert?"

"Yes?" he asked eagerly. "How may I service you?" The look he gave Fender was full of so much enthusiasm that he would obey any command that Fender gave. If Fender told him to jump off a bridge, he would consider it a great honor and do it. The interactions I witnessed were limited, but it was very clear that Gilbert's entire exis-tence was dependent on Fender's satisfaction.

"Her meal is different from mine." He shifted his gaze to Gilbert. "Why?"

Gilbert instantly breathed harder at the eye contact, faltering for a moment when he was the recipient of that stare, but not out of fear. Another reason altogether. "Sir, I just thought—"

"I'd been gaining some weight." I cleared my throat. "Thought I needed to cut back a bit..."

Fender stared at Gilbert for another moment before he slowly turned to face me, his dark eyes regarding me with suspicion.

Gilbert glanced at me.

Fender started to look angry, as if he knew I was lying. He turned back to Gilbert. "Melanie and I will have the same meals. Is that understood, Gilbert?"

Gilbert held his breath and nodded. "Of course, sir." He turned to leave.

"And that starts now."

Gilbert stilled then turned back around. "Sir, the chef—"

"We'll wait." He grabbed my plate and held it out to Gilbert without looking at him. His eyes were on me, still angry, like I would get punished for this when we were alone together.

Gilbert hesitated before he took the plate. "Of course... right away." He excused himself from the dining room in a hurry.

Fender pushed his food across the table in front of me. "Eat."

My heart raced so quickly in my chest, and my blood pressure immediately spiked. It made it hard to hear because of the loud thumping noise. My eyes even began to hurt. "I'll wait for your—"

"I said eat."

I immediately grabbed the fork and spun it inside the pasta, which was still steaming because it was just prepared by the chef. His lunch looked way better than mine had, and I could sense the taste before the food was even in my mouth. "I just didn't want Gilbert—"

"You're the lady of this house. You will eat as such. You will enjoy every single luxury that I've worked for. If you've gained weight, I haven't noticed. If you continue to gain weight, I still won't notice. Do you understand me?" He spoke to me like he did his men at the camp, issuing orders in expectation of complete obedience.

I gave a slight nod. "Yes."

He nodded to the food. "Chérie."

I still held the fork, the steam rising up and filling the air with the scent of fresh pasta with hints of olive oil and basil. I spun my utensil around and caught the noodles before placing it into my mouth, my tongue flooded with the incredible goodness that made me close my eyes for a brief moment.

His eyes were glued to my face, watching every little reaction I had like it was fascinating. That was how we spent the next few minutes, me eating and him watching.

Gilbert returned moments later with the food and set everything in front of Fender.

Fender ignored him and stared at me.

Gilbert studied Fender's face, hoping he would meet his look, but he never did. "I'm very sorry about the mix-up—"

"Leave us."

His face was hit with disappointment, his eyes falling along with his mouth. His hands went behind his back, he gave a slight bow, and then he dismissed himself, carrying himself without the same immaculate posture he usually possessed.

FENDER HAD BEEN in his office all day and through the night.

He was a different man now, so I felt welcome stopping by for a visit. Before I reached the door, I halted in my tracks.

Because Fender had just threatened someone.

"The only reason you're still breathing is because if I kill you, I have to kill Magnus too. So, trust me when I say my breath will be on the back of your neck, day in and day out, waiting for that trip, waiting for that simple mistake that will give me a reason to do what I should do right now."

I was so scared that I just stood there, too afraid to turn around and leave because my heels might tap against the floor and interrupt their...whatever this was.

He spoke again. "You've been warned, Liam."

Footsteps sounded a moment later, someone approaching the open doorway to his office. A man emerged and immediately turned right, heading to the front of the house where he could depart.

He didn't even notice me.

Oh, thank god.

My hand braced against the wall for support, like I'd been the one just threatened. I lifted my knee so I could pull off my heel and I wouldn't make a sound as I walked away.

"Chérie."

I stilled, my fingers against my designer shoes. Fuck. How did he know I was there? I lowered my foot back to the floor, took a breath, and then emerged into the open doorway.

He leaned against his desk, in his black sweatpants without a shirt, his feet bare. His muscular arms were crossed over his thick torso, and the large hearth on the wall adjacent to him blanketed him with a flickering glow. Those magnetic eyes were on me, pulling me toward him with an invisible force, the earthy brown color visible because of the way the firelight hit his features.

My fingertips came together in front of my waist as I entered his office. My heels barely tapped against the hardwood floors because I moved so slowly, prepared for him to scream at me for what just happened. "I wasn't eavesdropping. I came by—"

"I'm not angry."

"Really? Because you look angry."

His eyes kept their intensity, but a slow smile crept on to his lips. It happened rarely, like an animal assumed to be extinct emerging in the wild for a brief second before it ran off again. He was so handsome when he smiled.

I stared at it, knowing it would be gone any second.

Then it disappeared.

Gone. Like the fire just went out in the hearth.

He pushed off the desk and straightened as his arms came to his sides. "That's just how I look." He stopped when he reached the front of the seating area, as if he expected me to move the rest of the way and come to him.

I was in another designer dress, black and tight, the sleeves made of lace. An assortment of diamonds and jewelry had been placed on my nightstand, so I paired it with whatever I wore, looking ready for a special event even when I just sat around the house all day.

As I walked toward him, I watched the way his eyes took me in, absorbing me like paint on a blank canvas. The man he just threatened had left his mind the second he was gone. Now his thoughts were on me, telling me how beautiful I was without saying it, surrounding me with affection without even touching me.

Sometimes I forgot he was the boss. Because with me...he was just a man.

When I stopped in front of him, my hands immediately planted against his stomach, my fingers flinching because he was so hot, it was like touching a log in the fire. He was over a foot taller than me, and without the heels I constantly wore, our heights would be nearly incompatible.

His hand slid deep into my hair until it came around the back and fisted the entire thing. He squeezed it like a wet sponge he wanted to wring out. He dipped his head, looked into my eyes for a brief second, and then kissed me. It all happened in one fluid motion, but to me, it was as if time had slowed down, every action taking an eternity. His other hand wrapped around the small of my back, giving me a squeeze against him before his hand gripped both of my cheeks in a single palm.

He opened my mouth with his, gave me his slow breath, his tongue, and then he pulled away. He took away his kiss, his touch, his squeeze. He turned around and headed back to the desk, his strong back a sculpture of muscle. He was the perfect specimen for an anatomy class because every single muscle of his body was defined and chiseled, easily visible even across the room. He fell into the chair at his desk, where his laptop and paperwork lay along with his phone.

I approached his desk and stood there, the flames from the hearth hot on my skin, but not warm enough to replace what I'd just lost. My fingertips touched the edge of his desk, feeling the textured wood underneath my skin. It was hard and rough, just like him. "Everything okay?"

He leaned back in the leather chair, one elbow propped on the armrest with his hand in the air, his fingertips slightly rubbing together like there was a grain of sand there. His gaze darkened at the question. "Wait for me in my bedroom. I'll be there shortly." He dropped his gaze and straightened so he could turn his attention to his laptop.

His answer didn't disappoint me, because it was much better than the cold ones I used to get. I turned around and departed his office.

"Chérie."

I turned around when I reached the door.

His eyes were on me. "Be ready for me this time."

I WAS naked under the sheets when he came to bed.

He got on top of me and sank me into the mattress before his dick did the same inside me. He hooked my legs around his waist, folded me underneath him, and rocked into me deep and slow, his muscular arms anchored on either side of my head as he held his incredible weight on top of me.

My hands planted against his chest as I rocked with him, my legs pulling on his waist to reciprocate his movements. This seemed to be the only position he wanted to have me in because we rarely did it in other ways, but that was fine by me.

His passion was hotter than the fire, his words coming out in French, which was so sexy even though I couldn't understand a word of it. My hand slid into his short hair as I brought his mouth to mine, kissing him and feeling a little explosion inside my belly just from his taste. He made me writhe every time we were together, showed me how sex was supposed to be, that my experiences up until this moment weren't experiences at all. Just false imitations, like a knock-off handbag.

He suddenly slowed way down, his French endearments coming to an end. "Chérie."

My thighs squeezed his hips because I was desperate to keep going, so close to that climax that would make my hips buck entirely on their own, my brain haywire and electrocuting the rest of my body.

His hips stopped, his dick rock hard and sunken deep inside me. "Tell me." Sometimes in his intensity he looked angry, but he was just passionate, desperate for me. He started to rock his hips again, move through my copious wetness that forced the housekeeping staff to change the sheets daily.

My ankles dug into his ass as I pulled him inside me, wanting the thrusts to get harder. "I don't want to share you...ever."

He gave a quiet moan as he thrust into me harder.

"I want to be your only chérie."

He pumped harder, his eyes deepening into a new level I'd never seen before.

I got lost in the moment, got lost in the sweat and the heat, and I said what came to mind. "You're the only man for me..."

The moan he gave was so deep and sexy that I dug every one of my nails deep into his skin and came, watching him do the same. He held on to me so tightly my bones could break. He pounded into me mercilessly, grunting throughout. "Fuck, chérie."

HE LAY ON HIS BACK, slightly propped on the pillows, his thick arm around me and pulling me into his side.

I lay partially on top of him, my head on his chest with my arm draped over his hard stomach, looking at the fire in the fireplace. There was a big flat-screen above it, but he never seemed to have it on. The fire crackled just the way it did in the cabin, its warmth reaching us in the bed.

The sheets remained at our waists, and I wasn't cold because his arm cupped me all the way down to my ass, acting as a warm blanket.

He reached for his phone on the nightstand and looked through email.

I could see the screen, but it was all in French. Couldn't read a word of it.

He finished reading then set it on the sheets beside him. His rough fingers lightly touched my skin as he looked at the fire, one arm propped behind his head. If I didn't speak, he would never speak. He preferred silence, the conversations that went unsaid. Sometimes, his hand would glide to the back of my neck, his fingers delicately moving through my soft hair, handling me with a gentleness that continued to surprise me.

"How did you learn English?"

His fingers continued to move. "English is a requirement in French education."

"I wish French were a requirement in American education." Then I could understand what he said in bed, could understand what he said when he spoke to other people around me.

"I could teach you."

"Yeah?"

"Or have Gilbert do it."

I released a loud sigh. "No, not Gilbert." Even after I covered for him, he refused to speak to me. He continued his tirade of hatred. Sometimes people liked you no matter what you did. Sometimes people hated you no matter what you did. He fell into the second category.

Fender read between the lines, listened to words that were never spoken. "He doesn't hate you."

"He totally hates me. It's fine."

"You're the woman of this house. If he treats you as anything less, I will remind him that he works for you as much as he works for me." He turned his chin to look down at me, his fingers continuing to run through my hair.

"I said it's fine. Leave it alone."

"Why?" His voice deepened. "You think I'd allow anyone to disrespect you? Let alone in my own goddamn house—"

"It's fine because...I know why he hates me."

His fingers stopped moving. "Why, chérie? Tell me why anyone would hate a woman such as you? Beautiful like my rose garden, soft like its petals, quiet like the opening of the flowers in spring."

It was such a beautiful description that I faltered before I replied. It didn't seem like something a man like Fender would say, dark, rugged, marching through the snow in a bomber jacket with murder in his eyes. It only reinforced what I believed—that he was more than what he seemed.

I propped myself up on my elbow so I could face him, my hand planted against his muscled rib cage for balance. "Because he's in love with you."

Fender had no reaction. His eyes remained on mine, not blinking or moving.

"Did you...already know that?"

The silence continued.

I dropped my gaze and let the subject fade.

"Yes."

My eyes shifted back to his. "How long?"

"Years."

"Does that bother you?" I whispered.

He gave a subtle shake of his head. "As long as he does his job, doesn't matter to me."

"Am I the only woman to ever live with you?" I already suspected the answer, because Gilbert hated me for a reason, and that reason must be because I was special. I was different from the others.

"Yes."

My finger traced the lines between his segmented muscles absent-mindedly, my eyes shifting down to watch my movements. I didn't think about the other women who had been in his life because I didn't want to. I had no idea what kind of love life he had, if he'd had relationships, been married, just one-night stands; I really had no idea. I just knew he'd had a lot of sex—because he was good at it. "Can I ask you something personal? Or will you—"

"You can ask me anything, chérie."

My eyes lifted to meet his again, my finger halting. He gave me everything I wanted when he let go of my indiscretion. It felt like a relationship, husband and wife without marriage, the two of us together in passion and commitment. I couldn't lie to myself and pretend it wasn't the best relationship I'd ever had, even though it was wrong. "Do you have relationships like ours or...?"

"I've never taken a woman from the camp. I've never fucked a woman at the camp. I've never wanted a woman the way I want you, never been committed or monogamous. I've never had a woman the way I've had you, with nothing between us except each other. The women I occupy myself with are whores or socialites. But they feel the same to me, and the only difference is I pay for one and not the other."

My eyes dropped once again, looking at where my finger lay between two groups of muscle. His promiscuity was satisfied with a single woman—me. And I didn't see how I'd earned that. He was the one who was the fantastic lover. All I had to do was let him have me. "I understand why he hates me, then..."

AFTER I FELL ASLEEP, he carried me to my bedroom and placed me on the mattress. When he pulled the sheets and duvet on top of me, it woke me up, because the cotton was cold, not warm like his body.

I opened my eyes and looked at him over me.

He stilled as he looked at me. His eyes shifted back and forth before he leaned down and kissed me on the mouth. "Goodnight, chérie."

Before he could pull away, I grabbed his forearm. "Stay with me." I didn't want to stay in this cold room alone. I wanted to be in his bedroom, with the fire slowly dying down, with his immense size heating the sheets throughout the night. I wanted his big arms around me, acting as a cage that kept me enclosed in his safety.

His eyes didn't soften at the request like they did when I asked for him in other ways. "It's not you, chérie. Don't ask me again." He gently pulled his arm away from my grasp.

"If you want me in a way you've never wanted anyone else, then why?" I'd become entitled now that he gave me things I asked for, but this was something I wanted more than the trivial requests I made.

His eyes turned annoyed, like he just wanted to go to bed and not have this conversation. But he didn't bark at me. "I can't let my guard down around anyone. This is the final time I'll address it. Do you understand me?"

"No, I don't understand. Let your guard down?" I was actually hurt by the statement. "Does that...do you think I'd ever hurt you?" He'd put his gun on the dresser, and I never took it. I could find a weapon in any room and fight back if I wanted to, but the thought never crossed my mind. Not only was that not me, not who I was, but I had no desire to ever lay a hand on him.

He held my gaze for a long time, his eyes shifting back and forth, his breathing growing deeper. "It's not you, chérie. Not you."

FOURTEEN
HIDDEN DESIRES

Fender

I sat behind my desk with the phone pressed to my ear. "Hand it off to Jeremy's crew. They'll take everything back to headquarters." I hung up without saying goodbye, tossing the phone on the surface.

I had to return to the camp, so I rushed to finish up my affairs.

Gilbert entered with a couple folders. "Sir, Pascale just dropped these off at your request." He set them on the edge of the desk. "I've made all your arrangements for your departure. The president has requested a dinner with you when you return. Shall I go ahead and schedule that?"

"Yes."

"For three, it is."

"Four."

He gave a slight nod, understanding I referred to Melanie. "Of course." He gave a bow before he turned away.

My eyes drilled into his back. "Gilbert."

He halted without turning around, like he could detect what was on the horizon just from my tone. No one knew me better than he did because it was his job to know what I wanted without having to ask, to conduct his day based on my mood, to know when to disturb me and when to leave me the hell alone. He slowly turned around and came back to the desk, his arms by his sides rather than behind his back.

"Melanie will remain here. She's not permitted to leave while I'm away."

"And if she tries to run?"

He misunderstood me. "She won't. I just don't want her away from the estate when I'm not around." My men would keep her safe from any threat that could occur, but I felt more comfortable being in Paris while she was shopping or doing whatever kept her entertained.

Gilbert gave a nod. "Understood, sir."

My hand moved to the laptop, and I pushed it closed. "I'll be gone for a while, so I expect you to keep her company while I'm away."

He couldn't hide his look of disappointment. The feeling was too raw for him, too difficult to swallow. He was the consummate professional, remaining jubilant even in my worst moods, but this was the one request that was too difficult. "I have many assignments that require my attention, sir."

I hadn't really believed what Melanie said—until now.

"Gilbert." My anger remained bottled inside because of the affection I had for him. He made my life easy, and I knew the reason he was the best butler I'd ever had, provided an unparalleled level of care no one could replicate, was because of the way he felt. It never bothered me. I never cared. But now, it was directly affecting my life. "Melanie will be the countess of this estate, so you should treat her as such now. There will never be a time when I live here and she doesn't. If this is unacceptable to you, then you will need to make other arrangements."

He dropped his chin slightly and broke eye contact, visibly embarrassed that we were discussing his feelings without directly addressing them. He was put on the spot and forced to swallow a pill that would make him choke. His hands moved behind his back, and he cleared his throat. "I apologize, sir. I...I never meant for this to affect my professionalism."

If I were ever to trust someone besides my brother, it would be Gilbert. He had served me faithfully for a long time, kept his eyes peeled and monitored my men when it was never his responsibility, snitched on any maid who didn't meet his standards rather than have loyalty to the other people of his station. "I accept your apology. But if you have to apologize for it again, I won't." I gave him another chance when I wouldn't give anyone else another. But his loyalty earned him a do-over. His attraction had been obvious for a long time, when I walked out of the shower with a towel around my waist and his stare lingered longer than it should, when he stared at me from across the room at dinner parties, when he smiled so brightly the first time he saw me in the morning. Just as if he were a woman, it didn't bother me, didn't make me think twice.

"Thank you, sir. Won't happen again." He cleared his throat. "And I apologize if I'd made you uncomfortable—"

"You don't make me uncomfortable. Just don't make my woman feel uncomfortable in her own home."

———

I LET myself into her bedroom without knocking.

She was on the couch in her living room, reading. She finished her sentence before she lifted her chin and looked at me. When her eyes shifted in subtle surprise, it was obvious she expected to see me in sweatpants, not jeans and a leather jacket. "Going out?"

"Yes." I came farther into the living room and stared her down.

She held my gaze and stayed in her seat. "Where are you going?"

"Dinner."

Her eyes fell in disappointment, either because I was leaving her alone tonight or because she wondered who would be at that dinner. "Will I see you when you get home?"

"Yes. And you'll see me during."

I DROVE us into the city, and we entered my favorite restaurant. Reservations were six months to a year out, but when I walked in the door with Melanie on my arm, I was instantly escorted to a table without having to say a single word.

Menus were handed to us, my favorite bottle of wine was delivered to the table, and our glasses were filled.

Melanie sat across from me, her long hair in soft curls and pinned back on one side so her strands were down the opposite shoulder. Diamonds were in her ears and around her neck, and the designer dress she wore had been fitted to her exact measurements, not amplifying her beauty, but complementing it. Her eyes scanned the restaurant for a long time, taking it all in like she was beside herself to be in a place like this, dressed like that, with a man like me. She eventually brought her eyes down to the menu in her hands.

Which was in French.

"I'll order for you, chérie." I set down my menu and took hers, and the second they were at the edge of the table, the waiter rushed over. In French, I ordered what we wanted, and a baguette with butter was placed in front of us.

She looked around for a bit again, looking at the couples at the nearby tables, watching the waiters walk by, and then glancing out the window.

I drank my wine as I watched her, more fascinated by her than anything in this room.

When she was finished absorbing the scene, her eyes shifted to me.

Beautiful. Smoky. Rich blue.

She was still, her hands hidden below the table some-where in her lap, and she didn't reach for the bread. "I'm sorry. I just haven't been out in...a really long time." Every time she shifted her head slightly, the lights shim-mered in her diamonds. Her long, elegant neck was proud on her shoulders, her high cheekbones sharp like the perfect cut of a diamond. She was the most beautiful woman in this room. The entire world, in my opinion.

I drank my wine again, entertained by her beauty just the way I was entertained by a painting for hours. It was easy to fall into those eyes, to forget about work, forget about the past, to forget about everything.

Our food was delivered with lightning speed because everything in the kitchen had been put on hold until my dinner was finished. The steak and potatoes were placed in front of me as well as Melanie. Silently, the staff dismissed themselves.

"That was...fast."

I placed the linen across my lap and grabbed my silverware. "Because everyone knows I don't wait."

I DROVE us back to the estate, and we entered my bedroom.

Dinner had been for her, not me. But I enjoyed it because she was easy to be around. She didn't talk too much like most women. She didn't ask a lot of questions. She didn't meet my gaze fearlessly, always slightly intimidated by it. There were times when she looked at my arms, glanced at my chest, held my gaze with a slight burn in her eyes like she wanted me, and if we were alone, she'd be on her back with me inside her.

I stripped off my jacket and tossed it on the floor. The rest of my clothes followed.

She grabbed her zipper at the back of her dress and started to pull it down.

"Leave it on."

She flinched at my command and released the zipper.

I came up behind her and pushed her to the bed, grabbing her by the hips and lifting her up so her knees hit the sheets. When she pushed herself up onto her hands, I grabbed her neck and gently pressed her back down again. Her dress was pushed up over her waist, I yanked down her thong, and then I shoved myself inside her, keeping my hand against the back of her neck.

I moaned when I felt how wet she was, when I saw the damp stain on the material of her thong. She had been the most beautiful woman in that restaurant tonight. Every man knew it, even if he would never admit it to his woman, and every woman knew it, even if their man told them otherwise.

But I was the only one who got to fuck her.

With her moans muffled by the sheets, her back arched as far as it would go, I fucked her harder than I ever had.

———

WHEN WE WERE FINISHED, we lay in bed in front of the fire, her body tucked into mine like the sheets and the fire weren't enough to keep her warm.

I was the only thing that was enough.

Her body was light on top of mine, like rose petals. They weighed nothing, but they smelled like the garden, were soft to the touch. My fingers stroked her soft hair, gently wrapped it around my finger like a string. I could almost fall asleep like this.

Almost.

She released a quiet sigh, the same sound she made when she was on the cusp of drifting off. Her arm gave a gentle tug into my side as she used my chest as a hard pillow.

"Chérie?"

"Hmm?" She opened her eyes, turned her cheek to kiss my hot skin, and then lifted her body to look at me, her makeup a mess, her mascara running like fresh paint on a wet canvas. Her lipstick was smeared as if another color had transferred from the palette. But her appearance was still art to me, perfect in its imperfection, evocative. Every time I looked at her, it resonated deep in my soul.

"I'm leaving tomorrow."

Her sleepy eyes started to stir, and the gentleness of her relaxed face suddenly hardened. "Leaving? Where are you...?" Her words faded when her mind found the answer before she could finish speaking. "Oh." Her gaze dropped, her long lashes stretching over her cheeks.

"I'll be gone for a week. Maybe more." I didn't fit my life into a schedule. I gauged my surroundings and reacted to them. Having a schedule implied time was your boss. But in my world, I was the boss.

After she had a moment to process my departure, she looked at me again. "Can I come with you?"

I wished it were because she couldn't be apart from me, but I knew there was a different reason. Anytime her sister was mentioned, I felt the bones in my jaw work, like a machine without the proper oil to stop the grinding. She'd humiliated me, more than once, and it was obnoxious that she was still a wedge between us. Without her, our lives were perfect. But the second she emerged into our thoughts, Melanie's loyalty swayed. She pulled away from me. Her eyes turned sad. She couldn't enjoy the world I'd given to her on a golden platter. Releasing Raven was the best solution, but it would be catastrophic to my reputation. I spared her life twice and then let her go? The guards would be furious. The women would stage a coup. It would be fucking pandemonium. "No."

Her breaths immediately came out hard and strained. "Please—"

"No."

"Please. Let me see her—"

I snapped. "When I say no, I mean no. It's not a negotiation." My eyes drilled into her face like she was Liam, one of my disobedient men who needed a knife against his throat to be reminded who was in charge.

She couldn't hold the look and dropped her gaze. "I'm not asking you to let her go. I just want to talk to her—"

"You think I'd let the two of you be alone ever again?" I grabbed her by the neck and forced her gaze on me. "After the stunt you pulled?" My fingers gripped her throat but stopped just before I began to choke her. "You still have no idea what you did to me, do you?"

Her eyes shifted back and forth quickly as she looked into my gaze, pulling her body tight like she wanted to be as small as possible, but never looking at me like she was actually scared. She wasn't scared of me anymore.

"I had to sit there and wait for my men to return you. But would you return as my chérie? Or as a corpse? What would I have done if I lost you?" I lost my temper and pushed her down to the bed as I got on top of her, holding myself over her, bringing our faces closer together so she could truly grasp how much she'd hurt me. "What would I have done if I'd had to bury you? What would I have done if I'd had to live without you?" I forced myself to let go and get off her. My hands shook because I was so furious. I moved to the edge of the bed and planted my feet on the rug, my hands coming together, my arms resting on my knees. I closed my eyes for a brief moment just to wipe out the images in my head, flashbacks of events that I hadn't seen, Melanie trying to conquer a storm when I was the only one who could.

She didn't move for a long time, just lying there.

What the fuck did Magnus see in that bitch? She'd almost gotten my chérie killed. She should have died for that.

The mattress shifted and moved as Melanie crawled toward me. The insides of her knees hugged my ass as she wrapped her arms across my chest and over my shoulders. She held on to me as she pressed her face into my neck, her gentle breaths falling across my skin. "I promise I won't run again—"

"No. Don't ask me again."

She continued to hold on to me, her chest rising and pressing against my back, her hard nipples pressing into me every few seconds. "I'm sorry..."

IT WAS STILL DARK when I left.

In my bomber jacket and boots, I descended the stairs and prepared to depart out the double doors and get into the car that my valet had parked outside. It was raining. I liked the rain, so it didn't make a difference to me, and riding in the snow was no problem either. Ever since I was a boy, I'd had to survive. I had to get food in my stomach with no money. I had to find a place to sleep, even if it was in an alley. There had to be a solution to every problem. The rain, the snow, those weren't problems by comparison.

When I reached the bottom of the stairs, Melanie was there.

She was in her nightgown. Her lips were dull, and her eyes empty because she wasn't covered in makeup. She was exactly as she'd looked at the camp, and only a woman like her could pull that off and still be stunning.

Only my chérie.

I halted as I stared at her. Our conversation had concluded with her on top of me, riding me nice and slow, her tits in my face, showing me how sorry she was. My anger had evaporated, and now I looked at her with longing.

Because I would miss her.

And by the look in her eyes, she would miss me too.

Gilbert opened the double doors so I could depart and stepped outside under the portico roof. The rain was loud, splashing against the cobblestones, echoing as it pierced the pond in the center like bullets from a barrel.

She moved into me, her arms sliding inside my jacket, her head tilted all the way back because it was much harder to meet my gaze without her five-inch heels. "I asked Gilbert to wake me up...so I could say goodbye."

My hands scooped under her ass and lifted her up against me, her nightgown riding up so her ass hung out, but my men knew better than to look. I had her against me, right where I wanted her, with her face right next to mine.

Her arms circled my neck, and she rested her forehead against mine.

I held her there, silently saying goodbye, her body so light in my arms that I could hold her that way forever. *"Tu vas me manquer, chérie."* I kissed her, giving her my tongue, my hot breaths, my fingers kneading her ass.

"I don't understand..."

I gave her a slight smile as I rested my forehead against hers once more. "I think you do, chérie."

AFTER THE LONG JOURNEY, I arrived in the camp at sunset.

My men came out to meet me, taking my horse to the stables, grabbing my bag to carry it to the cabin before I arrived there, working like obedient dogs without needing a command. Not a word was spoken.

I was marched through the cabins then approached the clearing, flanked by two of my men. My eyes scanned the area, making sure everything was exactly as it should be, that the men were doing their jobs, that the women were doing theirs.

As I walked through the clearing, I could feel it.

Feel that stare.

Violent. Furious. Maniacal.

I stopped in my tracks and turned to give her mine in return.

She stood near the table, her ugly face contorted into a tight look that made her even more hideous than she already was. Her arms were by her sides, but her hands were curled into fists. Her nostrils flared as she breathed hard, as if she was a bull about to charge me, seeing red instead of black.

I took a step toward her. Silently threatened her. Promised to put that noose around her neck if she didn't look away.

But she didn't. The bitch fucking stared and stared.

She wouldn't give in, so she left me no choice but to turn away first.

And she should die for that.

There was only one reason she didn't.

One.

THE FIREPLACE BURNED in my cabin, the darkness pressing up against the windows like the shadows would slip through the cracks and put out the flames. My dinner plate was empty, the juice from my steak the only thing left behind other than a few crumbs of bread. My fingers rested on the top of my scotch, as if protecting it from someone who might want to steal it.

It'd been a long day, so I'd get to work when the sun rose.

Making an appearance was work in itself.

The guards never knew when I would arrive. Magnus didn't even know sometimes, not because I didn't trust him, but because I didn't know I was going until ten minutes before I left.

Magnus knew of my arrival but didn't speak to me.

Good.

He would depart in the morning, and hopefully, he would do that without a farewell. Our relationship had never been more tense, personally and professionally, and it was best if we didn't interact for the time being. Emails were intimate enough.

I stared at the fire, my thoughts going to the exquisite woman I'd left behind. My watercolor painting. The future countess. The only lover I'd ever had that I wanted all to myself. A woman who had been worth the patience. A woman worth all the high-end jewelry in my vault.

Footsteps thudded against the wood right outside the door.

My eyes stayed on the fire.

A knock sounded.

I drank from my glass.

He let himself inside, like my silent answer made it through the solid wood and into his ears. His hood was pushed back, his hair messy from being underneath the material all day except when he was inside a cabin.

I didn't give him a glance.

He stood there for a while, waiting for my coldness to thaw before he sat down. When that didn't happen, he did it anyway. He moved to the couch adjacent to my armchair, so we weren't face-to-face.

I didn't push the bottle into his hands. Offered him no hospitality. Gave no respect.

After a long silence, Magnus spoke. "Thank you—"

"Don't fucking thank me." My head snapped in his direction to regard him, my brother, who shared so much likeness but embodied so much difference. "I don't want gratitude. I want the respect that I lost when I granted your request."

Magnus held my gaze, his features as impassive as ever. "You're the boss. You don't need respect—"

"Without respect, there is only fear. Those girls work out of fear. The guards obey out of respect. Don't tell me you're too stupid to see the difference." I set my glass down with a loud thud, tempted to punch him square in the mouth. "What the fuck is it about this cunt? She's hideous."

Magnus's eyes flinched slightly, but he kept his mouth shut.

"If you moved mountains for a woman like Melanie, I'd understand. But she's not only unremarkable, she's disobedient, idiotic, and difficult. Fuck your whores in Paris. Fuck the beautiful women who want to lick your balls. But don't waste your dick and your reputation on a woman who's beneath you in every way imaginable."

He only took a breath and let it out. There was no other reaction.

"She's on her third strike, Magnus." No one even got one strike, but this bitch managed to secure three, and that infuriated me even more. "If she crosses that line, I'll kill her myself. If you care about this whore, keep her in line."

Magnus shifted his gaze to the fire. "Our production has exceeded the schedule—"

"I'm not done."

After a breath, he shifted his eyes back to me.

"Don't fuck with me again." He knew exactly what I was referring to without my having to address it.

"Charles paid—"

"I don't give a shit. He missed his deadline—"

"What happened to ruling with respect and not fear?"

My eyes narrowed on his face harder than they ever had. "He disrespected me when he missed his deadline—"

"You need to calm the fuck down, Fender. Greed and ego collapse regimes all the time. Don't let that happen to us. Because if you continue to operate this way, it will." Now his eyes showed the same anger as mine. "If you looked past your tyranny, you would see that I'm helping you. You would see that I've got your back through and through. You would see that I'm protecting you from yourself."

My nostrils flared as I breathed, processing his insulting outburst.

Regret didn't move into his features even though he had a few seconds to reflect on what just happened.

I was so livid that I actually quieted my voice rather than raised it. "How does protecting that cunt help me, Magnus? How does humiliating me in front of my men help me?"

Magnus held my gaze, absolutely still.

"Answer. Me."

The silence stretched, growing louder, our eyes boring into each other's. Then he looked away.

"Get out, Magnus."

FIFTEEN

THE LANGUAGE OF LOVE

Melanie

With Fender gone, there was a hole in my life.

All I had was my books, my thoughts, and TV entirely in French.

I slept alone in my bed, and while I did that every night anyway, I didn't smell like him. I didn't have that intimacy right before, our bodies wrapped around each other, his enormous size sinking me into the mattress. Without his whispers in French, without his hot gaze, I felt like nothing.

I felt like nothing without him.

I had no value. I was just some weak woman without a backbone. I was just someone who lived a life full of regret. The shadows took me, possessing my soul, making me relive the most painful moments of my life.

In the blizzard, begging for forgiveness that I would never receive.

She loved me still, would always love me, but it would never be the same.

Without him to chase away the thoughts, I was left to my own misery. I was left to reflect on my bitter regrets, to look further back than that terrible night in Paris, to think about all the things Raven did for me that I never appreciated. She was a better mother than our own mother had been, and I'd never told her that.

I never realized how shitty of a person I was until now.

Fender was the only thing that made me feel good about myself.

I TOOK my lunch in my room instead of the garden room. I didn't bother with my hair and makeup, because without Fender to appreciate it, there was no point. Sometimes I took a walk outside when the weather permitted it, but I mostly spent my time alone in my room.

I sat at the dining table and watched Gilbert serve my tray, a full meal with desserts and tea. Fender encouraged me to eat whatever I wanted, but I just wasn't hungry anymore. I barely ate half of whatever Gilbert brought me.

When he set down the tray, he didn't leave. This time, he stayed.

I looked up to meet his gaze, waiting for him to tell me what he wanted.

He took a deep breath with his hands behind his back. "May I join you?"

"Join me for what?"

"For lunch."

My eyes narrowed in confusion because the request came from nowhere. Gilbert and I hadn't spoken more than a few words to each other after Fender left. I'd given up trying to play nice with him, and once I stopped caring, it was actually easier to accept his hatred. "Why?" The question wasn't meant to be rude. His request was just a surprise.

He gave a shrug. "With His Highness gone, I don't have much to do."

"Um...okay."

He retrieved his lunch from downstairs and took a seat across from me. He had the small meal that I did, so Fender obviously fed his staff the way he fed himself. There were so many moments that showed his kindness and empathy, sometimes I forgot the other version of him that I despised.

I stared at Gilbert for a while, hardly able to believe he was actually there.

He sat with rigid posture and dined like he was sitting across from royalty.

It made me drop my elbows off the table and straighten my back.

We ate in silence for a while, hardly looking at each other.

I spun my fork in my pasta before I looked at him. "Did Fender ask you to do this?"

He hesitated at the question, his eyes still down on his food. He cleared his throat before he forced his gaze to rise and meet mine. "Yes."

"Well, you don't have to. I won't tell him." I'd rather be alone than have someone who hated me forced into my company.

His gaze dropped back down to his food before he took a deep breath. "I apologize for my behavior, Melanie."

I stilled at his apology, saw the sincerity in his gaze but could still hardly believe it.

"It was wrong of me. I didn't realize how much my personal feelings were affecting my professionalism until Fender addressed it. It's unacceptable, and I'm grateful he was able to forgive me. I hope you will as well."

I knew how terrible it felt to ask for forgiveness and not receive it. It was the most haunting experience. Isolating. Painful. "Of course."

HE TOLD me about his life in Paris, growing up in a middle-class home. Both of his parents were teachers. He had two sisters. He lifted the teapot and poured more tea into his cup then dunked his tea cookies inside before he took a bite.

"How did you start working for Fender?"

"I earned a butler position for a few ultra-wealthy families, taking care of their homes while they were away, things of that nature. It paid well and Paris is expensive, so I took the job despite the long hours. Fender was acquainted with those families, and when he heard all the positive things they had to say, he came to me privately and offered me the position. Said he wanted me to work for him exclusively. I'm loyal to my clients, so I turned him down. He went to my clients and paid them whatever they wanted to release me of my obligation, and I've been here ever since."

Fender didn't seem to accept no for an answer—ever. "How long have you felt this way...about him?" Maybe I shouldn't ask such a question, but the information was out in the open now.

To my surprise, he answered. He just didn't make eye contact as he did. "Within the first few weeks after I started working for him."

"That was four years ago."

He gave a slight smile that was packed with his sadness. "Yes...it's been a long time."

"That must be hard." I couldn't imagine working for someone you felt that strongly for every single day for years, knowing they would never feel the same way.

He dunked his cookie into the tea before he took a bite. "It was never really hard...until you."

I gave a slight nod. "I'm sorry."

"Don't be," he said quickly before he brought his cup to his lips to take a drink. "It was bound to happen sometime." He set the teacup back on the saucer then met my look, hostility gone from his gaze. "You're a very lucky woman. He's a good man."

"You think so?"

He studied me for a while, inhaling a deep breath as he considered his response. "I know how he earns his money. I know he's a criminal...and what kind of criminal he is. But I believe someone's goodness is determined by more than just their sins. Every day I've worked for Fender, he's been generous and kind, and even in his coldness, his loyalty is unquestionable. I've seen the softness beneath the hardness, seen the way he cares when no one else would. And with the kind of life he's had, the kind of suffering he's endured, the kind of revenge he possesses...I understand it. Whether it's right or wrong, I understand it."

"What...what kind of life has he had?"

He looked into his teacup and gave a slight shake of his head. "I'm sorry, Melanie. A butler always keeps his master's secrets. You'll have to ask him yourself."

GILBERT VISITED ME EVERY DAY.

Sometimes, he joined me for lunch. Sometimes, it was dinner. There was always this tension between us, because while Gilbert had dropped his hostility, he would never truly overcome his pain.

I had the man he wanted—and that would always hurt.

His love seemed so genuine that I actually felt guilty for being the one in Fender's bed.

Gilbert came into my room one night after dinner with a notebook and a book. He sat on the couch beside me, wearing a pajama set instead of his usual tuxedo.

I'd never seen him in anything other than his butler's uniform, so it made me stare at him longer than I usually would. He was lean and toned, a really handsome guy, probably Raven's age. The V in the front of his shirt showed his hard chest and some hair.

He opened the notebook and clicked his pen, crossing one leg and resting his ankle on the opposite knee. "Yes?"

"Sorry. I've just never seen you dressed like that."

"I assumed it wouldn't be a problem." He lifted his chin and looked at me for confirmation.

"No, not at all. Kinda nice, actually. Feels like we're friends..."

He looked back at his notebook—like we would never be friends. "Fender mentioned that you'd like to learn French."

"Yes, but you don't have to teach me—"

"It's no problem." He opened the book he'd brought with him, which held translations for words from French to English.

"Thanks. Sometimes Fender speaks to me in French, and I have no idea what he's saying." When he spoke to me in bed, it turned me on even though I didn't know what a single word meant. If I did know, it would probably be even sexier. "And when he talks to people, it'd be nice to know what's going on."

"What does he say?"

I looked away, feeling too guilty to say it out loud.

"It's okay," he said with a strong voice. "You don't have to hide your relationship for my sake."

So, he'd already deduced why Fender was speaking to me in French. "Are you seeing anybody?"

He turned to look at me, his pen in his hand.

"I mean, you don't have to answer that if you don't want to. I didn't mean to be rude."

His gaze remained stoic as he turned back to his notebook. "This moment? No. But I've had relationships on and off for the last few years. Sometimes serious. Sometimes not. When things are good, it does help my situation with Fender, but there's nothing that will ever truly make those feelings go away." He cleared his throat. "I trust that you won't share these things with him."

"Never."

He made some notes with his pen, writing out some common words. "Were you the one who figured it out...or was it him?"

I wanted to lie and spare his feelings, but I didn't. "I told him when I noticed, but he said he's known for years."

He inhaled a deep breath, and his pen steadied. After he recovered from the embarrassment, he continued to write.

"Have you considered leaving?"

He finished his notes then clicked the top of the pen. "I could never leave him. No one could ever run his life the way I do."

"I'm sure. But you have to think of yourself, Gilbert."

He gave a subtle shake of his head. "I would be miserable working for someone else besides him. With my other employers, there wasn't the same level of satisfaction."

"Are you ever...scared? You know, because of what he does?"

He shook his head again. "Fender is the most dangerous man in France. That also makes him the safest."

Whenever I looked out my bedroom windows, I could see the armed men near the gate, ready for the unexpected. At first, it was daunting, but I was getting more used to it now. Just as I got used to the faceless guards at the camp.

"Here's the basics. That way, you can at least greet people Fender introduces you to." He handed me the notebook. I read through the list, trying to pronounce each one, but I'd never practiced French.

"Americans butcher the French language." He released an annoyed sigh and helped me with each syllable, the pronunciation of each word. It was hard to look at a letter I've stared at my entire life but say it differently.

Together in front of the fire, we practiced.

When I grasped it as well as I could, he took the notebook back. "And what does Fender say to you?" He grabbed his pen so he could write it out.

"Um..." I tried to remember. When he spoke French to me, it was difficult to focus on the actual words because everything else drew my attention, like the look in his eyes, the deepness of his voice, what he was doing to my body with his. "*Tu es mon...* Something like that."

He wrote it down in his notebook. "You're mine."

The flush crept into my cheeks when I pictured Fender saying that to me, rattling the headboard as he proved that physically.

Gilbert had no reaction, keeping his feelings held inside like an uncorked bottle.

"*Tu es... moi... à moi...* I'm not sure. He said the words a couple times."

"Mine." He wrote it down.

"Oh..." So, everything he said was romantic. It wasn't dirty talk like I assumed. "*Tu es vra... magnifico?* I'm sorry, I'm probably not even close on that one."

Gilbert only needed a couple seconds to figure it out. His pen went to the page, and he wrote it out. "*Tu es vraiment magnifique.* You're fucking beautiful."

Like a movie in my head, I could picture him saying that to me, his hand around my throat, one arm behind my knee. The look in his eyes matched his words. His affection matched his aggression.

"I want you to memorize this and say it to him." Gilbert added another line to the notebook. *"Mon homme m'a manqué. Emmène-moi au lit.* When he comes home, that should be the first thing you say to him."

"What does it mean?"

"Roughly translated, it means, 'I missed my man, and now take me to bed.'"

Yeah, he would love it if I said that.

He closed the notebook and set it on the coffee table. "If my instruction isn't enough, we can have a professional come to the house. While English is a second language to most of the French, you will integrate into Parisian society much easier if you're fluent. Just because we speak English doesn't mean we want to. French is a much more beautiful language. You'll see."

A WEEK HAD COME and gone, and Fender didn't return.

I had no idea when he would.

I put on a purple long-sleeved dress from Louis Vuitton with some matching pumps, along with a few pieces of jewelry Gilbert had placed in my room. When he first showed me the jewelry box, I didn't touch anything because I'd never seen jewels like that in my entire life. Now, I put them on every day, always wearing something new because he had such a variety.

I made my way downstairs and found Gilbert in the main living room, carefully dusting a teapot with a soft brush, like it was a fossil found in the desert that needed to be handled with care. "Gilbert?"

He finished what he was doing then carefully placed the lid on top before he rose to his feet, in his tuxedo with his shoes as shiny as the paint job on a brand-new car. "Is there something I can get you, Melanie?" He removed the white gloves he used to handle the tea set as he approached me.

"Is that tea set really old or something?"

He halted in front of me, giving me that look that clearly asked, "Did she just really say that?" After he recovered from his shock, he finished with his gloves and held them at his sides along with the brush. "Yes...very old. This estate has been restored as minimally as possible to protect its history. A lot of the items in the house date back to the sixteen and seventeen hundreds, when Parisian society was bustling with parties and gatherings."

"Wow, I didn't know that. Fender doesn't...talk much."

Gilbert stared at me, his lips slightly pressed together in displeasure and his eyes a little dark. He didn't beam at me the way he did with Fender, and I'd just have to accept the fact that he never would. "Did you have a request?"

"Yes. Maybe the two of us could go shopping in Paris?" He was passionate about designers and fashion, the perfect colors on the right complexions, the accessories that elevated an outfit from simple to fantastic. "Then get lunch or something?" Raven and I never really had a chance to do those things because we went sight-seeing instead. My time with her had been short...before everything happened.

Gilbert's gaze dropped briefly before he found the words. "His Highness has requested that you don't leave the premises in his absence."

I was a bit disappointed but unsurprised. Without him present, there wasn't much for me to do. It was too cold to spend much time outside, and it'd been raining a lot. "Have you been in contact with him?"

He shook his head.

"Then how do you know when to prepare for his arrival?"

"Because I'm always prepared for his arrival." When his job was questioned, he was immediately defensive, like his occupation was the bread and butter of his life.

"Do you ever leave the house?"

"House?" he asked. "This is a palace, Melanie. Not a house."

"Sorry, I didn't mean—"

"And yes. I have my time off to do what I wish. I would normally leave in his absence, but since you're here, we both agreed I should stay put."

"Because you're the only one who speaks English?" Whenever I tried to talk to the housekeepers, they looked at me blankly then continued to work.

"Because the head butler is the only one who speaks to the master. Everyone else reports to me."

I didn't understand the hierarchy in this house, but that made sense. The rest of the staff moved in and out of the background, doing their jobs but trying to remain unseen. If Fender had to give orders to every single one, his day would be spent running a house rather than working. "Well, how about lunch?"

He gave a cut nod. "We can do lunch. Take a seat, and I'll join you momentarily." He turned to walk away.

I turned back around to admire the tea set, realizing that it could be hundreds of years old, that Parisian socialites may have drunk out of it and smeared their lipstick along the rim.

"And Melanie?" Gilbert turned back around.

I faced him.

"You look lovely in that dress. Purple is your color." He gave a slight bow before he departed.

"PRACTICING YOUR FRENCH?" He sat across from me in the garden room, which was surrounded by French doors made of glass, showing the water drops on the green leaves, the slight bop of the plants as the rain came down and made everything move. When spring arrived, I was certain it would be the most beautiful thing I'd ever seen.

I turned back to him. "Yes. That's all I have to do..."

"Good." He delicately placed his spoon in the soup then dragged the bottom against the side of the bowl before placing it in his mouth. With his eyes down on his food, he spoke. "I wanted to thank you for what you did with Fender a few weeks ago...just never got around to saying it."

I watched him, unsure what he referred to.

He lifted his chin and met my look. "When I restricted your food."

When that had happened, my actions were impulsive. I didn't do it so Gilbert would like me. I just didn't want Gilbert to get in trouble when he was a good servant in every other regard. I saw the way he breathed to serve

Fender, and seeing how angry Fender was, I wanted to preserve that relationship. "You're welcome."

"I know how this must sound, but…I did it because I want Fender to have the best of everything. I control every aspect of his personal life without him even realizing it, so it was natural for me to do that with you. I thought he would be displeased if you were bigger, so I wanted to address the problem without him even knowing."

"Why did you think he'd be displeased?"

He looked at his soup again and glided his spoon inside. "I know his taste in women."

"And what kind of taste does he have?"

"Tall, thin, model material. Perfection."

I wasn't tall, and I didn't find myself to be model material either.

"But while you're absolutely gorgeous, you don't quite fit into those requirements, so I guess I don't know everything about him…"

I looked down at my salad and pushed a couple pieces around, thinking about every moment when Fender looked at me—like it was impossible to take his eyes off me. Just his gaze alone showed more dedication than any man had ever given me in my entire life. He made me feel like the most beautiful in the world without even saying it. I didn't quite understand his fascination with me, because Gilbert was right. There were better options out there. "Can I ask you something?"

He took a bite of his soup and regarded me.

"What is it about him...that makes you feel this way?" This invisible divide between us always made us feel friendly but not friends. Maybe someday that would change. Maybe it never would.

He cleaned off his spoon before setting it on the linen on the table. The question seemed to make him lose his appetite, because he moved on to his tea and abandoned his lunch. "I'm sure you can guess, Melanie. You can guess better than anyone..."

I let the conversation die. If he wanted to answer, he could. If he didn't, that was his business. My food was no longer appetizing either, so I pushed it away and grabbed my tea and cookies.

"He's the most beautiful man I've ever seen...for one." He drew a deep breath then let it out slowly, like he was getting these heavy feelings off his chest. "I've never told anyone about this before, so it's both strange and cathartic to discuss."

"You don't have to. I just...was curious."

Gilbert watched me dunk my cookies into the tea before he continued. "The way he carries himself. The way he orders me around but never scolds me. He's a natural leader. He handles business like he'd been doing it for many lifetimes. He earns the respect of everyone around him without even trying. He says so much without saying anything at all. And his eyes...they're so deep and beautiful. He looks mad most of the time, but that intensity...it's so sexy. He's a man, you know? He's so...*manly*. I just love that. Strong. Powerful. Masculine. And while he's not affectionate, he's good to us. He's good to the people who are loyal to him. He's the most hardworking person I've ever been around. It's all those things, everything about him, every little thing..."

SIXTEEN

ALL THAT'S LEFT

FENDER

The sun was out.

The sky was clear, revealing the French Alps in the distance, the powder gleaming under the sunlight. There wasn't even a breeze, but the air was cold, absorbing the vapor that left my nostrils.

My stay had been worse than usual. Melanie was waiting at home for me when she used to be the reason I looked forward to coming to the camp. She had been the reason I'd stayed longer than I should.

But with her gone, my nights were lonely.

My boots smashed the snow underneath me as I crossed the ground, spots of soil breaking up the solid white cover. My men flanked me on either side, armed under their jackets, in case the guards staged a coup or one of the women was angry enough to come for me.

One woman in particular.

My black horse was ready for my departure. He was mine exclusively, and I was the only one permitted to ride him. He was well trained and obedient with a black coat that rebelled against the white landscape. A gorgeous horse deserved the right rider, and I paid a sum greater than a car to be that rider.

I always wanted the best in life.

My eyes left the steed waiting for me and settled on Magnus.

With his hood pushed back, he waited for me to approach.

We hadn't spoken after our tense conversation in the cabin. Wordlessly, he did his job, and I did mine. I didn't wait for an apology or an admission of guilt, and even if it did happen, it wouldn't change anything. The deep-seated loyalty I had for my brother was the reason he was still breathing right now.

I stared him down as I took the reins from the guard. "Leave us."

They all obeyed immediately—the way Magnus should.

Their footfalls died away as they entered deeper into the camp, moving through the cabins and approaching the clearing.

I held the reins even though Horus remained still.

Magnus stepped closer to me, my height but leaner in his arms and torso. His eyes remained guarded and cold, unapologetic about the last words he'd spoken to me. "I've had a few conversations with the Colombians about the increased production. We're working on a solution to our problem."

"I want a solution. Not an update."

"Solutions take time, Fender."

"We are men who don't *try*. We *do*. Remember the difference." I expected every man who worked for me to bust his ass like his life depended on it. That was how we took over the entirety of France and claimed it as our territory. When a streetwalker got their hands on our drugs and started their own pitiful organization, they were taken out. We didn't ignore them because their enterprise was laughable or because they were insignificant. We took on every single threat, no matter how small, just out of principle. Our business was run like a militia, with no exceptions. If you were going to bother to do something, do it the best. Something my father said when I was younger. The only advice I ever valued from that piece of shit.

Magnus's eyes shifted back and forth.

"Anything else?"

He inhaled a breath, deep and slow, like he kept back everything he actually wanted to say.

My eyes burned deeper into his. "Speak."

"Our operation is perfect. By scaling it up, we risk uncertainty. We risk a decrease in our product. We'll need to find more girls. The bigger something grows, the more difficult it is to manage. We have more money than we can spend in several lifetimes. When will it be enough, Fender?"

My hands immediately squeezed the reins because my brother was a broken record. Nothing he'd said in the past had changed my mind. Nothing he said in the present or future would change it either. "Never. It'll never be enough."

His expression didn't change, but his disappointment filled the air around us, an invisible energy. "You can't prove anything to someone who's dead."

I would never stop. Everything had been taken from me, and I wouldn't stop until everything was taken back. This was more than revenge. It was more than spite. It wasn't even about proving anything to a man I'd murdered near a stream.

It was about proving it to myself.

That I won.

That my mother won. My sister. My brother.

My family won.

I looked into his face and saw the only person I had left. "Do I need to remind you that you would be dead if it weren't for me? That you would have gone to bed for the last time and never awoken?"

His eyes narrowed slightly, growing more strained. "No."

"Then I shouldn't have to remind you that we're all that's left of our family name. I shouldn't have to remind you that no amount of money will make us forget that our home was once a dumpster in an alley. That we couldn't afford the doctor or the medication, so we had to steal to be able to get it. That we were jumped by full-grown men because we chose to take a different alley home. I shouldn't have to remind you of the suffering we endured because he decided to be a coward and make us cowards with him."

Magnus didn't drop his gaze.

"Don't make me remind you again. Don't make me remind you that I'm all you have left in this world—and you shouldn't take it for granted."

I DROVE in the fading light, the lights from the city becoming visible over the horizon. I had driven in silence most of the way, choosing to turn over my own thoughts endlessly as entertainment.

I hit the call button on the screen in the center console.

It only rang once. "Sir, it's great to hear from you. You're on your way?"

"A couple hours out."

"The house is ready for you—as always."

I didn't care about that. "Tell Melanie to be ready for me. She'll know what that means."

IT'D BEEN A LONG DAY.

But no amount of fatigue would make me want her less.

She'd been in my thoughts often, especially when I looked into the fireplace, remembering conversations in her cabin, remembering nights we lay together in my bed. I was obsessed with her the way I was obsessed with money. There was no amount that would ever be enough. All of her still felt like a shortfall.

The car was handed off to the valet, and my bag was retrieved by another staff member. The only person who spoke to me was Gilbert, because I didn't want to exchange pleasantries and give orders to twelve different people every time I came into residence.

Gilbert stood next to the open door, arms behind his back, standing tall and proud. His eyes watched me, full of excitement that could hardly be suppressed. "Glad you're back, sir. Wasn't the same without you."

I gave him a slight nod as I entered my home and wiped my dirty boots on the rug. My bomber jacket was dropped off my shoulders, and Gilbert was there to catch it.

He shut the main door as I headed up the stairs. "Shall I bring a tray, sir?"

I continued to the second and third landing. "Place it outside my door in an hour." I'd had a big breakfast before I left the camp, but many hours had passed, and I skipped lunch. I was hungry, but that need was dwarfed by another.

I made it to my bedroom and found her there.

Ready for me.

She was in black lingerie and heels, sitting on the edge of the bed like she'd been waiting there since I called. Her hair was in soft curls with a beautiful shine under the chandelier. The fireplace cast a glow across her cheek, brightening her already beautiful skin. Her makeup was sultry and heavy, perfect with her lingerie.

I took a moment to look at her before I approached the bed, pulling my shirt off as I went.

She got to her feet, standing in high heels.

My clothes and boots fell, like breadcrumbs across the hardwood floor and the carpet.

Her eyes took me in, trailing over my nakedness, slightly biting her bottom lip like she missed my heavy body on top of hers, missed my warm flesh, missed my big hands on her little body.

My hands gripped her hips, and I pulled her into me for a kiss, wanting her taste on my mouth, wanting her breath in my lungs, wanting her smell all over me.

But she pulled away. Her hands planted against my chest, and she pushed me back slightly, our lips close together but not touching.

I looked at her lips and then her eyes, knowing she had something to say to me, and I wished she'd spit it out quickly so I could have her after a long ten days without her. Ten fucking days.

She whispered to me in her beautiful, flowery voice, speaking in perfect French like she was fluent. *"Mon homme m'a manqué. Emmène-moi au lit..."*

I sucked in a deep breath between my clenched teeth. Flames rose up my veins and spread through my entire body. My hands gripped her waist deeply, squeezing her so hard that I was certain it hurt. When I let out the breath, all my muscles tightened, my dick hardened even more, and I released the first thought that came to mind. "*Chérie, je t'aime.*"

HOURS LATER, I grabbed the tray outside my bedroom, and we ate together at my dining table. She sat across from me, wearing a shirt she'd helped herself to from my dresser, and it fit her like a loose dress. Her lobes held solid diamonds, and whenever she tucked her hair behind her ear, they glimmered. The tears and screams had ruined her perfectly applied makeup, the mascara in dots underneath her lashes, streaks from the corner of her eyes like rivers down her face. But I preferred to see her with ruined makeup—because that meant I'd done a good job.

The food was excellent as always, but I didn't really enjoy it because I was too busy enjoying her appearance, appreciating the fact that she was really there with me. This wasn't a hallucination that my mind had created in my cabin. I didn't have to stare at the flames and see her face somewhere in between. This image of her was real.

Her eyes met mine. Sometimes they were down on her food, sometimes they looked out the window. She'd missed me while I was gone, and now that she had me back, she was nervous, intimidated by my presence. "How was your trip?"

"Fine." I expected her to ask me about Raven's well-being, but she was smart enough not to. "Gilbert teaching you?"

She nodded before she took a bite of her food.

"Your French is good."

"That's pretty much all I know how to say."

It was the most beautiful line I'd ever heard spoken, like prose straight out of a classic French novel. It was the single most erotic moment of my life, coming home to my woman and listening to her say those words to me. "You said it beautifully."

She gave a slight smile before she looked down into her soup.

"Gilbert been good to you?"

"He's been wonderful. We've had our lunches together, sometimes dinner."

"And he was pleasant to you?" When I'd realized Melanie's assumption about Gilbert was correct, that he did hate her, it made me angry. To have my own staff disrespecting the woman I'd chosen was ludicrous. It was disrespectful to me—and no one disrespected me.

"Very." She lifted her chin and studied my face, reading the anger in my eyes. "It's water under the bridge, Fender."

I'd never understood the expression because I didn't believe in it. Water was never under the bridge with me. The only time it was was with Melanie—because it was impossible to hold a grudge against her.

"What did you do at the camp?" Anytime that place was mentioned, her voice trailed off, like she was hit by the memories of the cold, the drugs, her sister.

"Make an appearance." I did my checks to make sure everyone was doing their job, but my presence was work enough. It taught everyone in my employ that I could show up at any moment, for any reason, and if anyone had their pants down, they'd die by my bare hands.

She finished her meal then set down her fork. "I asked Gilbert if we could go shopping together, but he said I'm not allowed to leave." She silently asked for an explanation, her eyes shifting back and forth between mine.

I held her gaze, waiting for the rest of the sentence or a question.

"You think I'll run away?" Hurt was in her voice, a slight change in her tone.

I studied that look for a long time, loving the fading light in her eyes, the way she needed my confidence to be happy. "No."

Her eyebrows furrowed slightly.

"I just don't want you out and about when I'm not in the city. The safest place in the world for you is right beside me. When I'm not here, second best is this palace. If you want to go shopping tomorrow, you may. I just expect you to be home by the time I'm finished with work."

I LAY against the pillows at my headboard, my legs straight and stretched out in front of me, my hands on her hips to hold but not to guide. I watched her move up and down, rolling her hips, getting slick with shiny sweat, her tight pussy taking in my tank of a dick like it was her honor to ride it.

She knew I liked it slow when she was on top. I liked to savor the feeling of her tightness around my length, how she remained so goddamn wet all night long, the little pants she made when she grew tired but pushed through it.

It allowed me to enjoy her in a whole new way. It made me feel like a king in my palace, to watch the most beautiful woman bed me like she was my queen.

She was my queen.

My countess.

When I was ready to give my final load, I grabbed her hips and forced her down, taking in my entire length as I came, the muscles in my thighs tightening, my arms bulging just a bit more, my throat constricting with the moan that I muffled.

My world was in constant chaos. The only quiet moments I had occurred when scotch was in my hand, but those moments were brief, fleeting. While she brought passion and fire into my life, she also gave me peace.

I'd never known peace.

My time with her wasn't spent thinking about my empire, the men I spared but should have killed, my brother and his idiotic qualms. My past had faded further into the background, become less present in my mind and soul.

She was artwork, and like the paintings on my wall, when I looked at her, I only thought of beauty, of ponds filled with lily pads, of pink roses in the garden covered in drops of fresh rain.

Those were the images that flashed across my mind the first time I saw her.

Peace.

When we were finished, we got comfortable in bed, her body curled around mine, using me as a hard pillow that probably gave her neck a crick. Looking down and seeing her spread across my enormous bed in front of the fire made me feel even more powerful. I had the money, the power, the world...and now, I had the woman.

She fell asleep instantly, her arm loosening around my torso, her breathing deep and even.

I let her stay for a while, until the fire had burned down, until the night deepened so she wouldn't wake up when I carried her to her bedroom. I slid from under her body, put on my boxers, and then carried her down the stairs to her bedroom.

The instant I stepped inside, it felt cold.

I got her into bed and walked toward her fireplace to get it started, to let the warmth make her bedroom feel like mine. When I moved to the living room, I saw her translation book there, along with a notebook filled with French phrases.

I stared for a while before I departed.

"Fender...?" Her quiet voice was raspy, like an hour of sleep was enough to make her throat go dry. She sat up and looked at the sheets as they fell down, realizing she was naked and her lingerie had been left behind. Then she surveyed the fire, slowly understanding where she was.

I stilled near the door, waiting for her unease to disappear when her surroundings became familiar to her. When she lay down again and closed her eyes, I would leave. I felt like a father making sure his child was tucked in for the night and unafraid of the monsters under their bed.

She didn't lie down again. She looked at me with disappointment. Hurt. Pain. Resentment.

I held her gaze and issued no apology.

Her eyes slowly fell, and then she lowered herself back to bed, pulling the sheets over her shoulder. Another argument was futile, and she finally got that through her head.

I turned back to the door.

"You say the safest place in the world is at your side."

I held on to the door but didn't step into the hall.

"I'm not by your side, Fender. I'm alone."

SEVENTEEN

THE COUNT OF MONTE CRISTO

Melanie

Fender worked in his office the next day.

I worked on my French, took a walk outside because the rain had passed, and when I asked Gilbert to tag along, he said he had too much to do since Fender was in residence. When I sat in the garden room for lunch, Gilbert only served one tray.

I looked at the empty spot across from me where Fender should be. "He's not coming?"

"Said he had too much to do. He's taking his lunch in the office." Gilbert excused himself.

I sat there alone. Now I was used to eating with either Gilbert or Fender, and without either one of them, it felt strange. There was only an empty chair across from me, a chair that I would never see because Fender's enormous size covered it like a cobblestone wall.

I eventually gathered my things onto the tray and carried it toward the front of the palace to his office. The door was open, and he was behind his desk, his food beside him, his dark eyes focused on the screen of his laptop.

I took a seat in the sitting room and placed my silver tray on the table, where it made an audible clank.

His eyes immediately shifted to me, intense and deep, like two drops of shiny oil.

I turned back to my food and waited for him to berate me, to order me out.

He said nothing.

I sat at the edge of the couch and took a drink of my tea before I turned to look at him.

He was back at work like nothing happened.

I BROUGHT my book into his office so I could read on the couch.

Sometimes he spoke on the phone, speaking entirely in French at a speed I would never be able to learn. Sometimes I could detect the subject of the conversation based on his mood, the way he barked out orders, or reprimanded whoever was on the line. Then he turned back to his laptop or looked through paperwork.

I had no idea what he actually did in here all day. He seemed like he just looked at paperwork and then yelled at people.

Maybe that was all a boss was supposed to do.

Gilbert stepped into the office then hesitated when he saw me on the couch. His hesitation turned to panic. "Melanie, you shouldn't be in here. His Highness needs to work—"

"She's fine." Fender spoke from his desk, his phone in his hands as he read something.

Gilbert stared at me for a few more seconds before he approached the desk. "Sir, I'm here to remind you of your dinner with the president Thursday. Is this still satisfactory, or shall I reschedule?"

"It's fine."

He gave a bow then departed the room.

Dinner with the president?

Fender set down his phone then came around the desk, in his sweatpants without a shirt. It seemed to be the attire he wore even when he had visitors in his office. He was in his home, so he didn't give a damn about professionalism.

He moved to the couch across from me. "What are you reading?"

"*The Count of Monte Cristo.*" I closed the book and set it on the table. "One of the few books you have in English."

He leaned back and spread his knees apart, his elbow propped on the armrest. The other arm was down and relaxed on his thigh. His jawline was prickled with hair because if he didn't shave every day, it would come in thick and dark. Even in his most relaxed position, his body was like a solid concrete wall that accompanied him wherever he went, and whether there was rain, snow, or a hurricane, it remained forceful. How did someone get that strong? "Are you enjoying it?"

"Yes, a lot."

"Good story."

"You've read it?" I asked in surprise.

He gave that rare, slight smile.

"I just... You don't seem like someone who reads."

"Because I'm a kingpin? Criminals aren't stupid, especially the ones who are good at it."

I never doubted he was smart. "You don't have a lot of free time, so I couldn't imagine you spending it reading... that's all."

"I don't read anymore."

"When did you read?"

"In school. I was in the top prep school in France."

I didn't know anything about his life before he was the boss. It was hard to picture him being anything other than this, the man who stomped through the snow in a bomber jacket and stared down anyone in his path with a spray of bullets. "You read a lot then?"

"Book a week."

He seemed to lack empathy and emotion, so it surprised me that he'd gotten lost in so many books in his youth. "Did you graduate?"

"No." His eyes started to turn cold.

Gilbert told me he had a hard life, but attending private school didn't scream struggle. "Gilbert mentioned you'd had a hard life. What happened?"

His open eyes remained glued to my face, a never-ending silence ensuing.

I suspected I wouldn't get an answer.

"Sorry, I just..." I didn't know what else to say.

"I had a hard life. Let's just leave it at that."

I looked down at the closed book in my hands, wishing he could confide more to me so I could understand why he was the way he was. Gilbert spoke so highly of him, and while Fender was actually gentle, affectionate, and kind, he was still a high-level criminal. He was refined and respectful toward me, treated me better than any other man in my life, but he did unspeakable things. Maybe what happened to him in his past would explain this dichotomy in his personality. "You can always talk to me, you know." When there was no response, I lifted my gaze and looked at him.

His appearance was exactly the same, as if he never drew his eyes away.

I started to ramble because that gaze was so unnerving. "Not that you have to. I just mean...I want you to know I'm here."

As if he didn't hear a word I said, he just stared. Eyes glued to my face with a level of attention I'd never received before, he studied me like he was too absorbed with the way my lips moved to take in anything else.

I LAY BESIDE HIM, tucked under the sheets, my thigh hiked over his hip with my arm against his chest. He ran hot, probably because he had muscle on top of muscle, so the sheets were down to his waist when they were pulled to my shoulder.

Every time I opened my eyes, he was staring at me.

Our faces were pressed close together on one pillow, and my fingertips rested against his chest, feeling the searing skin against my fingertips. Sometimes my palm glided to the area over his heart, feeling that strong and slow beat, like he could fall asleep.

But he never did.

No matter how comfortable we were, how tired he was from slamming his headboard into the wall, he never closed his eyes and drifted off. Wide awake and alert, he was more prepared for a run than sleep.

That look was intense and as deep as ever, even though we'd been wrapped up together for several hours at this point. The breaks in between were short because he never needed more than fifteen minutes to recharge and want me again. His desire was potent, and he was entirely focused on me.

The fire died down in the background, and instead of falling asleep so he could carry me, I decided to leave on my own. If I continued to fall asleep with my makeup on, it would cause a breakout, and I didn't want that. I rose and scooted to the edge of the bed, my back to him. "So, you're having dinner with the president?" I ran my fingers through my hair, and instead of sliding through silk, my fingers got stuck on the tangles and the sweat. "Is that like...the American president?"

"Yes."

I waited for further elaboration. When it didn't come, I got up and pulled on my clothes.

He eventually got up too, pulling on his boxers and standing tall in the bedroom, the fire blanketing him in a glow. With those dark eyes and that tightness in his jaw, he looked like he was part of the underworld, emerging from the flames in human form.

I came around the bed, sensing his chin turn as he watched me move past the fire. "Does this dinner include me?"

He stared for a long time before he walked up to me, his arm sliding around the small of my back and hugging me toward him, his chin dropping so he could actually look me in the face. His other hand went to my throat, getting a soft grip as his thumb brushed over my jawline. He turned my face slightly so he could press his face into my cheek. There was no kiss, just the closeness. "You're my woman, chérie." That was all he said before he silently excused himself to the bathroom. The shower turned on a moment later.

My eyes shifted back to the bed. The sheets were still warm. His scent was soaked into the fabric. My mind pictured me crawling back inside and refusing to leave. It was the closest thing I had to home.

But I left, walked down the stairs, washed off my makeup, and then crawled into the ice-cold bed.

Alone.

FENDER DROVE us into the city.

I wore something Gilbert had picked out for me, a skintight black dress, high heels, jewelry, and an overcoat to fight off the cold. My hair was curled but elaborately pinned to one side, the strands coming down one shoulder to expose the bare skin of the opposite one. My styling skills had improved, but I wasn't talented enough to pull that off, so Gilbert had someone do it for me. My makeup was done too, a striking smoky look that Fender appreciated the second he looked at me.

Fender handed over the car to the valet, and then he grabbed my hand, holding it aggressively as he guided me inside. It was the first time he'd ever grabbed me this way, his large hand encompassing mine almost completely.

When we stepped inside the restaurant, the staff immediately knew who he was but didn't speak a word to him. The maître d' came forward, gave a slight bow, and then indicated into the candlelit restaurant decorated in shades of rose gold, with crystal chandeliers. He led the way, bringing us farther into the restaurant and toward the rear where the windows were located.

The restaurant was a five-star Michelin-rated restaurant, so Fender was in a black blazer with a black shirt underneath, in dark dress pants and dress shoes. An expensive watch was on his wrist, and while I didn't know much about jewelry, I imagined it was worth more than the restaurant itself.

He dropped my hand and moved his hand to the small of my back, drawing me close so he could speak to me before we approached the table where a middle-aged man sat with a beautiful woman my age. "His mistress, not his wife." In the car, he'd told me how to address his wife, but that plan had now been canceled. "Mademoiselle is fine." When we approached the table, President Jacques Bernard rose to his feet to greet Fender with not only a handshake, but a gentle pat on the shoulder. They exchanged a few pleasantries in French before Fender introduced me. "*Ma petite amie*, Melanie."

I gave him a smile, extended my hand, and greeted him in French the way Gilbert taught me. "*C'est un plaisir de vous rencontrer, monsieur.*"

He gave me a smile before he leaned in and kissed each of my cheeks. "*Tout le plaisir est pour moi.*" He turned back to Fender. "*Où l'avez-vous trouvée, Fender? Elle est magnifique.*"

I didn't understand most of what he said, but I gathered that he addressed Fender, then called me beautiful.

Fender's only response was a slight smile. He moved to one of the chairs and pulled it out for me before he scooted it in and took a seat beside me. When we were all seated, he spoke in French, and I assumed he talked shop because Jacques turned serious and listened attentively.

His mistress, Kendra, gave me a couple smiles across the table but spent her time drinking her wine and helping herself to the sliced baguette in the center of the table. She was pretty much ignored the entire time, and she was so beautiful that there was no chance she actually enjoyed spending time with a man twice her age and a tenth of her attractiveness.

Fender and Jacques continued their intense conversation, the servers supplying more bottles of wine, taking our orders, bringing us appetizers we didn't even ask for. Fender had his arm around the back of my chair most of the time, sometimes on my thigh under the table, where his fingers purposely hiked up my dress slightly so he could touch my bare thigh instead. Sometimes he would grip me in the middle of the conversation, squeeze me just the way he did when he was on top of me, and other times, he was gentle, his fingers curling back underneath the dress so he could feel my panties. All of this happened without him losing focus on the conversation, listening intently then speaking passionately about whatever their conversation entailed. I'd learned a bit of French, but I had absolutely no idea what they discussed. Couldn't even guess.

KENDRA and I weren't included once in the conversation, so Jacques didn't even know I couldn't speak French. We said goodbye then left the restaurant. Fender was quiet on the drive, not saying a word to me.

I spent my time thinking about the mistress.

It didn't seem as if she even liked him.

Didn't seem as if he cared much for her either. She was just a beautiful young woman to fuck afterward.

What about his wife?

Would Fender do the same to me? When my beauty faded or his interest expired, would I be home while he brought my replacement to dinner? It shouldn't matter to me, but it hurt, picturing him sticking his hand up some other's woman dress possessively.

He left the city and drove down quiet roads into the countryside, pushing the car to high speeds because there was no such thing as a speed limit for him. His elbow moved to the center console, and his hand reached for mine without taking his eyes off the road. Gently, his fingers encompassed mine, holding them in his grasp rather than interlocking our fingers.

I stared at his touch. "What did you talk about?"

He answered immediately. "Work."

"He's...involved with the camp?"

"Indirectly."

That made my stomach sink like it was suddenly made of lead. In my naïveté, I assumed organized crime was small and localized. But now I realized how far those webs really stretched, how money could turn good men bad. My reality was shattered in that moment, because all the securities we took for granted weren't actually real.

Regimes didn't always fall. Sometimes they grew bigger and bigger.

When we returned to the palace, we immediately went to his bedroom. The fire was already going because Gilbert prepared for his arrival. The flowers in the vases had been changed, the bed had been prepped with turndown service, even French chocolates on the pillows.

Fender didn't care or notice any of that.

He dropped his blazer off his massive shoulders, yanked his shirt up his back and over his front, revealing the chiseled physique underneath. His shoes were kicked off, his bottoms were gone, and then he came at me hard.

His mouth collided with mine as he grasped the zipper at the back of the dress. He kissed me as he dragged it down in one fluid motion, getting it loose so he could yank it off me then grab one of my tits.

My body immediately smoldered at his fire, my breaths becoming pants, my nails becoming daggers into his flesh.

He yanked my thong down my ass as his lips dove to my neck next, sucking the skin, giving a slight bite to my shoulder, and then he scooped my ass into his arms as he lifted me off the floor, my heels still on.

He dropped me onto the bed, my head near the corner of the bed in the opposite direction from the pillows. His knees pushed my thighs open, and his body lowered onto mine, finding my entrance with his rock-hard dick and pushing inside with a masculine moan. One hand fisted the back of my hair, and he looked into my face as he rocked into me.

I moaned when I felt him, always surprised at his girth, never quite ready for it.

His kisses had been aggressive. His touch demanding. But once he had sunk inside me, his hips rocked into me slowly, and he took his time. We moved together, eyes locked on each other, and he pressed his lips to my cheek as he whispered to me. "*Chérie, tu es à moi. Tu es la seule. Je t'aime...*"

I could make out some not all. *Sweetheart, my only...*

IT WAS INSULTING that I had to leave and go back to my room.

Like a mistress.

I was there when he wanted, then excused when my use had expired. I suddenly felt like Kendra, just seated on the opposite side of the table, just a fuckable trophy. I sat up in bed and looked out the window for a moment before I sighed and got to my feet.

He was smart and intuitive, unlike most men, so he could discern words that were never spoken. His deep voice immediately addressed me. "What is it, chérie?"

Without looking at him, I gathered my clothes off the floor and picked up my heels where they'd been kicked away. "Nothing." The evening had been unforgettable, with gourmet food and first-class service, with a beautiful man who couldn't keep his hands off me until he'd been thoroughly satisfied. But I suddenly felt cheap. "Goodnight." I escorted myself to the door without giving him a backward glance.

"Melanie." His voice was quiet but contained so much power that it stopped everything in the room, even the flames in the hearth. His feet thudded against the rug around his bed when he left the bed and got to his feet.

I stared at the door, buck naked, my dress and thong in my hand. I was about to leave, like some kind of prostitute. My job was done, and now it was time to get out of his face.

"I asked you a question." His voice grew louder as he came closer to me, the anger becoming more palpable when he didn't get an answer. He barked orders and expected obedience, so it was naturally infuriating when that didn't happen with me.

I slowly turned around and looked up to meet his gaze, my anger rising when I saw the rage in his dark eyes. "So, that's just normal? A man to abandon his wife at home in favor of his mistress?" Sometimes I became so absorbed in Fender that I forgot he was a criminal who had the fucking president in his pocket. He had no values. He had no morals.

His intense eyes constricted as his eyebrows furrowed.

"Just changes his fucking mind at the last minute and takes his mistress instead?"

His expression didn't change, like he had absolutely no idea what I was saying. "It's common for a man to have a mistress."

My eyebrows heightened at his honesty. "And that's just perfectly fine?"

A long silence stretched, his eyes shifting back and forth as he regarded me. "I'm sure his wife is aware of that fact, yes."

I let out a long, drawn-out breath. "Wow...okay."

"It's common in French society. Not scandalous like in your country."

I pivoted on the spot and headed to the door, eager to get the hell out.

"Melanie." Now he did raise his voice, coming at me in a rage, grabbing me by the arm and yanking me back. He squeezed my arm as his dark eyes drilled into my face, backing me up into the wall so I couldn't get away. "Speak your mind. Now." He released my arm but kept me pinned in place, his hands pressing into the wall on either side of me, his thick arms as strong as steel bars in a cage.

I met his eyes before I dropped my gaze.

"Eyes. On. Me."

I sucked in a breath between my closed teeth and obeyed automatically. "Is that all I am to you?" My voice came out quiet, the hurt coming through. "A mistress? I'm the woman you fuck in your bed, but I'm not the woman who sleeps there. When my beauty fades, will I be replaced with a Kendra? Is that the kind of life I can expect?"

He was absolutely motionless long after I confessed my fears. His eyes stopped shifting back and forth, turning still like the rest of him, like he didn't even need a breath. His palms remained planted against the wall. He moved in closer, getting right in my face. "You insult me." His palms dragged down the wall until his arms dropped by his sides. "Get out." He turned away and walked back to the bed, his muscular back tightening and shifting with his movements.

I breathed hard as I remained in my spot. "Whatever..." I turned to the door and yanked it open.

"Improve your French." He turned back around and stared me down with a smoldering look of hatred. "Because you suck at it."

———

"SIT." Fender pressed his hand into my shoulder, forcing me down onto the bench.

"No...please." Tears ran down my cheeks as I watched the executioner drag Raven across the snow and to the noose that waited for her. I grabbed on to Fender's jacket and tugged. "Please do this for me. Please spare her."

He turned away and looked at the blood in the snow from the previous victim. "I can't stop this."

Raven dragged her feet and turned to me, tears down her cheeks. "Melanie, help me!"

I pushed against his hold and fell to the snow. "No!"

The executioner forced her onto the box and tightened the noose around her neck.

"I'm sorry!" Tears blurred my vision, so I could barely see. "I'm so sorry! Forgive me."

The executioner tightened the rope and then kicked the box from underneath her.

She dropped and swung on the rope.

"No!" I sat in the snow, convulsing with sobs that cracked my chest.

The executioner readied the knife and stabbed her in the stomach.

She gave a grunt when the blade pierced her, her blood dripping to the snow.

I fell to the earth, buried my face in the snow. "All my fault...all my fault...no..."

I jumped up in bed, gasped for breath, and tugged at the sheets like they were piles of snow. Tears were hot on my cheeks. There was a fire in my fireplace, but there were no torches hanging on the wall. The room was chilly, but not stinging with cold. My palms dragged against the sheets to feel the silk instead of the powder. "A dream... It was a dream... not real." The room started to infiltrate my vision, the shape of the bed, the windows covered with curtains.

My bedroom door opened, and he came inside, a dark silhouette.

I immediately jolted, spotting his dark outline and seeing the executioner.

He moved to the bed quickly. "Chérie, why are you screaming?" He sat at the edge of the bed and reached for me.

I jumped away, my heart racing so quickly I thought I'd have a heart attack. I clutched my chest as I hyperventilated.

Fender stilled and watched me, his dark eyes visible in the light of the fire. "It's me, chérie... It's me."

I took in his features and felt my breath start to slow. But the tears didn't stop.

He gently reached for me again, this time his hand moving to my shoulder. His fingertips squeezed me lightly, his thumb brushing across my skin in a soothing motion. "A dream...just a dream."

My breathing slowed once the threat was gone, when I understood it wasn't real. But the tears amplified, the regret constricting my throat like I'd swallowed a baseball bat. "I wish I were dead." I cupped my mouth to stifle the sobs. "I did this...I fucking did this. I hate myself. I can't even look in the mirror because I hate what I see." I dropped my gaze to the sheets, imagining the snow that looked and felt so real. Her blood was staining the ground, her guttural noises loud as the knife pierced her intestines. My eyes closed as the image radiated across my mind, causing my breath to halt in agony.

His hand moved into my hair to stroke me gently, to try to calm me in silence.

His touch just made me feel worse because I enjoyed it. I shouldn't enjoy it. I shouldn't want him there. I pushed his hand away and left the bed altogether, moving into the living room. I took a seat on the couch with my arms crossed over my chest and stomach, just trying to get through this emotional agony that was as potent as physical pain. It attacked my brain, my heart, everything. It was like losing blood in the snow, like I was the one in the noose. I closed my eyes and just tried to get through it.

The cushion shifted as he sat directly beside me. His hand didn't move into my hair again. He didn't touch me at all, just the way he used to in the cabin. "Why can't you look in the mirror?" His voice had been harsh in our fight earlier that evening, but now it was soft like rain-drops on a rose petal. "Why do you hate what you see?" He waited for me to answer his question, and when that didn't happen, he gently prodded again. "Talk to me, chérie."

I opened my eyes and looked at him, tears on my cheeks, my lips, in the corners of my eyes. "She's there because of me. She wouldn't let me leave alone because she loves me so much...and she would do it again even if she knew what would happen. She would give up her life for mine in a heartbeat." I shook my head, my voice cracking with tears. "And I shit all over that. What kind of person am I? I'm living in this fucking palace and fucking the guy who keeps her there. I just abandoned her... She would never abandon me."

He watched me with those dark eyes, his features expres-sionless. For the first time ever, he dropped his gaze and looked at the cushion between us. The intensity was gone from his gaze. He looked like a different person—just for an instant.

I looked at the coffee table and forced the tears to slow, forced myself to calm. Otherwise, I would get a migraine from this grief.

"Chérie." His voice was cloaked in such affection, it was like he physically touched me, physically reached his hand out and grabbed mine.

I turned back to him.

"People think life is complicated, that we wind up in situations because of a series of decisions. People think they happen to life. But in reality, *it* happens to *us*. Life happened to both of you, Melanie. You can blame it on yourself, but you were targeted before you even knew it, and it was going to happen, regardless. Maybe that would have included her. Maybe it wouldn't have. No way to know. Because life isn't complicated. It's very simple—and random. To assign guilt is pointless."

"It's more than that—"

"If Raven were in your position now, here with me, do you think her behavior would be any different?"

"Yes. She never would have slept with you. She never would have—"

"She's sleeping with Magnus, so I don't believe that. There's literally nothing you can do for her. You can't run. You can't go to the police. All you can do is accept your reality. And you aren't a bad person for enjoying it too."

I dropped my gaze. "But I'm weak. I'm a weak person." I was just baggage to her when we tried to escape. If I were smart, I would have understood my surroundings and not had been captured in the first place. If I were strong like Raven, I wouldn't need Fender to make a fire.

"I don't see what you see, chérie. I see a beautiful, kind, lovely woman. If you were anyone else, Gilbert would be unemployed right now. If you could die by your sister's side, you would. You're a woman who likes to be taken care of, and you shouldn't apologize for it. You don't deserve to feel guilty for being who you are. I love taking care of you. I want to take care of you every single day. I want to give you a life that you deserve. I wouldn't want you any other way. That's just how I am—and I won't apologize for it."

I looked at him again, seeing the confidence in his gaze, seeing a man who overwhelmed me with sincere compliments. "You're the only one who has nice things to say about me."

His eyes softened until they turned sympathetic. "Because I'm the only one who really knows you, chérie."

My eyes started to water as I looked at him, for a variety of reasons. "If you really feel that way about me...please do this for me. You were right when you said I can't run to her. I can't go to the police. My sister would never give up on me if the situations were reversed, and the only way I can save her is if you agree to do this for me. So, if you feel anything for me...please."

He held my gaze for a long time, his eyes still, his breathing nearly unnoticeable.

"I will always feel this way. I will always suffer. I will always wake up with nightmares of her with that rope around her neck. She will always be in the back of my mind, consuming my thoughts anytime I'm alone...even when I'm not alone." My hand reached out to his, and I squeezed it between both of mine. Two tears dripped from my eyes and down my cheeks simultaneously. "Please...I beg you."

His eyes slowly shifted away, looking at another point in the living room.

"You're the boss. You can do whatever you want—"

"I told you I don't negotiate. I don't make exceptions—"

"You took me."

"That's different. The guards know exactly why I did that. To take her is a different scenario, especially after all the grief she's caused—"

"The exception is not for her. It's for me." I squeezed his hand tighter. "She's always going to fight. She's always going to cause grief. Your life will be easier when she's gone—think about it that way."

He fell silent and didn't look at me again.

"You're my only hope, Fender."

At the sound of his name, he turned back to me, his gaze hard.

"Take care of me. I'm asking you to take care of me." I knew I was so close to changing his mind, securing the one thing I wanted more than anything else in the world. My hands shook as they held on to him.

He stared for a long time before he spoke. "She will always stand between us. She will always haunt you. That is the only reason—"

"Thank you." I jumped into him, my arms latching on for dear life. My body moved into his lap, and I clung to him like a lifeline.

He didn't hug me back, remaining still as he felt me bury my face in his neck and cry. His arms eventually wrapped around me, his hand moving into my hair, pressing a kiss to my shoulder. His hand gently pulled me back so he could look at me. "Don't misunderstand me. I'll remove her from the camp, but I won't let her go."

I was disappointed but unsurprised. "Then where will she go?"

"On the estate in the guest quarters. You can go visit her, but she'll never be permitted to enter our residence. Guards will watch her at all times. She'll have everything she needs to be comfortable, but never freedom. That's the extent of my generosity."

She would just be a prisoner again, but in a luxurious setting. Raven would never accept that. "If the police will do nothing if she goes to them, and she's no threat to you, then why not just release her?"

He stared me down long and hard, like the question angered him. "Because I don't like her." His tone darkened, his expression hardening and turning his countenance angry. "Appreciate my generosity. Because I'm being very generous, more generous than I've ever been in my life—for you." He stared me down in expectation.

My arms remained wrapped around his neck, my face close to his, my ass in his lap on the couch. I knew Raven wouldn't accept imprisonment in any format, but she would be taken care of, we would see each other every day, we would be safe for the rest of our lives. She would accept it eventually. She would appreciate what I'd done for her—that I saved her. "Thank you."

EIGHTEEN
THE CATACOMBS

FENDER

I spoke to Magnus on the phone inside my office. "Jacques has lifted the importation embargo from Colombia, so we can get what we needed through another medium." All it took was some wining and dining, making the president feel like a major player in the game, to get what I wanted. Money wasn't the only thing that mattered to him. Ego was even more important.

Magnus held his silence.

He was already on thin ice with me, so I didn't appreciate his disapproval. "You have nothing to say?"

"If we lift the trade agreement, what's to stop copycats?"

"Our guns." I hung up because I couldn't stand his bullshit a second longer.

Gilbert stepped in a moment later. "Sir, where will you be taking your lunch—"

"Here." I tossed the phone across the desk.

"Of course," he said with a nod. "Shall I tell Melanie you wish to be alone for the rest of the day?"

My immediate reaction was to dismiss her, but I didn't mind having her around, even if we didn't speak. Her presence was soothing to me. Her beauty distracted me. Made me forget about bullshit. "She's always welcome."

He gave a bow then departed.

When I'd woken up that morning, I wanted to take back my offer.

I shouldn't have caved.

I allowed her to make me weak. I allowed her to turn me soft. But when I heard her nighttime screams, I came running without hesitation. I watched her tears pour down her face and wished I could take it all away. I wished I could give her only joy. I wanted to take care of my chérie, and watching her fall into despair told me how much I'd failed.

I fucking failed.

Now I couldn't take back what I promised. I couldn't go back on my word to her. I had to see this through, pull out that obnoxious bitch and replace her with someone else, only to have her live on my property, to be fed and clothed for the rest of her life.

And I had to foot the bill.

But there was no other way.

Raven was the thorn in my side, the cinder block in the road, the bullet lodged deep into my flesh.

Heels tapped against the hard floor outside the open doorway, growing louder as Melanie approached. She had a slow gait, taking her time as if she had nowhere to be or whoever expected her presence would wait a lifetime.

I'd wait several lifetimes.

My back was sunk into the armchair, my fingers curled into a fist against my chin, my elbow on the leather armrest. My eyes took her in as she stepped inside, holding a book in one hand, wearing a pale blue dress with matching heels. Her only responsibility as a resident was to wear the beautiful clothes I provided, the diamonds, the finer things in life that most people didn't even know existed.

She halted on the rug and examined me. Her eyes absorbed my appearance, my mood, everything about me. That told her everything she needed to know. She silently took a seat and opened her book to read.

Not speaking a word to me.

My eyes didn't turn back to my phone or laptop because they were glued to her cheek, seeing the way her hair naturally fell forward when her chin dropped, and she had to push it back, only for it to fall once more. Her beauty was paralyzing to me, like the strongest nuclear weapon on the planet. In silence, it could obliterate every thought that came to mind with an invisible power.

I'd always be angry about the compromise she'd forced me to make.

But it was worth it.

I WORKED THROUGH LUNCH. Took phone calls. When Magnus called back later, I picked up then hung up immediately, just to make my anger palpable. I could have ignored the call for the same effect, but I wanted it to sting.

I sank back into my chair, thinking things over, and my eyes focused on her like she was a painting on the wall right in front of me. My eyes lingered a long time before I shut my laptop and moved to the couch across from her.

When she heard me, she looked up from her book. She regarded me for a while before she closed her book without inserting a bookmark and set it on the table. She was still reading *The Count of Monte Cristo*. It was a long book, so it was no surprise that it was still in her hands. She straightened with the poise Gilbert had instilled in her then dropped her chin to regard her hands on her knee, her fingernails painted with French tips.

The fire continued to burn hot in the hearth because Gilbert had silently entered the office and continued to feed it without either one of us noticing, being the shadow on the wall that had no real presence. It was another day of rain, and it was audible even though we were on the ground floor. The raindrops splattered against the windows, leaving tears on the glass that streaked down like the ones on her cheeks last night.

I leaned forward with my forearms on my thighs, one hand encompassing the other. Whenever I was with her, my mind turned empty, devoid of objects, light, feelings. Normally, it was saturated with more shit than I could contain, but she brought me peace that was akin to nothingness. To not think, to not feel, it was like meditation.

She lifted her chin and looked at me. "When will my sister be here?" It was a question she'd probably wanted to ask since last night, but she could only restrain herself so long.

Peace was shattered. "When I return to the camp."

"When will that be?"

"When I decide to return." I never made plans further than a few days into the future. Life was uncontrollable, so I just went with it, not against it.

Disappointment filled her gaze. "Like in a few weeks?"

My eyes narrowed on her face.

She quickly dropped her look. "I'm sorry. I'm just...I'm afraid she'll be dead by then."

"Magnus saved her neck twice. No reason he wouldn't do it a third time."

She inhaled a deep breath and slowly released it, her eyes closing briefly. When she was ready, she looked at me again, showing me those brilliant blue eyes that were like sapphires to complement her diamonds. "I'll feel a lot better when she's here, but...I don't think the nightmares will ever stop."

"Nightmares are part of the human experience." I had them often, the same premise happening in different ways. Sometimes I was a grown man who came into my family home and stopped my father from killing my family, beating him with my bare fists before making him eat his gun. Sometimes I was the helpless teenager that was just skin and bones, and there wasn't a damn thing I could do for my family—not even Magnus. Decades had passed, and it still haunted me like it was yesterday. I gave my father a death no one deserved, but that failed to bring me peace.

She was the only thing that did.

She looked down again, her little fingers moving together slightly. When she turned her head, it showed how slender her neck was, the little vein that rose to her jawline, the soft and delicious skin that tempted my tongue. "You have nightmares?" She looked up again to see my reaction.

"Yes."

"Maybe you wouldn't have nightmares...if I were next to you."

My expression didn't convey my annoyance. I remained as stoic as ever, but I knew exactly what her endgame was.

"Because if I were beside you...I don't think I would." She approached the situation differently, coming from an angle she hoped I wouldn't see.

Chérie, I see everything.

She waited for my response, and the longer it didn't come, the more her eyes sank. "You can trust me—"

"I don't trust anybody." Like razor blades, the words left my mouth and sliced through the air. "It has nothing to do with you. How many times do I have to say it?"

Her eyes winced, like I'd just cut her deeply. "You said the safest place in the world is with you. How am I supposed to feel safe if I'm down the hall in a freezing cold bed—"

"Then I'll fuck you there. Problem solved."

She winced again.

My anger was inconsolable at this point. When I gave her a little string, she wanted the entire rope. She tugged and tugged, having an entitlement she never earned. "You ask me for more when all I should be getting is your gratitude. You should be on your fucking knees thanking me for the sacrifice I made for you." I couldn't keep my voice down like usual. It was one of the rare times when I actually yelled right in her face, when my ferocity hit her shores like a goddamn hurricane. "You have no idea what it will cost me. I woke up today wishing I could take it all back, but I'm a man of my word, so I won't break my promise to you."

She breathed hard as she absorbed the wind and the hail, eventually dropping her gaze entirely because the intimacy between our eyes was just too much. Bumps formed on her skin like she was cold, and she absent-mindedly crossed her arms over her chest to protect herself from my wrath.

I was used to yelling at people—but not her. There was no regret, only more anger because she'd forced me to do what I'd rather avoid. My obsession with this woman was obvious to everyone, including her, but I wasn't a fucking pushover. I wouldn't give in to every demand she asked for, not when I already gave her the world.

She didn't rise and depart my office. She remained in the same position, just breathing.

I leaned back into the couch and curled my fingers into a fist, my elbow propping on the back of the couch with my hand on the back of my neck. My other arm was stretched across the back of the couch. I rubbed the back of my neck and the bottom of my hairline, my fingers running through the short strands. I waited for her to storm off and not speak to me for several days.

"You're right."

My fingers stilled at her admission.

She smoothed out her dress then got to her feet. When she approached me, she hiked up her dress before she lowered herself right between my knees.

I stared at her. Breathless. Still. Focused.

Her palms moved up my sweatpants to the band before her fingers hooked inside the fabric of my boxers. Then she dragged them both down, assisted when I lifted my hips to get the clothes off my ass, and she pushed everything to my ankles on the floor. "I should be thanking you." She craned her neck forward and started at my balls, pressing gentle kisses there.

The surprise waned, and my hand fisted her hair, keeping it from her face as I guided her onto my length and pushed her down, getting my dick in her throat, moaning when I felt that tongue. "Yes, chérie." I closed my eyes briefly when I felt her warm mouth, when I listened to her make a slight choking sound. My hand gripped her neck, and I forced her down over and over, making her take that dick harder than her pussy did. Tears formed in the corners of her eyes and she gasped, but I guided her at the aggressive pace I demanded, and she didn't resist. "Thank me good and hard."

THE CATACOMBS WERE ONCE a national land-mark to the French. Tourists could pay a fee to explore the underground tunnels that stretched for miles and miles, admire the skulls in the walls, the underground city of the dead.

Until the Chasseurs bought it.

I wasn't the only man acquainted with the political aristo-crats of this country. Paris was known as the city of love, the Eiffel Tower a symbol of light and heart, the bakeries selling chocolate croissants that couldn't be replicated elsewhere.

Little did people know that monsters lived in the shadows.

That it was one of the most corrupt cities in the world.

I descended through the tunnels until I came face-to-face with Bartholomew in the great hall, an enormous cavern with an ancient city in the rear. The Chasseurs were there, drinking at their tables, entertained by the French whores that were paid to pay a visit.

Bartholomew was on the throne, and his eyes were instantly on me when I entered, as if he expected me the moment I approached his territory, his spies everywhere.

His chin was propped on his closed knuckles, and with a bored look, he watched me approach.

There was another throne beside him—but it was empty.

I stopped in front of him.

His eyes were still and cold.

Mine were hard and black.

The standoff ended when he spoke. "You lifted the regulations. Congratulations."

He knew everything the moment it happened—as did I.

He continued his bored expression, losing interest in me the second I stepped into his presence. "You better be here to deal us in. Otherwise, you're here to brag, and no one likes a bragger."

"Once we ramp up production, we'll offer you a partnership. Not sure when that will be, but soon. Get ready."

His body didn't shift or move, but a slow smile spread over his lips. "Now we're talking."

"YOU OFFERED them a partnership when we haven't even figured out a way to implement this?" Magnus asked incredulously. "I'm in negotiations with Hector, but nothing has been guaranteed. To increase our supply, he'll have to make changes, and those changes could get a competitor's attention. Fender, we don't make promises we can't keep—"

"I made him no promise. Instead of sitting around finding all the reasons why something won't work, find the reasons why it will work." I tossed my jacket on an armchair in my bedroom as I paced.

"I'm being realistic, Fender. Maybe you should try it sometime—"

"Maybe you should grow some balls and stop being a little bitch." I hung up and slammed the phone onto my nightstand. "*Mauviette...*" I yanked my shirt over my head then dragged my hands down my face as I approached the bed. When I heard her quiet footsteps and the creak of the door, I knew I wasn't alone. I dropped my hands and turned my stare on her.

She flinched at my look, her hand still on the door like she intended to sneak away when she realized my foul mood.

My stare continued, eyeing the black satin nightgown that showed her soft thighs. She was barefoot, looking petite when she didn't have those five-inch heels to compete with my height.

"Everything okay?"

I turned away and undid my jeans before I kicked off my shoes. "Get in bed."

She hesitated before she entered my bedroom. She got on the bed then slid under the sheets as she watched me finish getting undressed.

When I was naked, I got into bed beside her. But my mood was too foul for sex, at least right now, so I lay beside her and stared at the fire Gilbert had prepared before I returned home.

She didn't come close to me, giving me my space. After minutes of silence and separation, she moved closer to me and wrapped her body around mine, giving a slight shiver when her body thawed at my heat.

My arm wrapped around her as I cradled her to me, loving her body up against mine even if I wasn't inside her. Her skin was so soft, her smell so fragrant, her hair like gentle fingertips against my skin.

Time passed with our eyes on the fire, watching it dance beautifully, slowly dying down as it cannibalized itself, eating the fuel that sustained it. My thoughts were on business, but particularly, my uncooperative brother. He claimed to be the voice of reason, but he felt like the voice of sabotage.

Melanie propped herself on her elbow and faced me, some of her hair falling forward onto my chest. Her hair had grown longer over the months, becoming more beautiful with its increased length. It was extra rope to wrap around my fingers when I held on to her, like reins to the most beautiful mare.

And I was her stallion.

"Where did you go?" Her fingers moved farther up my stomach to my chest, lightly pressing into me like she wanted to feel my hard muscle push back.

"Met a business associate."

"That didn't go well?"

"That was fine. But I spoke to one of my men when I came home...and I didn't appreciate the conversation."

"What did he do?"

I turned to look at her, questioning her with my eyes.

"I just...want to know more about you." Her voice trailed away in its timidity, as if she were afraid she would provoke the hurricane again. "You don't talk about anything personal, so..." Her hand continued to rub my chest.

"You know everything about me, chérie." She knew me better than anyone—besides Magnus—without realizing it.

"Really?" she asked. "Because I don't even know your last name."

"A surname tells you nothing about who I am."

"Then what does?" she whispered.

My hand slipped underneath her hair and cupped her cheek, her skin cold to my touch, like the fire and my warm body still hadn't thawed her entirely. My thumb brushed against the corner of her mouth as I stared at those full lips, dark with lipstick, with a gentle shine of gloss. When I looked in the mirror, sometimes I saw the imprint of her lips on my neck. When I looked at my dick after she sucked me off, I could see it around the base of my length. It stained the sheets, stained the pillowcase when I shoved her face down to get her ass higher into the air. "This." My eyes lifted to her eyes again. "The way a man treats his woman...tells you everything that matters."

Melanie

He sat in the center of the couch in his office, his bottoms snug around his ankles with his bare feet planted to the floor. My panties were somewhere on the rug. His thumbs were pressed against my hips, and his fingers kneaded my ass as I rose up and down, my tits dragging against his chest.

His eyes were always on mine, always watching every reaction I made, every breath I took. His strong hands guided the pace, making sure I kept it nice and slow as he preferred. Whenever I was on top, he never wanted it hard and aggressive. He wanted it to stretch it out forever, for us to breathe as one person, to make the moment last forever.

My arms hooked around his neck, and I kept my head close to his, moaning in his face, my bent knees on his thighs while I arched my back as best as I could. I'd come into his office to read and feel his presence, but he marched over, dropped onto the couch, and before I knew it, I was on top of him, riding him like he'd just come home after being gone for weeks.

I clung to him as I started to rock hard and fast, driving myself into another climax that made my eyes burn with tears, made my perfect makeup run.

He watched me come, his eyes gaining in intensity as I came and clenched his dick. "*Je t'aime, chérie.*" His fingers dug into my ass harder, and he brought me down with force, releasing inside me with a clenched jaw, the cords in his neck bulging with tension. He gave a masculine grunt when he finished, his dick throbbing inside me before he gave my ass a hard smack with his big hand. "Fuck, chérie."

I was comfortable on top of him, even though I knew we were finished because his dick finally began to soften. My arms remained around his neck, and I rested my forehead against his as I caught my breath, my nipples softening when the heat was over. The office smelled like a wood-burning fire, sweat, and sex.

His eyes maintained their intensity, like everything I'd given him wasn't enough. It would never be enough. His arms wrapped around my back and tugged me harder into him, locking me in place like he didn't want me to leave. He probably had a million things to do, but he'd rather be naked and wrapped up with me, still buried inside me like a car in a garage.

Moments like these made me forget the truth. I wasn't a prisoner in a labor camp who caught the eye of the king-pin. I was at a bar with my friends. He walked over and bought me a drink, and after weeks of hot sex and midnight secrets, he asked me to move in to his mansion so we could be together always.

I wished that were the truth.

His arms loosened around me like the opening to a cage—so I could fly away. His hands glided to my hips, where his fingers gently caressed me underneath my hiked-up dress. His dark eyes looked me over, examining the beauty that had stolen his attention and religiously kept it.

My arms dropped from his shoulders, and my hands moved to grip his shoulders so I could use his mass as an anchor when I got up. But I stayed. I looked into his dark eyes and stayed. I looked into his hard face and realized I didn't know the man who had given me intimacy so deep, it changed my perspective on my situation every single day. "Can I ask you something?"

His eyes turned guarded, deflecting the question I'd yet to ask.

"You said I could ask you anything."

"You know how I meant that, chérie. You can ask me about my lovers. You can ask where I've slept. You can ask me anything a woman would want to know about her man. Everything else...off the table."

"Why?"

His eyes turned hard like stones.

"Is it because you don't trust me?"

His eyes remained rigid and in place, but slowly, they eased up a little.

"You said you don't trust anybody, but how can someone live that way?"

"It's easier than you think." He broke eye contact and shifted his gaze away, looking at the fire that smoldered down to hot coals. Flames reflected on the surface of his eyes, the brightness making a sun appear in the darkness of space that surrounded it.

"There has to be somebody..."

Seconds trickled past before he spoke. "My brother."

"It doesn't seem like you're close. He's never come to the house."

"Trust is an elemental connection between two people that isn't affected by companionship or conversation. It's unconditional. Regardless of what happens in this unpredictable life, that remains predictable." His eyes shifted back to me. "We're very different men. We believe in very different things. But those virtues and ideologies are irrelevant when it comes to us. There are times when I want to break that trust, but I never would. And I'm sure the temptation has happened for him as well. But it never happens. It will never happen." He stared me down for a while. "That's what trust is."

I WAITED for Fender to leave and retrieve my sister.

It never happened.

I trusted his word. I knew it would happen.

I just wanted it to happen now.

Fender had left early that morning and hadn't returned. He didn't tell anyone where he was going, not even Gilbert, and I knew better than to ask. If he departed for the camp, he would tell me, so that meant he was doing something in the city.

I explored the house again, examining the paintings in bedrooms on floors that no one ever frequented except for Gilbert and the housekeepers. I made my way to a large room with hardwood floors and mirrors on one wall. Exercise equipment was spaced out everywhere, heavy weight plates on the floor and dumbbells in the corner. Everything was big and heavy, so this must be where Fender did his workouts. He must have done it early in the morning before I woke up

I went downstairs for lunch and took a seat at the dining table in the garden room even though I wasn't hungry. There was just nothing else to do, not when Fender wasn't home. When I saw him in his office, he didn't usually talk to me, and I didn't understand his phone calls in French, but it was still comforting to be near him.

I didn't want him to leave me here alone.

But when he returned, he would have Raven.

And I could see her all I wanted.

"Everything alright, Melanie?" Gilbert carried the teapot and filled my teacup. "Your eyes are sad." The steam immediately rose from the cup, a translucent white color that filled the room with the smell of peach. He set the teapot on the surface in front of my lunch.

My elbows were on the table, and my chin was propped on my closed hand, ignoring the table manners I should exhibit. When he didn't scold me, I knew he was cutting me some slack because of my somberness. "Fender said he would retrieve my sister from the camp, but that was days ago, and he still hasn't gone..."

Gilbert positioned his arms behind his back as he stood at the head of the table, dressed immaculately in his tuxedo, a slight shadow on his jawline. "You're worried he won't keep his word?"

"No. I just... The wait is killing me."

"Well, her quarters have been prepared. He asked me to oversee the project. Perhaps that will make you feel better."

My hand dropped from my chin, and I straightened. "He did?"

He nodded. "Would you like to see them?"

I abandoned the lunch Gilbert had served and got to my feet. "Yes. Please show me."

Gilbert hesitated, glancing at the hot food that had just been brought from the chef's kitchen.

"Hot or cold, it's still delicious. Don't worry, I'll eat it."

WE MADE our way across the property to another building that was identical to the main palace, just a tenth of the size. It was two stories, probably the size of a single home in my old neighborhood. There were gardens around the perimeter with a patio that showed the lawns and the main palace.

It was nothing like the cabin she had now.

Gilbert allowed me inside, and we stepped into a living room with elegant furniture facing a TV. There was also a piano in the corner. The curtains were parted over the windows, giving a view outside.

It was beautiful.

Nothing like a prison.

We explored the guesthouse, stepping into her bedroom, where she had a large bed all to herself. She had a master bathroom with a full tub and a shower, a vanity to apply her makeup. Clothes were in the closet. Not nice things like what I had. But they would keep her comfortable.

Gilbert followed behind me. "Fender makes a promise, he keeps it. You shouldn't doubt him ever again."

I turned back around and regarded him.

His expression contained mild offense.

"I didn't doubt him. I'm just anxious."

"Why would you be anxious if you didn't doubt him?"

My arms crossed over my chest, and my eyes narrowed. "Gilbert, I understand your loyalty to that man, but let's not forget that my sister is working in a labor camp every single day that he doesn't go back. She could be killed at a moment's notice. I'm entitled to be anxious—so get off my ass."

I SAT on my couch and watched TV in French, hoping to catch on to their conversations. It was such a hard language for me because I'd never been exposed to it prior to my trip to Paris. In high school, I took Spanish... and didn't retain a word of it.

A knock sounded on my door, telling me Gilbert had entered my bedroom.

I kept my eyes on the TV, still annoyed with him from earlier today.

He cleared his throat as he stood at the end of the other couch.

I still didn't look at him.

"Melanie, I'd like to apologize. I think my feelings may have gotten the best of me."

I turned away from the TV and met his gaze, seeing the guilty look on his face. "You think?"

He dropped his gaze, the features of his face sagging like he aged a decade in a second.

"Please accept my sincere apology."

"I'm not going to tell Fender."

"I already knew that, Melanie. I'm sorry because I was being biased and insensitive."

My anger was impossible to grip, so I let it go. "It's okay, Gilbert."

He came closer then indicated to the cushion beside me. "May I?"

"Sure."

He took a seat then grabbed the notebook on the coffee table. "Working on your French, huh?" He nodded to the TV.

"Fender said I sucked at it, so…"

"Yes, he asked me to teach you even when he's in residence." He grabbed the pen and clicked it. "Any luck with this?"

"Nope." It was some kind of soap opera, and while there was a lot of yelling and then a lot of steamy scenes right afterward, I couldn't make out the transitions in between. Other than simple words that I had already learned, the rest was indecipherable.

"French is a difficult language for a novice. And we speak so quickly that it's hard to grasp."

Whenever Fender spoke on the phone, his words tumbled out like a waterfall. In English, his words were seldom and purposeful. Maybe it was because it was his second language.

Gilbert crossed one leg on the opposite knee and got comfortable against the cushions.

"Is he home?"

"Yes. Just had dinner."

If he wanted to see me, he would have come to me. He wouldn't have ordered Gilbert to continue his instruction. He was either in a bad mood or still had work to do.

His work outside the camp seemed to be dinner with important figures and nighttime strolls with shady characters. I knew which one it was when I wasn't invited.

Gilbert went on with his instruction, teaching me a couple phrases I could use at dinner parties, and then tried to help me figure out what was being said on the TV show, so I could follow along. "I think regularly watching French TV will help. They say immersing yourself in a culture is the quickest way to learn a language. But since you don't go out, this is the next best thing."

The most French I'd learned was what Fender said to me, so that was true. "He said I sucked at French, so I'm obviously not understanding what he says to me."

"And what does he say?"

I tried to think of something new, something I didn't recognize. "Cha... chatti—"

"*Chatte*, probably."

"*Chatte parfaite.*"

He chuckled as he wrote it down. "*Chatte parfaite.*"

"What does it mean?"

He lowered his eyes and cleared his throat. "Perfect cunt..."

"Oh..." Sometimes I didn't want Gilbert to translate because it was a bit awkward, but I didn't have a phone or laptop so I couldn't figure it out myself.

Gilbert moved on. "What else?"

What other dirty things did Fender say to me? "Uh... something like... *te baiser... dans le cul...* I'm not sure if that's right."

He didn't have a reaction as he wrote it down. "He wants to fuck you in the ass."

My eyes immediately paled at Gilbert's words. I was sure Fender would do a good job, but I was not interested in that...at all. My cheeks started to redden a little bit when I knew exactly what he said, what he wanted me to know that he'd said it. I pushed past it to dispel the awkwardness. "He also says... *Je t'aime, chérie.* He says that a lot, actually."

Gilbert went absolutely still, the point of his pen pressed to the white paper, a drop of ink growing bigger and bigger the longer he held it there. With eyes wide open, as if he realized he forgot to turn off the stove in the kitchen, he didn't even breathe.

"What?"

He unclicked the pen then dropped it on the notebook, like he was finished for the night. He leaned forward and set the notebook there, his forearms moving to his thighs, his hands coming together.

The silence was suffocating. "Gilbert, what does it mean?"

He inhaled a deep breath before he cleared his throat. He got to his feet, straightened, and then tucked his hands behind his back before he departed the living room.

"Gilbert?" I got to my knees and faced the back of the couch, watching him walk out. "I don't understand. What the hell did he say?"

He halted in his tracks, his back to me, one hand gripping the other wrist. His entire body lifted with the breath he inhaled then slowly sagged as he exhaled, his shoulders dropping farther than they'd been a moment before. "I love you, sweetheart." He took a step forward and continued his route to the door. "That's what it means."

MY LEGS WERE CROSSED with the book in my lap, the pages open to the next chapter in the story. The fire was warm against my legs and knees, even though it was several feet away from me. My eyes took in the words, but occasionally they would flick up and look at the fire.

Fender sat at his desk, making phone calls, working on his laptop, so comfortable with my presence it was like I was absent.

When the fire died down, Gilbert entered and quietly fed the fire with more logs.

He didn't look at me.

When he brought lunch, Fender received his tray first at the desk. "Anything else, sir?"

Fender's eyes remained glued to his screen. "No."

Gilbert nodded before he turned around and crossed the room, his shoulders still low, his eyes hollow. When he returned with my tray, he set it down without making eye contact with me then departed without a word.

He didn't hate me.

He was just heartbroken.

I closed the book and stared at the food he'd brought me, having no appetite because my hunger had been replaced by guilt. My fingers traced the edge of the pages of the closed book as I stared.

"Chérie."

I lifted my gaze, not realizing Fender had moved to the couch across from me.

He stared me down, shirtless in his black sweatpants, his bare feet on the rug. His stare was endless and depthless, like he could do this for hours, days, an eternity. "What is it?"

I moved to the plate that held the tea sandwiches, one of my favorite items that the chef prepared. I set it on my thigh then picked up the freshly made bread without a crust and brought it to my lips for a bite. "Nothing." I'd been quiet and withdrawn for two days, unsure what to do with the information Gilbert had revealed to me.

"I don't trust people who lie to me."

I stopped chewing at the assertion and lifted my eyes again.

His stare had darkened with sheathed ferocity.

"I just... It's been over a week since you said you would remove my sister." My first impulse was to lie because the truth wasn't an option.

His anger slowly defused, and he accepted my lie as truth. "I'm leaving the day after tomorrow."

My eyes focused on his face as my heart clenched with a jolt. "You are?" Being reunited with my sister was what I wanted more than anything. Knowing she was safe, even as a prisoner, was better than her working in the snow, being the target of the executioner and the guards who despised her.

He gave a nod so subtle it was hard to catch.

"Thank you..." The end was near. My sister would be here, her hands in mine, her arms around me. I was so deliriously happy by the image in my mind that my eyes actually watered. My hand returned the half-eaten sandwich to the plate, and I set it on the table.

He didn't give another nod.

My spare time could be spent with her in the guesthouse, talking the way we used to, reading together, just being together in the same room. My mind drifted away into memories that hadn't been formed, the two of us eating on the patio deep into spring, swimming in the large pool on the grounds in summer, living a luxurious life.

"How's your French?"

My eyes immediately shifted back to him, my heart tightening for a whole different reason.

He didn't blink, his eyes shifting back and forth as they pierced into mine, penetrating my mind for the information he wanted.

That was what he wanted me to understand.

He wanted me to know how he felt.

What would happen once I understood? What would he expect from me?

My words broke the silence. "He taught me a few more things. We watched a soap opera, and he translated for me." I held his gaze and waited for him to catch my lie like he did every other time.

His eyes continued to drill into me, piercing the surface and digging deep inside.

I held my stance, controlled my breathing, and hoped Gilbert hadn't already told him the truth.

Because I'd be screwed.

A full minute of tension passed. "Your French better stop sucking soon, chérie."

———————

I STEPPED out of the office to use the restroom, but I had an alternate agenda.

I located Gilbert in the grand foyer, speaking to a housekeeper in French, giving orders that implied he was dissatisfied with her work. When they were finished, he turned around and halted when he came face-to-face with me.

There was anger in his eyes, out of his control, and then it dimmed to unbridled pain. He inhaled a deep breath, getting a hold of the reins connected to his heart. When he spoke, he had a controlled voice that hid his resentment. "How can I serve you, Melanie?"

Gilbert and I were never close and we would never be close, but his sadness hurt me. I was the reason his heart had been broken, having something that he could never have, that no amount of affection and loyalty could earn him. "Can I speak to you in private?"

He immediately glanced down the hallway to where the office was located to make sure we were alone. He gave a subtle nod toward the drawing room and closed the door behind us. It was full of stocked bookshelves and a seating area for entertaining. He pulled a book off the shelf, to cover his ass if we were caught. "Yes?"

"Please don't tell him what you told me."

His eyes didn't look the least bit confused because he knew exactly what I spoke of. "He wants you to know, Melanie. I can't hide it."

"I understand that. Just...buy me some time?"

Now his eyes narrowed in disappointment. "You don't feel the same way." His resentment was palpable, that I had the love of a man he adored, and I didn't want to treasure it the way he would.

"He told me he's returning to the camp in two days. I just need to get Raven here first. Please, just give me two days. I can't risk losing her, not when I'm this close." My hands came together in front of my chest, silently pleading for him to betray his own boss and help me out.

He turned away slightly and released a long sigh, carrying the burden before he even took it. "Two days."

I closed my eyes. "Thank you...thank you."

"I'm only helping you for one reason."

I looked at him again and lowered my hands.

"Because you better be prepared to say it back once I tell him."

TWENTY

BIRTHDAY DRINK

FENDER

I sat in my office and stared at the fire, a glass of scotch on the desk, my temple resting against my closed knuckles. My mind shifted from one topic to the next, thinking about the hour I would leave for the camp in the morning, imagining Raven's face as she was taken from the cabin for the final time, Magnus's reaction, the men's reaction to my weakness. Then I thought about my other responsibilities that required my attention. And of course, Melanie, the woman I would leave behind.

I saw her face as I stared at the flames.

She'd been quiet and withdrawn for the last two days. Her sister had been on her mind consistently, which changed her behavior toward me. I hoped having Raven here wouldn't steal all of Melanie's focus.

She'd better have nothing but gratitude toward me.

Gilbert entered my office and didn't draw my attention until he was in front of my desk. "Sir, is there anything I can get you before I retire for the evening?"

My hand dropped to the screen of my phone, and I tapped it with my finger.

It lit up, reminding me how late it was. "No."

Gilbert gave a bow. "I'll see you in the morning."

"Gilbert."

He straightened. His expression instantly fell, turning serious. At attention, he kept his gaze locked on my face.

"Melanie will not learn French watching TV. She will learn by what I say to her. Understood?"

Gilbert held my gaze for a while before he gave a nod. "Understood."

"Her French better be flawless by the time I return."

He gave another bow. "It will, sir."

SHE WAS PINNED UNDERNEATH ME, my arms hooked behind her knees, her body shaking slightly with my movements. Her head was on the pillow, her eyes on me, her beautiful face erotic when it was tinted red, when her lips were parted in her moans and screams. Her eyes never shone brighter than when we were together like this.

This was not the way I took my whores. The last thing I wanted to see was their faces. All I cared about was their asses and tits.

But Melanie's face was her most beautiful feature.

It was the face in my dreams. The face in my fantasies. The face seared onto the inside of my eyelids. On the road through the wilderness, she was in the landscape, on the side of the mountains I passed. She was in a glass of scotch. In the flames that danced in the fireplace.

When we finished, I didn't want to leave.

It was the first time I'd wanted to stay.

For the entire night.

But my eyes wouldn't close. My heart wouldn't slow. I had to depart in a few hours, and I needed to sleep before the drive. I lay there for less than a few minutes before I got out of bed and pulled on my bottoms.

I'd come to her bedroom so the sheets would be warm after I left, so she would fall asleep immediately and not realize the moment I was gone. But she was wide awake, as if she knew what was about to happen.

She sat up and moved to the edge of the bed, her large tits perky and proud, her long legs over the edge with her foot on the bed frame that surrounded the mattress. Hair messy, makeup smeared, she was gorgeous.

It was hard to leave.

I moved to the bed beside her, looking down into the side of her face, the thin line of mascara that had dripped with a previous tear. My hand moved to her thigh, my fingers surrounding nearly the entire thing.

"When are you leaving?" Her eyes were down on the rug, her features somber with sadness.

I loved that she hated my absence. I loved that she needed to sit in my office while I worked just to be near me. I loved the way she made me feel, like she'd be lost without me. "In a few hours."

"I'll set an alarm so I can say goodbye."

My hand moved into her hair and pushed it behind her shoulder, revealing the feminine curves of her high cheekbones, her slender jawline. "Sleep, chérie." My thumb brushed across her bottom lip, feeling my lungs suck in a gulp of air when her beauty left me breathless. "I'll see you when I get back."

"When will you be home?"

I sucked in another breath as my thumb stilled against her bottom lip, cherishing her choice of words. This palace was her home. It was the place where we both belonged. "I don't know." I never knew. I never made plans, because plans could be tracked and traced.

Keeping everyone on their toes was how I kept my power.

"Be careful..."

I felt my lips lift with a slight smile. "Always." My hand cradled her face and neck, and I turned her toward me, giving her a soft kiss that lasted for several seconds. My eyes closed briefly as I enjoyed it, as I felt that lightness in my stomach, that tightness in my chest. I opened my eyes and saw that hers were closed, that she loved the kiss the way I did. I pulled away and kept my hand on her neck. "*Je t'aime, chérie.*"

Her eyes opened and met mine, her lips lightly parted from the kiss. While her eyes showed affection and desire, there was no recognition, like she had no idea what I just said.

I left her on the bed and rose to my feet.

A knock sounded on the door.

My entire body tightened at the sound. My muscles prepared for an invisible fight, and I instinctively moved in front of Melanie so she would be blocked from view.

"I'm so sorry to disturb you like this," Gilbert said as he opened the door. "But it's urgent. Magnus needs you." He kept his eyes closed as he held out his personal cell phone, doing his best to protect my privacy.

I snatched the phone out of his hand and pressed it to my ear. "Are you okay?" I could still feel the weight of his body in my arms when I'd lifted his lifeless form off the bed. I could still remember the feeling of ineptitude when I dropped him on the stairs. I could still remember looking behind me as we ran for our lives, making sure my little brother was still with me.

"I'm fine." He took a second to breathe into the phone, as if my question put him off.

"Then what is it?"

"She escaped."

My eyes narrowed on the wall in front of me.

Gilbert silently excused himself and stepped into the hallway but left the door open, so he'd be prepared to take orders.

I didn't need to know who she was. "When?"

"A few hours ago."

The anger in my veins was instantaneous. "Then why the fuck did you wait a few hours to tell me?" With flared nostrils and bulging veins, I was a bull that had found its waving red target.

Melanie threw some clothes on then approached me.

I held up my hand without looking at her and marched into the hallway. "Why, Magnus? Why the fuck didn't you tell me the second this happened?"

"Because she knocked me out with a goddamn pipe, and I was unconscious," he snapped. "I have a fucking concussion and a migraine that can't be fixed with pills. The men found me and went after her. The second I realized what happened, I called."

I marched into my bedroom and grabbed my clothes. "Where is she?"

"They don't have her yet."

"I'm on my way. And when I get there, she'll hang. You can't save her this time, Magnus."

His silence lingered like he wouldn't say anything. Just hang up and get back to work. "I know."

I hung up then pulled on my clothes as quickly as possible before I kneeled and got my boots on, the veins in my neck bulging, my gums aching because my teeth were so tightly clenched together.

This bitch had humiliated me—again.

I stood up and grabbed the phone. When I turned to the door, Melanie stood in the doorway, in a wrinkled nightgown with one strap down her shoulder, hair and makeup in the same mess I'd left her in just a moment ago.

But that beauty meant nothing to me now.

The stress on her face had turned her ugly, because she already knew exactly what had happened based on my conversation with Magnus. "What's...what's going on?"

I grabbed my bomber jacket and forced my arms through the sleeves as I threw it on my body. I stared her down as I walked to the door, silently commanding her to get out of my way.

She didn't call my bluff and moved aside.

"She ran." I moved down the hallway and to the top of the stairs.

Gilbert was down below, shouting to the valet. "Get the car around. Now!"

Melanie was quick behind me. "You mean Raven?"

I stopped on the second landing and looked at her over my shoulder.

Her face turned white like the snow at the camp.

I kept going, taking the stairs two at a time to get to the bottom floor as quickly as possible.

"Fender! Wait!" Melanie came after me, tripping at the bottom, but Gilbert caught her. "Please!"

I was at the front door.

"Please!" Her sobs were so loud they echoed in the foyer, like a storm on the roof that shook the entire house.

Time was of the essence, and I didn't have it to waste. I didn't want to console her. But instead of stepping over the threshold and into the pouring rain, I turned to face her again.

She got to her feet with Gilbert's assistance then came to me, barefoot, teardrops on the floor like muddy tracks from the rain. "Don't kill her. Please...please don't. I'm begging you." Her pupils were bloodshot red, her eyes puffy, her cheeks wet and black from the rivers of makeup that traversed down to her chin. "You were going to remove her from the camp anyway, so just—"

"No."

Her chest started to rise and fall harder, her breathing becoming labored with terror. "I would never forgive you—"

"I don't need you to." I'd give this woman anything she wanted, but not this. "She humiliated me—again."

"She's just trying to survive—"

"My answer won't change. Not this time."

Her hands covered her mouth to muffle her sobs, and her entire body shook with uncontrollable tremors. She slowly moved to her knees in front of me, her face in her hands, her cries like wails.

"I will find her. And she'll face the Red Snow." I left her there on the floor and stepped into the rain where my car waited. But her tears came with me, a cacophony inside my mind, a sound that would haunt me forever.

I MADE the trip in record time.

I pushed the car through the damp streets, rode my horse through the snow, and arrived at the camp close to noon.

My reins were tossed to a guard, and I landed in the snow, my eyes scanning the area for signs of activity. The camp was as quiet as ever, the girls in the clearing, like there hadn't been an escape overnight.

I marched deeper into the camp until Magnus caught me.

He pushed his hood back and regarded me since the girls couldn't see him. His eyes were bloodshot, like he'd taken that pipe pretty hard to his head, but other than that, he looked fine.

"Where is she?"

Magnus squinted his eyes as the sun shone on his face. "Haven't found her."

Heavy heartbeats passed, thudding in my chest like hooves from a horse. "How is that possible?"

"Hounds followed her tracks close to the river then lost the scent. The storm hid her horse tracks—"

"She's on horseback?" My voice rose, spit flew from my mouth, my vocal cords nearly popped in half. "How the fuck did she get into the stables?"

"I don't know. The bolt was cut—"

"Cut?" I asked incredulously. "What the fuck did she cut it with?"

"I don't know." He continued to give the same meaning-less answer, his eyes staying on mine even though the sun made them water.

"You don't know?" I stepped closer to him, forcing him to step back. "I'm sick of that answer, Magnus. You're supposed to be in charge while I'm away, but the second I leave, all hell breaks loose." Bartholomew's voice came back to me, telling me to cut my brother out and replace him with someone far more suitable...or kill him. I pushed the thought away as quickly as it entered my mind.

His arms hung up by sides, bloodstains on the fabric from the wound at the back of his head. "We'll find her. The men and hounds are still looking—"

"If they can't track her, that means she crossed the river."

Magnus gave a subtle reaction, a quick blink. "She and the horse won't survive if that's true."

"Unless she crossed at the perfect spot." My eyes drilled into his face, looking for a trace of a lie. I refused to believe that Magnus would betray me for a woman, let alone a woman who looked like a hag compared to Melanie, but now I wasn't so sure. It was the second time she'd escaped, this time with a horse, and now she couldn't be tracked. "Magnus."

He held my gaze, confident in his stare, like he had nothing to hide. "No."

His loyalty to me was far greater than the obsession he had for this woman, so I accepted it without a second thought. "She would never know where to cross in the dark, so if she crossed in any other way, she was swept downriver. The men will continue the search for three days. If she doesn't pop up, we'll assume her body is irretrievable. Whether she's dead out there or dead in here, makes no fucking difference to me."

THE HUNT CONTINUED past three days.

Moved into four.

I wanted to hang her body on the noose so the girls could see it.

Could see what happened if they ran, if they disobeyed, if they did anything other than process that coke.

But it never happened.

She couldn't be found.

I sat in my cabin in front of the fire, drowning my anger in scotch. The executioner made an announcement to the girls, that she'd frozen to death and her body was stuck under a waterfall where we couldn't reach.

That should be enough to scare them from making the same attempt.

The door opened, and Magnus stepped inside, pushing his hood back, his eyes less bloodshot now that the concussion had passed. He moved to the other chair beside me and stared at the fire.

I drank my scotch like he wasn't there.

"I'll leave in the morning."

My eyes remained on the flames, thinking of Melanie at home in her bedroom, knowing that her sister was dead. Her sister's death had been cleaner out in the wild rather than from the noose, but she was gone all the same. Good fucking riddance. "I'll return to Paris in five days."

Magnus gave a slight nod before he grabbed the bottle and poured himself a glass. One of us was usually at the camp at any given time, but sometimes there was a day or two where the overlap failed. The guards weren't stupid enough to cross us.

He brought the glass to his lips and took a drink, his tired eyes focused on the fire, heavy with stress.

My chin was propped on my closed knuckles, letting the fire envelop my body with heat Melanie used to give me. When I returned home, I wasn't sure what I would find. Even if I didn't kill her sister, she might not want anything to do with me.

What would I do then?

Magnus turned his gaze to me, silently waiting for me to meet his look.

I was still pissed off even though he had nothing to do with it, so it took me a few minutes to reciprocate.

He held up his glass slightly. "It's Mom's birthday."

I stared at his glass for a while, not realizing the date because so many other things had been on my mind. I lifted mine and gave a slight tap against his. "Happy Birthday, Mom...wherever you are."

TWENTY-ONE

KNIFE IN THE STOMACH

MELANIE

It was like a knife in the stomach.

Raven was dead.

I knew it.

Magnus wouldn't be able to protect her, not this time.

I sat in the living room in front of the fire, tears coming and going as I looked out the window onto the estate and the landscape that extended for miles. "Why couldn't you have just waited one more fucking day..." Tissues were balled in my fingers, damp against my skin. There were no smudges of makeup, not when I'd stopped bothering to make myself look nice.

I used to wait on pins and needles for Fender to come home.

Now I couldn't care less.

Deep in my heart, I knew Fender had a gentle soul and an innate kindness, so there was hope that he wouldn't go through with it. He might spare her—for me. He might lock her back in her cabin as her punishment.

He did love me...after all.

Gilbert knocked on the door and let himself inside even when there was no response. He moved into the living room and regarded me, with features soft with sympathy. "Melanie, Fender has returned to the palace. Thought you'd like to know..." He gave a slight bow then stepped away.

I stayed in my spot on the couch because I dreaded the answer Fender would give.

If he told me she'd been hung in the Red Snow, I'd throw myself out the window to make the pain stop.

I couldn't face that reality, so I stayed curled up in the corner of the couch, a box of tissues beside me, a dull headache behind my eyes that had been there for almost a week. My fingers loosened on the tissue in my hand and brought it to my nose to wipe the snot that had dripped through my stressed sinuses.

An hour later, the bedroom door opened.

I knew it was him, and instinctively, I pulled my knees closer to my chest and took deeper breaths, preparing for the hardest moment of my life. The room instantly felt warmer when his presence approached, when his energy rivaled the heat of the fire.

I kept my gaze averted.

He stepped into the living room and stopped near the coffee table.

He stared...and stared.

I kept my eyes down, my breathing becoming a bout of hyperventilation, tears forming in my eyes once more.

"Chérie."

"Don't...fucking...call me that." Tears poured down my cheeks, and I pulled my knees closer. My hair was oily because I hadn't showered. My skin was dry because I stopped moisturizing. I'd descended into darkness and couldn't get back up.

He moved to the cushion beside me and took a seat, his eyes on my face like I was in full makeup and a beautiful dress.

"You could have just brought her back like we agreed on. That's all you had to do." My words were muffled by the hard tears. "If you think you can kill her and still have me, you're wrong. She's all I have..."

"I didn't kill her."

The breath died in my throat and never reached my lungs. My face turned to look at him head on, to see those dark eyes regarding me with his eternal affection, like he still saw beauty in my plain face and sorrow. "Did you... Is she here?" My voice cracked with happiness, imagining her downstairs, waiting for me. My hands reached for his, squeezing them in gratitude.

"We never found her."

My hand immediately loosened on his, my dream shattered. "What...what do you mean?"

"We searched for four days. Never turned up."

"So...so...she got away?"

His eyes turned sympathetic. "She's dead. Her body went over a waterfall or she's buried somewhere in the snow, and that's why the hounds can't find her."

"Or...she escaped."

His eyes narrowed. "You've been out there before, chérie. There's no chance of survival—"

"You don't know my sister." If anyone could find a way, it was her. If the guards hadn't caught up to us, she might have made it to safety. She already tried to flee once, so she'd learned from her mistakes and perfected her getaway. "The only reason you couldn't find her is because she outsmarted your men and your hounds." I couldn't dim the pride that burned brightly inside me. The storm almost killed us, but Fender didn't understand that my sister was the storm. They were at her mercy— not the other way around.

A subtle look of irritation came over his visage. "If that makes you feel better, chérie."

I WASN'T BLINDLY HOLDING on to hope.

I knew she was alive.

I knew Magnus helped her in some way.

More days had passed, so I wondered if she was in Paris. Or maybe she took off elsewhere so Fender would never find her again.

But I knew she would never leave me behind.

Fender and I had returned to our previous relationship in the cabin, where he came to me for sex, but I refused. He would never make me. He would never threaten me. He would just sit there and stare.

I read my book in front of the fire in my bedroom, and Fender joined me, sitting in the armchair, entertained by my face. I did my makeup once again, wore the clothes Gilbert provided for me because the misery had passed.

She was out there...somewhere.

Like Fender wasn't there, I read my book and listened to the sound of the fire. Hours passed, and nothing was said. I turned the page, now halfway done with the book. I'd stopped reading when he was gone, too grief-stricken to do anything but cry.

His deep voice broke the silence. "Chérie." The command in his voice was impossible to ignore. It rang with an inherent power, like the blood of kings ran through his veins.

It forced me to meet his gaze.

He was shirtless in his sweatpants, and his eyes intensified when I met his look, like simple eye contact was enough to fulfill the intimacy he craved. "If you believe she escaped—"

"I do." I believed it with my whole heart.

"Then nothing has changed between us." The flames illuminated the side of his body, making his muscles glisten with power. But no amount of light could ever brighten those midnight-sky eyes.

I dropped my gaze.

He moved from his armchair to the seat right beside me, the pressure of the cushion completely changing when his weight was added. His hand moved to my thigh, and he came closer to me, close enough to kiss me if I would allow it. "*Je t'aime, chérie.*" His hand cupped my face, and he pressed his forehead to mine. "*Tu es mon amour. Pour toujours...*"

Now that I knew the meaning of his words, listening to them was a different experience. He loved me. He would always love me. Forever. But I pretended not to understand, like he was just begging for forgiveness.

Last time, he'd looked into my gaze in the hope I understood his words. This time, he didn't, as if he just said them because they were words sitting on his tongue. He moved my hair back and pressed kisses to my neck, slowly moving down to my shoulder, tugging the strap of my nightgown down so he could kiss me there. His kisses turned harder, and his hand cupped my bare tit when the fabric slid down farther.

My eyes closed, and I enjoyed every single touch, every single kiss, all of his romantic affection that no other man could ever reproduce with the same quality. My head tilted back, and I almost got swept up in his current.

My palm moved to his chest and pushed him back, ending the rain of kisses.

He moved with the touch, obeying my request without hesitation. But his eyes were filled with a new level of disappointment and fury.

"If you want me...you have to promise me." My palm remained pressed to his chest even though he didn't move toward me again. I could feel his steady heartbeat increase, growing faster and harder. I stared at my hand for a moment before I looked at him again. "That's the price you must pay." My hand left his chest and returned to my lap. "And it's nonnegotiable."

His eyes remained still and cold. Silence passed without an outburst, without him losing his temper. He inhaled a breath, slowly let it out, and closed his eyes for a moment before he regarded me, as if he was ready to listen to my demand.

"You have to promise me that you or your men will never kill her. No matter what she does. No matter the situation."

His stare remained cold and hard, his breaths increasing slightly. He turned his face away and looked at the fire, all the muscles of his body thick and tight at the same time. Veins bulged slightly every time he used his arms, because any tension at all was enough to make them stress. The light of the flames danced on his face, high-lighting his flawless complexion, the fair skin against the dark hair.

"If you really think she's dead, what does it matter?"

He watched the fire a little while longer before he turned back to me.

"Give this to me...and we can be what we were before."

He inhaled a deep breath, his nostrils flaring as he exhaled. He didn't want to give it to me, but if he loved me, he would. He would accept the humiliation she had caused and moved on. "I promise, chérie."

ONCE HE WAS INSIDE ME, his anger disappeared.

His hand fisted my hair as he rocked into me, his body pressing mine into the mattress, his deep breaths blanketing my skin with his desire. He spoke to me in French, told me I had a perfect cunt, that I was the most beautiful woman in the world, and that...he loved me.

He said it with deep conviction, with masculine force, with hands that gripped me so tight it was like I was a balloon that might fly away. He took me like I was air to his length, the water to his throat, the blood to his heart.

He took me in that same position over and over, sometimes banging my headboard into the wall, sometimes taking it slow, like he needed to kiss me more than thrust into me, like his big hands needed to gently touch me everywhere.

How could a man who loved like this be cruel?

How could he be two different people?

Unless he'd always been the same man—the man that I knew.

He just forced himself to be something else...for whatever reason.

Hours passed before the grand finale. Our sweaty bodies lay together on the bed, the duvet kicked to the bottom and only the sheets behind. The fire had died down at some point, but he kept the entire bedroom warm.

He lay on his back, his head turned toward me beside him, one hand resting on his chest.

He watched me.

I was on my side, meeting his look with tired eyes. When I closed my eyes, he would leave. He always waited for me to drift off before he left, in the hope I wouldn't notice and I would sleep through the night without him.

I closed my eyes, feeling the fatigue pull at me, the relief that I'd gotten what I wanted.

I opened my eyes again to reach for the sheets beneath me.

But stilled when I noticed his eyes were closed.

Slowly, his breathing changed, turning deeper and lighter. The muscles of his body relaxed. His tense face softened into an expression I'd never seen before, almost like a boy in his childhood bed.

I WOKE up when I felt his body shift off the bed.

My eyes opened, and I saw him at the edge, looking down at me.

I assumed it was sometime in the middle of the night, but my eyes immediately squinted at the brightness from the sun.

It was morning.

He watched me with his typical hard gaze, but he didn't look angry that he'd slept in my bed through the night.

I stretched slightly, cold now that he was gone.

He grabbed the sheets and the duvet and pulled everything on top of me. "It's early. Keep sleeping." He leaned over the bed and gave me a kiss, his hand cupping my face as he did so.

When he pulled away, my fingers grabbed his wrist, not wanting him to leave, to shatter this moment.

He trusted me.

I'd made him give me a promise he didn't want to keep... and he still trusted me.

He stayed above me, his eyes searching mine for meaning.

I kicked the sheets back off and pulled him toward me again. "Make love to me before you go..."

TWENTY-TWO

BETRAYAL OF BLOOD

Fender

It was a promise I didn't want to make.

But it was the price I had to pay to get what I wanted.

And it was worth the cost.

Because Melanie was priceless.

Whether Raven was dead or alive, it didn't matter. She'd humiliated me again, but that didn't matter either. The only thing in my life that really mattered was the woman in bed beside me every night.

The woman who slept beside me all night.

The woman who completely lowered my guard to let her in.

It was hard to believe that it happened, but once it did, the weight left my shoulders. The pressure was off my entire body. The invisible weight of the past had somehow evaporated altogether.

I lay in bed with my chérie on me, her leg tucked between mine, her arm around my waist, her makeup a mess all over the pillow. Her eyes were closed, but she wasn't asleep. She rested after the hours spent wrapped up together, sometimes her on top, but mostly me on top of her.

My chérie was another painting to add to my collection, costing a price in a currency that I never used to pay for things. Euros, diamonds, and gold weren't enough to afford her. I had to pay with a sacrifice.

But now I got to live in this painting, got to admire it when no one else was allowed to see it at all. My finger-tips gently glided down the back of her arm, feeling her rose-petal-soft skin, feeling how warm she was because of me.

That moment was shattered by Gilbert.

"Sir." He knocked on the door. "I'm sorry to disturb you, but Magnus is here to see you."

My fingers stopped their caress.

Her eyes opened.

I left the bed and pulled on my sweatpants before I opened the door. "What does he want?" He shouldn't bother me at this time without good reason, and he shouldn't still be Paris either. I closed the door and walked with Gilbert down the hallway.

"He didn't say, sir. But he has a woman with him..."

I halted in my tracks and looked into Gilbert's face.

He held my gaze. "That's all I know, sir."

My heart worked harder than it ever had, experiencing a spike in anxiety that I hadn't felt since adolescence. Betrayal seared into my skin like a branding iron. Fury unlike any I'd ever known struck me like lightning.

I continued down the hallway and made it to the top of the stairs.

Magnus was there, near the bottom of the staircase as he waited for me.

And there she was several feet behind him.

Raven.

I gripped the rail as I looked down to the foyer, seeing the woman I despised in my very own house...like a fucking guest.

She must have felt my stare because she lifted her chin to meet my eyes. Instead of her typical venomous fury, she actually dropped her gaze as quickly as possible, like she was truly afraid of me.

When I took the first step, Magnus glanced up at me.

I looked at him in a way I never had before.

Like I didn't know him.

Like he was a stranger.

A liar.

I took my time walking down the stairs, using the moment to condense my anger, to cool my hatred before I released fury from my nostrils like a goddamn fire-breathing dragon. It was a long walk to the bottom, and our eyes remained locked on each other, a silent conversation happening between us.

I reached the bottom and reserved my stare for Magnus only.

She was insignificant to me.

He was everything to me.

Magnus stepped back, sensing my rage in the silence, and he had the humility to drop his gaze and break eye contact first.

I spoke in French, so that dog wouldn't understand. "You lied to me."

Magnus wouldn't look at me.

I stepped closer to him, barely able to restrain my rage. "You looked me in the eye and fucking lied." The betrayal was almost too hard for me to accept. It was too disturbing. Too painful. "For a woman. An *ugly* woman."

Magnus lifted his chin again, dressed in jeans and a shirt, his appearance different when he wasn't in the garb of the guards. He didn't look confident either, basking in his guilt for what he'd done.

"Now, you bring her into my house—like a wet dog that's going to track mud everywhere."

"There was no other way." He finally spoke up, his chest rising and falling with his deep breathing. "You can't see past your hate. You can't see past your stubbornness. I had to save her, and asking you wasn't an option."

"So, you lied to me instead?" I stepped closer, my eyes so hot they were burning my own face. "You love this woman?" That was the only thing I would understand, because I knew the irrevocable feeling all too well.

Magnus was quiet, his eyes holding my fire. "No."

What a disappointing answer.

"But I feel deep affection for her..."

I had no fucking idea why. "So, you come here to show me what you've done? To come clean and ask for forgiveness? Don't bother. I will never give what you seek." He was all I had in this world—and he stabbed me in the back. He helped her escape. He told her the way. He let her beat him in the head just to mask his lie. Pathetic.

Magnus turned quiet.

"Leave."

He didn't move.

"I told you to get out—"

"I'm here for her sister."

All feeling left my body. My extremities turned numb. My heart even stopped.

"I'm here for Melanie." He wasn't the strong man I'd seen on a daily basis. Now, he was torn between his two loyal-ties—split in half. It made him half the man.

My eyes immediately glanced to the puppet master behind him.

She immediately looked away.

My eyes shifted back to Magnus. "No." I stepped back.

"Brother." Magnus rushed me. "I'm not asking you this as your business partner..."

I turned back to give him my full stare.

"I'm asking you...as family." He inhaled a deep breath then held it, pleading with his gaze. "I'm asking as your brother."

"That's rich, Magnus." This woman was a constant prod in his back, making him stick out his neck for my blade. Pussy-whipped and pathetic, he was almost unrecogniz-able to me.

He held his stare, not blinking, exuding his desperation. "I never ask you for anything."

He'd betrayed me, made a fool out of me, but when my little brother asked for something, it was impossible to deny him. Perhaps the feeling that connected us had never been loyalty. Perhaps it'd been love. "I do this... then I owe you nothing. Ever."

Relief flooded his gaze, and he gave a nod. "Yes."

I held his gaze a moment longer before I took the stairs, making the climb all the way back to the third floor, down the hallway, and into the bedroom where I left her.

Melanie was fully dressed and on the edge of the bed, prepared for whatever happened downstairs. When she saw me walk inside, she immediately got to her feet and walked to me in her heels. "Everything okay?" Her hands immediately went to my arms, and she came closer to me, surrounding me with her affection.

Before Magnus had entered my home with his dog, my life had been perfect—a painting. But that woman never failed to interrupt my life, whether it was here or at the camp. She was the thorn on a rose stem, pricking you when you tried to smell the petals. She was the storm clouds that passed over a sunny day.

"Fender?" She squeezed my arms and brought me back to reality.

"Magnus is downstairs—with Raven."

Her fingers immediately released my arms as her eyes popped wide open. "Oh my god..." She stepped back and cupped her mouth, her eyes still on mine, processing the revelation. "I knew it... I knew she was alive."

"She's alive because Magnus helped her." She cut the bolt on the stables? Why did I believe that horseshit? Her scent was lost because she perished in the river? I felt like a goddamn idiot. My trust overrode my common sense.

She dropped her hand from her mouth, her joy so bright, it was like daylight through the windows. "Why are they here? For me? I have to go see her..." She moved past me to the door.

I grabbed her by the arm and pulled her back to me. "Chérie." I got her close to me, looking into her bright eyes and seeing the excitement she couldn't contain. "Magnus has asked me to release you. I've agreed."

Slowly, her excitement faded away, her breathing rising.

"Go down there. Hug your sister. Tell her you want to live here with me. And that will be the end of it." Magnus had asked me to release her, and I obliged. But I only obliged because Melanie wouldn't leave me even if I let her go—and there was nothing her sister could do about it.

Melanie looked at me and didn't say a word.

I stared at her. Waited for a nod. Waited for some sign of agreement.

She dropped her gaze and looked at her hands as they came together in front of her waist. She did that any time she was nervous. Any time she was unsure of herself. She fidgeted in place, swallowing, her eyes filled with a sheen of dread.

The longer I stared, the clearer her decision became.

Magnus had betrayed me.

Now, the woman I loved had betrayed me.

The second one hurt a lot more. And that was how I knew how deeply I'd fallen for her. My prized painting would leave my palace. Her side of the bed would be empty. Her quiet presence in my office would feel like a loud absence. The passion would snuff out like the fire in her bedroom. The millions I'd spent on her jewelry would be thrown into the vault to collect dust. The dresses, gowns, shoes, would be stuffed into a closet so I'd never have to see them again. Our time together had been short, but her vacancy would haunt me like a ghost. A million knives pierced me, but my gaze remained as stoic as ever. "Go." I stepped to the door and left her there.

"She's my sister—"

"Go." I kept going, walking out the bedroom door, down the hallway, and to the staircase. The last thing I wanted to do was watch her walk out of my life when I'd expected her to stay with me forever. She said she would never leave me, even if she could, but that was a lie, another lie from someone I trusted, and I was too blind to see it. But I forced my indifference, my coldness, and turned off every feeling inside my chest and made it empty, and I walked down the stairs to where Magnus waited.

Her heels tapped against the wooden staircase as she emerged. "Raven!" Her voice cracked in emotion, echoing in the foyer, showing the depth of her love that she never felt for me.

Raven moved forward, ignoring me. "Baby sister..."

Melanie ran the rest of the way then collided with Raven, the two of them holding each other, crying, whispering to each other.

Raven held her like a mother held a child, supporting the back of her head and rubbing her back, closing her eyes like she was so unbelievably happy to be reunited with the person she loved most.

Magnus watched them together, his eyes less intense when he watched Raven's happiness.

Raven pulled away and cupped her cheeks. "Let's go home."

Melanie nodded.

Home. *When will you be home?* Her voice came back to me, her beautiful eyes on me as she sat beside me on the bed where we made love through the night. I thought I was home.

Raven took her hand, and the three of them headed to the door.

I watched them go, arms by my sides, powerless to do anything because I wouldn't go back on my word. When I made a promise, I kept it...unlike everyone else.

Melanie stopped at the door then turned back to me.

My eyes burned into her face, hoping she would reconsider and stay with me. Momentarily, the peace she gave me returned, the quiet happiness that she provided to my broken soul.

Guilt. Pain. Remorse. It was in her blue eyes. But there was nothing else.

"Goodbye, chérie."

TWENTY-THREE

TEARS OF MISERY

MELANIE

Magnus parked in front of the apartment building.

I looked through the rain-splattered glass and saw the window to Raven's office, the one that had a distant view of the Eiffel Tower. We vacated the car, and my beautiful dress was ruined by the rain that poured down on us. I moved to the stoop that led to the stairs, but when I turned back around, Raven wasn't behind me.

She stood with Magnus in the rain, like neither one of them cared. "Go ahead without me."

I nodded before I glanced at Magnus, the enigmatic man who only had eyes for her. While she looked at me, he stared at her just the way Fender stared at me. With that dark intensity, that possessive stare, that all-encompassing feeling that made you feel watched even through a solid barrier.

And that was the moment I knew.

Those same dark eyes. That same brown hair. That same powerful presence. That same silent command.

Magnus was his brother.

I went up the steps and to the third floor where Raven's apartment was. The door was unlocked, so I let myself inside, seeing that it was exactly the same as the day we left. Her coffee mugs were in the glass cabinet. Her pink dish towel with the Eiffel Tower printed on the front on the kitchen island. Pictures of her friends from college on the fridge. I moved forward to the window in the living room and stared out across the apartment. The same man I remembered sat at his desk with his laptop in front of him.

It was hard to believe it'd only been a few months...when it felt like an entire lifetime.

I moved through the apartment and approached the window that gave a view of the city's most famous cultural landmark. It was still daylight, so when the sun fell, those lights would shine the way I remembered.

My eyes dropped down to Raven and Magnus on the street.

They talked, standing several feet apart, sharing no affection but a connection that I could see with the naked eye.

I had no idea what to do with myself, so I took a seat at the desk and watched the rain pelt the glass in front of me, the sound comforting but also heartbreaking.

Because I used to listen to the rain for hours while I was in bed with Fender.

When he slept beside me.

I inhaled a deep breath as the tears burned my eyes, suddenly feeling everything at once. The second he was gone, it was like a gaping hole inside my heart. Blood flooded in, and my heart couldn't beat the same anymore. It ached every single time. It struggled with every beat. Brought more pain every time it tried to keep me alive.

I didn't want to leave...but I had to.

If I stayed, I would never see Raven again. She would never forgive me for wanting to be with him. Our relationship would break apart, and we wouldn't see each other anymore, even if we were free.

And she was the person I loved most in this world.

My cheeks mirrored the window in front of me, my tears drops of rain. My dress was soaked and my skin was cold, but once I took it off, it would really be over. I would be back to my normal clothes, my normal makeup, smelling like cheap perfume and crappy hairspray.

I wouldn't smell like him anymore.

It would be like it never happened.

The apartment door opened and closed.

I inhaled a deep breath and quickly worked my fingers over my face, wiping away the tears, fixing the running makeup, doing my best to hide a heartbreak I shouldn't feel.

Her footsteps sounded up the stairs. "Melanie?"

"In here." I forced a smile that was so numb I couldn't feel it.

But I didn't have to because she looked as devastated as I did. She sat on the chair beside me and inhaled a deep breath, releasing it as a long sigh. She didn't have tears the way I did, but the heartbreak glistened in her eyes. She cleared her throat and pushed it away like it'd never been there in the first place. Her hand reached for mine and she held it on my thigh, looking into my face as the rain poured down outside, as the sound became louder against the rooftop and the window.

"You okay?" I whispered.

After a long pause, she gave a nod. "Yeah. You?"

"Yeah..." It was the first time I'd breathed air as a free woman, but I felt like I would never be okay again.

CPSIA information can be obtained
at www.ICGtesting.com
Printed in the USA
LVHW111445140521
687356LV00016B/644